A *brilliant* SPRING

KATE SMOAK

DEDICATION

To every one of you incredible
readers. Thank you.

– Kate Smoak

CHAPTER
ONE

ELISSA

My mother's copper hair, once perfectly sculpted, is now frizzy and unkempt, with pieces sticking up out of her bun. The powdery florals of her Chanel No. 5 assault my senses as she sobs into my jacket, her shoulders shaking. The hairs on the back of my neck stand up and a cold sweat breaks out over my body at our oddly intimate embrace.

"He…he…he didn't make it."

My world stops spinning. Harold didn't make it. What does that…

"They had to take him to surgery…to clear a blockage…and he had another heart attack on the table, and…"

My mother's wails echo down the cardiac wing hallway. "What am I going to do?" she cries. The shrill squeaks of busy hospital professionals' shoes fill the background as doctors, nurses, and orderlies flow around us like a river, moving from room to room and to the nurses' station. Beeps, whirrs, and a mumble of voices surround us as I stand frozen, rigid, with my mother's arms crushing me.

"Uh, Mrs. Black?" A tall, handsome nurse wearing light green scrubs appears behind my mother. I feel her stiffen and her arms drop from around me. She delicately wipes the tears from her face as she turns around, trying to appear composed.

"Would you like to see him now?" the nurse asks softly. My mother gives him a curt nod and follows him down the hallway. After a few feet she stops short, then turns to look at me.

"Elissa," she hisses incredulously. "Aren't you coming to say your goodbyes to your father?" Her eyes narrow, but her sniffling breaks the sternness of her look.

"Uh, maybe in a second. I need a minute." Isn't that what the funerals are for? The goodbyes? A warm hand rests on my shoulder, giving it a small squeeze when another nurse bustles by us, tugging her stethoscope off her neck and hooking the earpieces in her ears. I turn to Brandt and his eyes are shadowed with uncertainty. "I'm fine," I whisper to him.

"Are you sure? It's okay to be sad, or, you know, not okay." His eyes flicker across my face, looking for any signs of sadness or devastation, but I'm fine. A little numb, maybe, and a little angry over the fact that I'll never get my father's respect like I deserve, but who am I kidding. That was never going to happen anyway. I pull my phone from the purse slung over the crook of my arm and message Riley.

Me: *Harold's gone. Had two massive heart attacks. One during surgery and croaked.*

"Wow, a little insensitive," Brandt says, a hint of judgement colouring his voice. I shrug off his comment.

"Riley knows me. I don't have to pretend with her." A second later my phone beeps.

Riley: *Do you need me to come down there? U okay?*

I smile at my bestie's unwavering support. I message her back saying I'll be home soon, grab Brandt's hand, and follow the path my mother took down the hallway of gloom to see my dead father.

• • •

He looks…swollen. The person lying in front of me looks so unlike my father. The man before me is calm, relaxed, and peaceful. But…yes, somewhat swollen. The doctor said that it's a side effect of the surgery. Collette is leaning over the bed, arms stretched out and hands wrapped around my father's hands, sobbing uncontrollably, and it's unbearable. I don't think I've ever seen her shed a tear my entire life, so to say it's uncomfortable is an understatement.

It hits me at this moment that these two people in front of me right now are people I don't even recognize. My mother has actual feelings, which I assume she's having because she now doesn't have a husband to rely on, and not because she truly loved him. She loved the money. And her pool boys.

But the biggest stranger is my father; he always has been. And now, that's all he'll ever be. A stranger. It's odd that I feel nothing. Well, that's not entirely true. I'm angry, sure. But only because I'll never have that moment. The one in the movies, where the father finally says, "I'm proud of you." I'll never have that.

I tear my eyes away from my mother and father and look around the bleak little room. It's painted a dull, murky, blueish gray that just looks deathly. And that's all I smell, death. Maybe that's all in my mind, but it's what I smell. Well, death, and that weird, antiseptic, clean-but-doesn't-feel-clean smell of hospitals. The long greyish curtains around the bed are pushed up against the wall, hanging beside an end table that has a vase of fake sunflowers, in a weak attempt to brighten up the morbid room.

I shuffle my feet awkwardly, and Brandt's shoulder nudges me from behind. I lurch forward, his action catching me off guard. I catch myself a step closer to my mother and she looks up at me, tears brimming in her eyes, their light blue looking more turquoise because of the bloodshot red tinting the whites.

Her hands fall away from my father, a Kleenex wedged and sopping in one palm, and she stretches her hand out to reach for mine. I'm frozen, not sure what to do or how to comfort her. Brandt's large hand rests on my shoulder blade and he nudges me forward again until I'm within my mother's reach.

Her long, slim fingers weave around my hand and squeeze, and the moisture from her tears and snot slides against my hand. I resist the urge to gag. Her eyes lock onto mine, and her lips quiver as a small, warm, genuine smile stretches across her face.

"Thank you for being here," she whispers. My heart does a flip, and I'm not sure why. I gently squeeze my mother's hand back before slipping out of her grip.

"We're going to head out now," I say. "Do you need a ride home?" Collette shakes her head, her bangs swishing across her forehead.

"No, thank you. I have the driver downstairs waiting. Have a good night, you two." My mother stands up and brushes the wrinkles out of her skirt. Her heels click on the tile floor as she steps into me and wraps her arms around my stiff body. I'm frozen in place, my arms rigid at my sides, as my mother's embrace stifles me. My breathing quickens and becomes shallow, my heart rate spikes. She releases me, and her cold hands slide down my arms as a tight smile appears on her face.

I step out of her reach, backing away until I bump into Brandt's hard chest. His arm snakes around my waist and I offer my mother a silent nod before we turn and leave the room. I can feel Brandt's heavy gaze lingering on me as we walk toward the elevator. I sigh.

"I'm fine. I promise." But my words seem to do nothing to assuage his concern. His arm tightens around my waist, tugging me closer to him. We step into the elevator, surrounded by nurses, patients, and doctors. I lean in a little closer to Brandt and rest my head on his shoulder.

• • •

We step off the elevator, this time in my building, and we head for my apartment. Before I have a chance to unlock the door, it flings wide open and two thin arms wrap around my neck.

"Are you okay?" Riley asks softly. She steps back, her hands gripping my biceps as she looks me over, making sure I'm not hiding any feelings. Her eyebrows raise before dropping in satisfaction. "Yeah, you're fine. So, was it awful seeing him like that?" A shiver ripples over her, causing me to shudder.

"Uh, I really don't want to talk about it right now. I want to hear about you. How are you doing?" Riley's face falls, and her eyes shift away from me and land on Brandt for a moment before she spins on her heel and turns away, sauntering over to the couch.

"Fine," she says, her tone clipped. I roll my eyes and follow her to the couch to sit down beside her.

"He knows, I told him." Riley's head swivels to face me, a red flush coursing under her skin as tears well in her eyes. Her jaw ticks.

"You. Told. Him? Elissa, it wasn't your news to share!" Seeing the hurt in her eyes makes me feel small. I sigh, my shoulders drooping as I collapse on the couch beside her, cradling her hands in mine.

"I know, but I had to tell him. We're trying to do this thing right, which means no more lies," I say as my eyes dart to Brandt. Riley relents, and her body relaxes into the couch. She tugs her knees to her chest. "So, what did Rhys say?"

Riley bites her lip and gnaws for a moment before answering. "Well, he didn't say much, but he said so much in so little. At first, he was huffy and smug because he thought I wanted him back," she scoffs. "As if. But when I told him about my *situation*, he didn't even ask if it was his. He demanded a paternity test! Like, why else would I be here if I thought it wasn't yours? You know? Why would I tell him about a random hookup's baby? Sometimes I swear he's not the brightest — sorry, Brandt."

He shrugs nonchalantly as he rummages through the cupboards, clinking glassware together as he looks for something. A moment later, his hands are holding glasses and a bottle of white wine. His large, strong hands un-cork the bottle and he pours two glasses of white, then goes to the fridge and returns with a bottle of sparkling water, pouring it into the third glass. He brings the drinks over, passes one to each of us and sits over on the chair in the corner, closest to the television.

"I just…I understand why he wants a paternity test. I do. But for that to be the first thing, and only thing, out of his mouth just hurts. I love —" her voice breaks as she tries to grab hold of the emotions bubbling up inside her. I rest my palm against her thigh and give a gentle squeeze.

"It'll be fine. Like I said, I'm here for you and the little nugget, whatever happens." Riley's soft hand slips over top of mine and squeezes back as her eyes stare into mine, full of love and…hope.

CHAPTER
TWO

RILEY

When Elissa and Brandt excuse themselves for the night and slip behind Elissa's bedroom door, I'm left alone, sitting in silence. I sigh and look around the room, taking in the quiet and loneliness I feel in this moment, preparing myself for the pending life I'm sure I need to get used to. Being on my own.

I stare into the colourful red, green, yellow, and blue lights that glow on the bare Christmas tree in the corner of the room, opposite the chair Brandt was sitting in. A few opened presents sit under the tree, waiting to be put away. I sink into the couch more as I stare into the glow of the lights on the tree until my surroundings melt away and I'm back at Rhys' apartment.

Bundled up in my black peacoat and woolly white infinity scarf, I fluff my straight black hair and toss my head as I roll my shoulders back, straightening myself into a confident pose. My shiny red nails glimmer in the sunlight streaming into the lobby of Rhys' building as I reach for the button to buzz up.

"Hello?" His familiar voice echoes in the tiny room, wrapping around me in a warm embrace. My insides melt at the warmth that seeps through the intercom.

"It's me," I say. "We need to talk. Can I please come up?" I wait for Rhys to say something, but nothing comes. The silence stretches for a full minute or so, and I'm about to give up when the buzzer sounds, and the door unlocks. My hand wraps around the handle, the cool metal stinging the palm of my hand, and I pull on the door with force, as if it's going to lock in an instant because Rhys changed his mind.

I take careful steps to the elevator, mumbling under my breath. Mumbling about what I want to say, what I should say, what I need to say. I mumble imaginary counter-arguments he might give me, but also the happy, hopeful answers a tiny piece of me clings to, even knowing it's unlikely. Realizing I probably sound and look like a crazy person stalking the stretch of hallway to the elevator, I pick up my pace and hit the elevator button before anyone has a chance to see me.

When the elevator comes to a stop, my heart hammers in my stomach. The pulse is so strong, it's making me nauseous, and this time I can't blame the pregnancy.

Goosebumps prickle on my skin as I near his door, raising the tiny hairs on my arms and the back of my neck. The hallway suddenly feels a thousand degrees warmer as beads of sweat form and roll down the centre of my chest. I take a steadying breath, running through all the words I need to say to Rhys, and raise my fist to knock on the door.

It swings open before my hand connects with the heavy metal door. Rhys steps back, opening the door wide so I can slip inside. I peek out of the corner of my eye and damn, does he look good. His black hair is darker and slicked back like he's fresh from the shower, and as I pass him, the warm, comfortable smell of Old Spice tickles my nose. He's wearing basketball shorts, no shirt. His broad shoulders are exposed and so are the delicious bumps that ridge his core down to his...

Focus, Riley. I clear my throat as I kick off my boots and bend over to tug up my socks, which have slipped off my feet partially. I shrug off my jacket and turn to hang it up when I see Rhys' face staring at me in amazement, but not in a good way. Almost like he can't believe I'm getting comfortable.

When I'm finished, he brushes past me and another cloud of his body wash fills my lungs. My heart aches to capture that scent for later. He pads toward the couch and sinks into it, sprawling his arms across the back and showing off his mouthwatering shoulder muscles as they pinch and bunch together. I have to tear my eyes away in order to focus and make my way to the living room, where I delicately sit at the opposite end of the couch.

We both sit in silence; only the ticking of the clock makes noise. Finally, Rhys sighs. He leans forward, braces himself on his knees, folds his hands together, and turns his head to face me.

"What is it, Riley?"

My tongue freezes in my mouth. My whole body ices over and my heart rate slows. I hear my breathing get laboured, and I'm momentarily paralyzed. My mouth drops open, but snaps shut again a second later. I'm losing all the words I had prepared. I'm just sitting in front of him like a mute fool. Rhys sighs.

"Riley, I don't know if I want to get back together, okay? There's just —" My hand flies into the air to stop him. *Excuse me?*

"I'm sorry. You think *I* want to get back together? Me? The one who was dumped, ruthlessly, and then callously used just weeks later because you thought I was an easy fling? Fuck that." And suddenly, part of me changes my mind — I don't want him to know anything that's going on. My mind is telling me to move my feet and just leave. Forget him and his ignorant bullshit. But my feet and body remain rooted in place. *No, Riles. He deserves to know. Scratch that. He needs to know; he doesn't deserve shit.*

I shake my head and clear my thoughts.

"I'm pregnant." I wait for a response, but there's nothing. He's just staring at me with hard eyes. I tilt my head, furrowing my brows. "It's yours," I confirm. More silence. He finally moves, leaning back into the couch with a rigid posture. His muscles are tight, and his neck is straining. I can tell he's uncomfortable.

"I want a paternity test." His words sink my heart like the Titanic. A paternity test. I mean, yeah, sure, but how can he not believe me?

"But you never used a condom when you hooked up with me last; it's yours." He says nothing, gets up from the couch and walks over to the door, holding it open.

"I'll call you when I set up an appointment to get this done. You can leave now." My mouth drops open. Doesn't he want to know anything else? I'm floored, and I can't think straight as I float up off the couch, move toward the door, and slip on my boots and shove my arms into my jacket. I stop in front of Rhys, looking at him, but not really seeing. My stare is vacant, and I can't believe the conversation, or lack thereof, I just had with him.

My mind is reeling and blank all at once as I step outside onto the sidewalk. I bunch my coat up around my neck to keep me warm, and I realize that I left my scarf at his place. Well, I'm not going back now. The icy wind bites at my cheeks as I walk down the road, staring up at the skyscrapers as I stroll, the late afternoon sun glittering on the snow. People bustle and flow around me as I take my time walking back home.

My eyes flutter closed as my head falls to the back of the couch, and I'm back in my apartment when I open my eyes. It feels like a lifetime ago that this happened, but it's been only hours since I told Rhys. My shoulders collapse as I exhale a heavy breath and push myself off the couch. My feet shuffle me to my room, and I slip behind the door, closing it with a soft click. My hand slides down the wooden grain of the door as my other hand releases the handle. I press my forehead into the door frame and exhale, then flip the switch on the wall and light fills the room.

I grab my phone off my bed, plug it into the charger, and sift through the clothes on the floor to find my pajamas from this morning. Once they're on, I switch off the light and climb into bed. As I slide between the cool sheets and the duvet, sadness envelops me as well, and I realize that I'm in this on my own. I'm all alone. Elissa will be too busy with the company and Brandt, and who knows about Rhys.

I roll over and pick up my phone, and I squint into the glow. I scroll through my messages and find the one person in the world that I need: my mother.

Me: *I miss you. Love you.*

A few moments later, her reply comes in.

Mom: *I love you too, baby. Xx*

I click my phone off, place it back on my nightstand, and stuff my arm underneath my pillow. My other arm slides down and wraps around my barely bloated belly.

I'll love you just like my mother loves me. I'm all you'll ever need.

CHAPTER THREE

ELISSA

Brandt and I excuse ourselves after talking with Riley and making sure she's doing all right. When I close the door to my room, giant, muscular arms wrap around me from behind as his face nudges my hair out of the way to place kisses down my neck. My skin pebbles under his touch, instantly heating the rest of my body.

"Mmm, Brandt. Not yet, let me go shower. Wash off the smell of disinfectant and death."

"C'mon, Eli," he whispers in my ear. "Let me cleanse you with my tongue. I promise it'll be more fun." Heat simmers below as his words stoke a fire inside me. I spin around in his grasp, loop my arms around his neck and crush my lips against his, pulling him into a deep kiss. When I pull away, his eyes are still shut and I worm my way out of his grip, then grab his hand and pull him to the washroom.

"I never said you couldn't join," I say coyly, batting my eyelashes at him and quirking my lips deviously. He follows me to the washroom like a magnet, and I strip as I go, letting an item of clothing flutter to the floor one by one. His eyes are on me, dark and full of lust. His breathing shifts to heavy, quick breaths. I'm fully naked as I reach the shower and turn on the water, and it springs to life overhead like a waterfall.

Brandt's standing just inside the washroom door, his muscles flexing and moving as he removes his clothing, and I can see the strain in his pants. He unzips his pants and lets them drop to the floor, then steps out of them and pushes them aside with his foot. His biceps flex as he grasps the waistband of his boxers and drops them, letting his long, thick, hard cock bob free. My eyes are pinned to it, and I lick my lips, desperately wanting to take his length in my mouth.

He struts over to me, his muscular thighs clenching as he walks, until his warm skin is softly pressed against mine and I can see our chests are rising and falling at the same pace. He steps closer, forcing me to take a step back into the shower, and the hot water runs down my shoulders and head as I step under the spray. Steam billows around us, fogging up the glass walls of the walk-in shower. I gasp from the heat beating down onto my back, and reach for the tap, but Brandt beats me to it, turning down the temperature just a smidge.

With a knowing smile, he says, "We're going to need this to keep us cool." His stormy green eyes roam all over my naked body. I feel his eyes travel from my clavicle down to the swell of my breasts, his gaze caressing the peaks of each mound. Down further, he watches my toned stomach clench under his stare. He slowly drops to his knees, kissing my stomach as he goes. He kisses the apex of my thigh and hip, his tongue flicking along the wet skin. His mouth trails lower as his hand heaves my leg over his shoulder, pulling me closer to him.

I lean against the wall for more support as he kisses back up my leg from my knee, nipping and sucking as he goes, all the while looking up at me through heavy-lidded, sharp eyes. I stare down at him as my pulse races and my breathing matches my pulse. A quirk of his lips tells me he's enjoying this slow torture. I roll my hips forward, trying to egg him on; convincing him to put his mouth on my throbbing clit.

He pulls away and I feel cold. A small smile spreads across his face.

"What?" he asks, his voice an innocent, playful growl.

"Please, Brandt." I jut my hips forward.

"Please what, Eli?" he grumbles into my skin, nipping my thigh between words. I've never been more thankful to be in a shower because it's embarrassing how wet I am right now. I'm sopping, drenched, and eager.

"Please taste me," I say breathlessly. Something flashes in his eyes, and his smile widens. He grabs my ass with a tight grip and places soft kisses along my pelvic bone. His tongue sneaks out and he places wet kisses on my skin as he travels lower. He finally makes it to just above my clit, then stops. "Ugh! Please, please," I moan, wiggling my ass and hips desperately. A chuckle rumbles out, and suddenly he dives into me.

His tongue rolls along my clit before sucking it in. He buries his head into me, pressing his nose flat against my pubic mound. His teeth glide over my bud and pulse on it lightly, making an electric current shoot to my toes. His thick fingers find my opening as he runs them along my seam. He gathers some of my moisture and thrusts two fingers inside, hooking them to press against the spongy wall.

"Brandt," I moan. I feel his smile curve along my pussy, and he thrusts into me harder. His tongue draws circles around my clit as his fingers drag along inside me, stroking me into a frenzy. One of my hands twists into his hair as the other braces against the cool tile wall for support. A tingle creeps over my body and my toes curl. I chant his name over and over as I speed toward the finish line. My insides tense as I get ready to come… "*Yes*," I moan. The sparks are shooting all over my body now, and my eyes roll into the back of my head when suddenly…he stops.

When I open my eyes, incredulous, he's standing, and my foot is back on the ground. He's pumping himself, his jaw clenching as he uses his other hand to wipe my arousal off his face. "You're not coming just yet," he growls at me. I'm heaving breaths when he reaches out, spins me around, and presses me against the freezing glass wall. My face squishes up against the wall, my cheek obscuring my vision slightly. Brandt's fat, hard cock slips against my clit, and he rolls it around, collecting the natural lube.

He lines himself up, pressing the crown of his dick into me, just one inch to start. My insides are screaming for him to ram his dick inside me and make me come. "Please, *please*, Brandt. I need you. Now." I'm begging. I need this man like never before. He pulls back a bit but then slams into me, catching me off guard, gasping for air. "*Yes…*"

Brandt freezes. Not a single muscle moves. *What's going on?* Then it hits me. It feels too good. Way too good. He's just gone bareback into me for the first time. I revel in the feeling of his skin rubbing against mine. When he still doesn't move, I rock my hips.

"Fuck, Eli. Stop for a minute or I'm gonna blow," he growls. I look over my shoulder as the water beats down onto my back, and I see him, tensed, eyes clenched shut. I roll my hips again.

"I'm on the fucking edge. I need you, Brandt." Something inside him breaks because he slides out and thrusts back into me, and hard. He bucks into me like a savage beast, grunting as his fingers curl around my hip and press in deep. I feel my skin bruise from his grip, but fucking revel in the painful pleasure. He pistons into me, one hard thrust after another. His thick, rock-hard cock drilling into the exact spot to make me come. Fireworks start to explode behind my eyes. "Yes, Brandt. Yes. *Yessss…*" I moan like a bad porn video, but I can't help it. The way his cock fills me up and hits the right spot every damn time…it's too much.

My legs quiver as I spasm around his cock, squeezing him like a vice grip. He grunts out a choppy moan as he finishes, plastering my insides with scorching hot come. As he's coming down from his orgasm, his thrusts slow, and he leans forward, placing kisses on my back, shielding me from the downpour of water.

He withdraws and helps me stand up straight. My cheek is sore, and no doubt red, and my vision slowly returns in my right eye. Brandt's shoulders slump as he takes a deep breath, like he's been waiting to let out this pent-up energy. His come dribbles down my thighs and I squeeze them together to stop the weird sensation. His hand grabs mine and he pulls me under the water.

He turns to grab a loofah, lathers it up with soap, and drags it along my body, wiping it between my legs. "The least I can do is clean up my mess," he chuckles in a low, gravelly voice. My skin burns, but with what, I don't know. I can't describe what's burning me inside right now. But it's something I don't mind. It's something that feels right with Brandt.

We climb into bed after the shower — naked, at Brandt's insistence — and his arm sneaks behind my back and drags my body across the bed, tucking me under his arm. My head falls onto his chest and with his other arm, he hooks my leg over his. "Stay put," he grumbles, his voice full of possession. But then he places a soft kiss on my forehead, sighs, and I feel his body relax.

I'm frozen in place, unsure of what to do. Scared to move. I've never cuddled before. My head bounces as his chest rumbles with laughter.

"You can relax. Nothing's going to happen."

I draw in a deep breath and let myself relax with the exhale. I do this a few more times and settle in, moving my body to make myself more comfortable. Brandt's hand trails up and down my side, a light stroke. And somehow, this feels right.

CHAPTER FOUR

ELISSA

The next few days flew by in a blur of steamy, passionate sex. I don't think Brandt or I left my bedroom for longer than ten minutes, and that was just to pick up takeout at the door. Brandt didn't even have a change of clothes on him, so we stayed naked the whole time. The days were spent fucking on every surface, snuggling and watching movies on my computer, and consuming our calories in bed. The nights were spent with our bodies intertwined in various positions, sweating and panting, and cleaning up in the shower.

As Sunday afternoon finally rolls around, Brandt clambers out of bed after another salacious round and shuffles around the room, collecting his articles of clothing. All the muscles in my body ache from the three-day sex binge. They're fatigued and in serious need of recuperation and rest, but I don't want Brandt to leave. *What is wrong with me?*

Brandt is bouncing on his feet, tugging his jeans over his massive thighs, and the metal zipper grinds as he zips up. I shimmy out of bed, pulling the silky white sheet with me and wrapping it around my swollen, sore chest. I kick the sheet around until it falls behind me and saunter over to Brandt, my hand resting on his shirtless pec. My nails rake along his chest as I rise to my toes to kiss his soft, plump lips. His beard scratches against my jaw and I giggle like a schoolgirl.

His brows raise, questioning why I'm laughing. My finger traces along his strong jawline, scrubbing into his thick, bristly stubble.

"It's scratchy. Someone needs to shave." I place a kiss on the corner of his jaw, and I feel it clench underneath.

He grabs my wrists from his chest, lowers them, and gently pushes me away.

"You need to stop, or I won't be able to leave."

"Thus fulfilling my plan," I reply, a small, sly smile sparking on my lips as they roll between my teeth. Brandt drops my hands, and he tugs his black t-shirt over his head, ruffling his hair. My hand reaches out and runs through his wavy golden hair, brushing back the locks that have fallen over his face. "Are you coming back later?" I ask. He gives me a strange look, one that I can't quite describe — almost pained, maybe?

"No," he breathes out. "Since we have to go into the office tomorrow, I was thinking of spending tonight at home and catching up on some things before tomorrow."

My heart deflates, wondering how, in the span of a week, I've become so reliant on being beside him. "But tell you what," he continues. "I'll pack a bag." He leans his head in to place a kiss on my lips. "And I'll come stay the night after work." His lips brush against mine again as he says this, and a warm shiver rolls up my spine. His lips linger against mine, waiting for an answer. I feel his lips twist into a smile as I nod, my nose dragging against his.

His arms slip around my waist, and he pulls me into a tight embrace as his lips press into mine. The kiss starts off soft and gentle, but quickly turns heated as his tongue lashes across my lips. My mouth opens and his tongue plunges in, licking every corner of my mouth. I moan into his lips, and he growls back as I feel the pressure growing in his pants. He breaks the kiss and steps back.

"Time for me to go, or I won't be leaving," he chuckles. "See you tomorrow, Eli. Good night." He turns and leaves me standing in the middle of my room, naked and wrapped in a sheet, and a heated wanting between my legs. Needing to find relief, I pull out my favourite purple clit-sucking toy, although it's not nearly as satisfying as having Brandt do it.

I've finally managed to put on my plush, grey housecoat and pad out to the kitchen in search of sustenance. The dishes clatter as I grab a bowl, spoon, and a box of cereal and place them on the counter. I open the fridge to grab the milk, closing the door with my heel. I pour the cereal into my bowl, but some sugary squares fall onto the counter.

I pick them up and shove them into my mouth as I pour milk over my cereal.

I make my way back to my room, prop up my pillows and crawl into bed. The cereal is crunching between my teeth when a tiny figure appears in my doorway. Riley's face wrinkles and she grimaces as she comes into my room.

"Holy fuck, it smells like a brothel in here."

I laugh out loud, and hard.

"Good. That means we did something right," I reply.

"You need to change your sheets and grab an air freshener because it is disgusting in here." Riley's eyes scan my room with disgust as her nose wrinkles and her lips pucker. I stifle the laugh bubbling in my throat.

"Are you sure it's not just the pregnancy hormones that are heightening your sense of smell?"

Riley's eyes flit to mine, her brows furrowing.

"What do you mean?"

"Uh, have you not done any reading? Pregnancy hormones generally heighten your senses, particularly smell." Her head bobs slowly, and I can see the wheels turning in her head before she shakes it.

"Yeah, this is not a pregnancy thing. This is 'you're a disgusting sex addict and need to clean and sanitize your room' thing."

I can't contain my laughter any longer. I throw my head back, and Riley gives me a look that says I have three heads. I can't help this feeling, I'm just joyful. For maybe the first time in my life, I feel at peace. And I know it comes at a weird time, seeing as my father has passed, but…I don't know. I'm light and airy. Maybe my head is just foggy from all the sex.

"So, any word on your father's funeral arrangements?" Riley asks, abruptly careening me back down to earth and shattering my good mood. I groan, gritting my teeth.

"No idea what's going on with that. I'm assuming my mother will reach out when I need to show up." Riley's cautious glance flicks over me as she sucks on her bottom lip. "What? Just say it."

A hard swallow rolls in her throat. "It's just…when do you find out about the will? Since you have access to your trust fund and have no reason to be cut off anymore now that your father's gone, are you planning on staying with the company?"

I sigh. Riley asks a great question, but one I'm not totally prepared to answer at this moment. I shrug noncommittally, giving her a nondescript answer. Her feet drag along my floor as she steps further into my room, and her hair flies around her as she flops onto her back on my bed. A smile twists on my lips when I see her face contort. A wave of disgust washes over her, nose twitching and face going pale when she realizes that she's just laid down on the stinky, sex-tainted sheets.

Riley springs to her feet, dancing around, wiping herself off like she just found a spider crawling on her. Another hearty laugh bubbles forth from me. Tears sting my eyes as I watch her prance around, shaking off the creeps, and I swipe at a stray tear rolling down my cheekbone. Riley finally stops dancing, stomps her feet, and shakes out her hair. "Well, I'm going to shower, now that I'm covered in your sex filth." She turns and skitters out of my room, slamming the door behind her. Milk dribbles from my mouth as I giggle, spilling down my chin and onto my cushy robe.

I place my empty bowl on my nightstand, the spoon clattering in the bowl, and slouch out of bed. I dig my fingers under the mattress and tug the corners of the sheets out, rolling them into a ball as I pull, and toss them into the corner of my room. They flutter to the ground in a pile, like a heap of snow. After I finish making my bed all fresh and new, I take the sweaty, cum-stained sheets and blankets straight to the washing machine at the end of the hallway near the foyer.

When I return to my room, I jump, startled by Riley laying on her stomach on my freshly made bed, flipping through a magazine. Her legs are crossed behind her, swaying. Her eyes are dull and a ghost of sadness floats in them. I study her, taking in her small, fragile body, a body swelling with a new human life, so soon after being hospitalized for malnutrition. My insides curdle as I fret over how this pregnancy is going to affect her eating disorder struggles. Riley is one of the strongest people I know, but even the strongest people have an Achilles heel. I sigh, my head dips, and a soft smile sprawls across my face. I skip over to where Riley is laying and jump onto the bed beside her, snuggling into her side.

CHAPTER
FIVE

BRANDT

I'm almost at Rhys' place on this snowy Sunday afternoon. I was at home for a total of fifty minutes before Rhys called me, completely freaking out. So, after I showered and put on some clean clothes, I bundled up again and headed to his place. The last few days with Elissa have been fucking glorious. I've never felt so satisfied and fulfilled in my entire life. Finally, the piece that was missing has clicked into place. I finally have her, all of her.

When I get to Rhys' place, I kick the snow off my boots on the brick wall of the building before entering. Rhys' place is only a block and a half away from Elissa's.

It's so tempting to go back there and stay in bed with her for the rest of the day. Hell, the rest of the week. I wrestle with my subconscious to stop myself from walking over there right now and just crawling into bed with her and making love.

I only need to knock once and Rhys has the door open, standing there in a sleeveless tee and basketball shorts, his choice of loungewear. His black hair is wild and sticking up everywhere. It looks like his hands have been pulling and tugging at it. His eyes are sunken, with dark circles staining the skin beneath them, and the stench of a distillery taints his breath. He's a wreck, and I can only think of one reason: Riley.

"What's going on? You look like shit," I say, my large hand clasping at his shoulder. He shrugs off my hand and stares at me with dead eyes.

"Fuck you, man." He shoots his words with poison. His face falls, and the wrinkles around his eyes soften. "Sorry, there's just a lot on my mind right now." I nod my head, but don't press. He doesn't know that I know what's going on and I'm not about to tell him, either. If he wants to talk, he will.

I stalk over to the couch, passing Rhys, and drop into the cushions. He collapses face-down into the loveseat across from me, his arm thudding on the ground as his lungs push out a groan. Even his apartment smells like rot and decay. I open my mouth to tell him to pull himself together and clean his apartment, but he speaks first.

"Riley's pregnant," he moans into the couch's velvety dark brown cushion. His head lifts off the couch, turns to face me, then slumps back down into the cushions. I tense. I'm not quite sure what to say, which probably works in my favour, seeing as I already know this tidbit of information, but have no idea how to play it off.

"Oh," is what leaves my lips. Rhys groans again and buries his head further into the cushions. "What are you planning on doing?" I ask tentatively. His head pops up to face me again, his jaw clicking.

"I don't fucking know, man. Like, how do I even know it's mine? We've been broken up for almost three months. She's probably slept with a bunch of people by now," he growls. His fingers curl into a fist and it drags along the floor as he swings it, avoiding eye contact.

"You really think she's been sleeping around? Dude, she was in fucking recovery. Grow a pair and own up to your fucking mistake. You were the stupid one who randomly hooked up with her without a rubber." Rhys groans again, grumbling something under his breath that I can't quite make out. "Stop being a pussy."

"Well, I'm not doing anything without a paternity test." My jaw hardens at Rhys' inability to be a man and take responsibility. I knew my best friend could be a jerk and irresponsible sometimes, but I didn't realize just how much of a jackass he really is. He's the one worried about Riley sleeping around, as if he hasn't been since they broke up?

"You're pathetic, man. I think you're just using a paternity test to hurt Riley. You're fucking miserable without her, and you have been since you dumped her."

He pushes himself up into a sitting position and plants his feet on the ground like he's bracing for an attack.

"C'mon man, you expect me to think she hasn't been sleeping around?" I stare at him. His face is blank and his eyes are vacant.

"You're telling me that you weren't sleeping around either? I find that hard to believe. Knowing you, you were burying your dick in some wet cunt the second you dumped her. We both know who you are." Rhys' face blanches, and he looks away from me, his jaw clenching so hard it makes his scalp shift. "Oh, and what about how far along she is? Doesn't that line up with the fucking backslide you had with her?"

Rhys' colour is bubbling under his skin until he finally bursts.

"I haven't been with anyone since Riley, okay? No one. I still fucking love her, man. But I'm so unbelievably pissed at her still. And I can't trust that it's not my baby." His shoulders drop as he slumps back into the couch, his head hitting the backrest. He shoves his hands through his messy black hair. We're both basking in the silence for a moment when his eyes pop open, narrow, and he sits up straight, glaring at me. "How the fuck do you know all this? I didn't mention how far along she was or about us hooking up at all." His voice grows tense. I sigh, shrugging my shoulders.

"Elissa told me. We're sort of…back together."

His eyes widen, and his head drops down as he stares up at me under furrowed brows.

"When did this happen?" he grumbles. I look away, shrugging my shoulders again. "Brandt, when did this happen?" I heave a sigh.

"I guess around New Year's." I wait for the yelling or admonishment to come, but he says nothing. He stares at me with hard eyes and sighs.

"Well, good for you, man." He's silent and still for another moment before he propels himself off the couch and makes his way to the bathroom, then slams the door shut. Feeling the tense air only thicken more, I decide to leave, giving him time to cool down.

"I'll leave now, man. Let me know if you wanna shoot some hoops later," I shout at the closed door. Rhys makes a *hmpf* sound, and I hear the hot water screech on as I leave his apartment.

• • •

I'm looking down at my phone as I walk into my building and I bump into something, or rather, *someone*. They land on the ground with a thud and a feminine cry. Startled, I look away from my phone and peer down to see the top of a familiar blonde head sitting in front of me. I extend my hand, holding it out to help her up. Her hand slides into mine, her black nail polish shiny in the lobby light. Her fingers grip as I tug on her, lifting her off the ground. Lexi's blue eyes find mine and her gaze softens.

"Hey, you," she coos.

"Hey," I say, a little colder than I mean to.

"I saw *her* the other day. Glad you two worked it out."

"Thanks…" We stand in awkward silence when my mouth opens. "Sorry for…well, about everything. I really didn't mean to hurt you."

"I know. And I appreciate the apology." Her crimson-stained lips twist into a sad, soft smile. "Well, I better hurry up. I'm late for a date," she says with a wink.

"Have a good night, Lexi. And good luck."

"You too."

• • •

When I'm finally in my apartment, I kick off my shoes, toss my coat on the hook, and stalk to the kitchen, swinging the door to the fridge open to grab a beer. The top pops off, and I toss it across the counter; it skids across the cool stone until it clunks into the sink. I take my beer and head to the couch, dropping into the cushions and grabbing the remote off the coffee table, switching on the Raptors game. I lean back into the couch and rest my feet on the table. And for a moment, everything feels right in the world.

CHAPTER SIX

ELISSA

I groan as my phone goes off, ringing directly into my ear because it's shoved under my pillow. My hand curls around the phone and my thumb slides across the screen to accept the call.

"Mmello?" I mumble into the phone.

"Elissa, is that any way to greet your mother? I taught you better than that!" A shrill voice screeches through the line. My eyes fly open, and I shoot up to a sitting position. "It's six in the morning. Shouldn't you be up and getting dressed for work already?"

I groan at her chilly words.

"I don't go into the office until nine. I still have at least an hour to sleep," I grumble into the phone. In the background, it sounds noisy, like a bunch of people are murmuring and moving about. Clinks and scrapes and all kinds of ruckus. If I didn't know better, I'd say it sounds like my mother is getting ready to throw some kind of party.

"Well, get up. I am calling to inform you that we are having your father's funeral service today, at eleven sharp. I expect you to be at St. Patrick's just before ten. The company's publicist has written a eulogy for you to speak. Please look presentable." *When do I ever not look presentable?* I roll my eyes, knowing full well she can't see me, so I stick out my tongue like a child for good measure.

"Yes, Mother," I croak, and the line goes dead.

I tap the email app on my phone to send Lori, my assistant, a note to say I won't be in today. But, when my inbox loads, there's a company-wide email letting all the staff know of the funeral today at St. Patrick's Church, in downtown Toronto. The board has apparently elected to close the whole building in honour of Harold. With a heavy sigh, I slink out of my bed, my feet hitting the cold hardwood floor, and shuffle off into the bathroom to get ready for this long and torturous day.

• • •

Riley slides out of the car first, smoothing down her black mid-thigh dress and fluffing her black curls. Her hair has grown out over the last few months and is no longer in a lob anymore. I like the new look; the long, curled strands frame her heart-shaped face. It suits her.

Her warm breath billows in the cold air as she waits for me to get out of the car.

"Are you coming, hun?"

"In a second," I murmur to her. The driver looks at me from the rearview mirror.

"Ma'am, where would you like me to park?"

I sigh. "You don't need to call me 'ma'am,' Arthur. I've known you since I was ten. You can just call me Elissa." A small chortle bubbles out of me. "But if you want to go and grab a coffee, I'll message you when we're done." Arthur nods his head and I slide out of the black sedan. When my red heels hit the cold pavement, a powerful urge to run, and keep running, overwhelms me. As if sensing my flighty moment, Riley hooks her arm through mine, and she leads us up the steps of St. Patrick's Church.

The tall, beige stone stairs lead to a flat patio before continuing toward the front wall of the church, with its three sets of double doors, each decorated with crosses. I stop and stare up at this magnificent church. One large arched window stands tall, stretching up the face of the church, with two shorter ones on each side. Underneath the windows is a row of small, narrow, arched cutouts that look like they were retrofitted with more modern window panes.

The main building has two wings on either side, with more cutouts that also look to be paned after the fact. Each tall peak of the building is topped with a stone cross. Ivy coils up the right side of the building, weaving across the beige bricks. I take a deep breath, squeeze the crook of my arm on Riley's, and we head into the church together.

The church is quiet as hushed, reverential tones murmur and bounce off the walls. Whispers are mixed in with the natural hum of the church's atmosphere. When Riley and I get to the main entrance for the chapel, I notice my mother right away. Her copper locks coil into a tight, neat French twist, and her bangs are perfectly curled and fluffed. Her makeup is minimal, but flawless as always. And, even with the makeup, her eyes are still puffy, and the creases of her nose are splotchy and red. My heart pangs as I feel a rush of guilt settle in. *Maybe my mother is actually sad about Harold passing.*

When my mother spots me, a wide, warm smile passes over her face and she steps toward me and Riley, the clicking of her heels echoing in the chapel. I feel dozens of pairs of eyes on us as she nears, arms wide open, tissue wadded in her hands. Her arms clasp around me, pinning my arms to my side and pulling me in for what feels like a genuine hug. My arm bends upward awkwardly, and I pat her side.

"Hi, Mother," I say, keeping my tone level.

"Hi, baby," she says, then steps back and looks at Riley. She pulls her in for a hug as well, and places a kiss on Riley's cheek. "Good to see you, Riley. So glad you made it."

Riley gives my mother a tight smile. "Of course, Mrs. Black." My mother stands tall, but a tiny flash of shock crosses her face. A thick, warm arm snakes around the right side of my waist and the familiar cool richness of Brandt's wintry scent wraps around me like a blanket. I feel him lean down, and when I look at him, he places a soft kiss on my lips. My insides instantly heat and my heart hammers in my chest as our first public display of affection is here, at my father's funeral.

My mother clears her throat. "A-hem." Her shrill, prickly voice interrupts the moment.

"Mrs. Black, I'm deeply sorry for your loss." Brandt's words are like warm butter as he steps forward and offers my mother a kiss on her cheek. She whispers a "thank you" and gives me a look. A look of what, I'm not quite sure, but it *almost* looks like approval.

"Well, I better get going and see that the priest is ready to go. Elissa, please join me in a moment to grab your speech." She turns away with one last smile and saunters off to find the priest. Riley slinks off to find a seat in a pew near the front. I turn my gaze to Brandt.

"Thanks for coming," I murmur. His face brightens as his lips twist into a soft smile.

"Well, I wouldn't be here if Harold wasn't a partner, and the email that was sent out made it seem like this was mandatory for all staff," he says, chuckling quietly. My heart swells at the sound of his laughter and the crinkles at the corners of his eyes.

"Well, I suppose I should find my mother and this speech I'm supposed to recite," I grumble with a roll of my eyes. Two warm hands clasp my face and I find two beautifully dull green eyes staring back at me (I'm choosing to believe they're beautifully green because of my colour blindness, and well, just look at the damn man). His gaze never wavers as he looks into my eyes and draws my face closer to his. My hands find purchase on his chest, and I don't realize I'm holding my breath until his lips touch mine, and I gasp for air.

His tongue swipes across my lips and I instantly grow hot. I realize this is wholly inappropriate, kissing like this in a church, but I can't stop. His tongue flicks and rubs against mine, and I resist the urge to deepen the kiss. My hands slide along his silky smooth charcoal suit, grasping the lapels, ready to dive in, when he breaks the kiss. A sly smile sprawls across his face as his eyes look past me.

"Oops…sorry, Father," he murmurs in my ear. And I nearly snort. My hands fly to my mouth, stifling the noise threatening to come out. A devilish glint sparkles in his eyes as he straightens his jacket and places a kiss on the side of my head. "See you soon." He maneuvers around me and stalks off, stopping a few times to talk to some of our coworkers before finding a spot near the front with the rest of the board members.

Air rushes into my lungs as I try to calm my nerves and prepare to find my mother for the eulogy I will need to deliver. Hopefully, it will be believable. I look around me, taking in the beauty of the church. The cathedral's tall arched ceiling features beautiful pendant lights dangling down over the two main rows of pews. In between the outer wings of pews and the centre ones are tall cream and white marble pillars. Discreet speakers adorn each pillar along with tasteful, but ornate, flower arrangements — red and white roses and sprigs of baby's breath.

Beautiful stained glass windows line the outer walls of the chapel, each depicting a different biblical scene, and little stonework pictures hang on the wall of the stations of the cross. The altar is smooth white granite and is lined with a white cloth with golden crosses on either end. The air smells of burning candles and that unique scent that all churches have. You can never quite name what it is, but they all smell the same.

Despite the reason for gathering, I feel calm. I feel…at home here. It feels warm and inviting, so unlike my father. It's ironic that such a cold and distant person is being celebrated and mourned in a place that is so warm and welcoming. I grimace as I shake myself from my thoughts and head toward the front of the church to find my mother and the publicist.

CHAPTER SEVEN

Elissa

My knuckles bloom white as my fingers crinkle the pages in my hand. The words on the page, I just don't comprehend. What the publicist wants me to say makes my stomach turn. My mother stands off to the side, talking to the publicist as they give me time to review the speech. My teeth grind together, the bumpy surfaces scraping together.

Thank you all for coming today. My father, Harold Black, was a generous, hardworking, loving father.

Vomit bubbles in my throat.

He was the heart of Black & Wells Publishing and Press, the backbone of the media empire he created in his early days after university. Harold worked incredibly hard to provide for his family, but also for his employees. He thought of every single one of his employees as an extended family member, which is why the turnout today is a testament to his character...

Oh. My. God. It's like a commercial, an endorsement for my father, even after death. While it's true that he treated his employees well, there's no way everyone is here because they thought this highly of him; the board mandated them to be here. I drop my hands, the pages still being squeezed in my clenched fists. How am I supposed to deliver this eulogy, to say these words about my father, words that I just don't believe?

My body feels like it's being wrapped in iron chains, slithering around my body and coiling tightly until I can't move or breathe. It's like the walls are caving in on me and I'm struggling for air. My blood boils, and I'm crushed by fighting emotions. Anger and nerves battle it out and the urge to run surges in me when I hear a door click open behind me. I'm torn away from my thoughts. I turn around and Riley is standing at the door, a look of worry on her face. Her eyes are glassy, she's pale, and her perfectly sculpted brows pinch together.

"Are you okay?" she asks in a hushed tone. I nod my head, take a deep breath, and give her a weak smile. Her shoulders drop as she visibly relaxes a little. Some colour returns to her face. "Okay. Because I need to freak out and you're the only one I can do it with."

I cock my head, giving her a concerned look, and she deflates. "My parents are here." I immediately understand her dilemma. My heels echo as they click on the floor of the small room until I'm in front of her, wrapping my arms around her, the pages wrinkling against her back. She lets go of a heavy sigh and melts into my embrace.

"It's going to be okay, Riles. You don't have to tell them anything yet. You still have some time until you'll start showing." My voice cracks as I try to keep my volume low so that it doesn't carry through the room and to the ears of people on the other side of the door. After a few moments, she sighs, and I rub her back. "Let's go. I need to recite this junk."

Riley pulls away from me, holding me at arm's length as she stares into my eyes. Her flawless eyeliner never fails to amaze me. Her eyes waver as they look back and forth into mine. "You know, you don't have to read the eulogy if you don't want to. Just give me a sign and I'll hold your hand and we'll run out of here. 'Grief stricken' they would probably play it off as." I chuckle and shake my head, and she chuckles along with me. Her hands grip mine, and for a moment, I am calm.

• • •

The funeral procession started off well enough — it was all very polite; people coming over to my mother and I in our pew, greeting us, offering their condolences. I'm not sure who put together the funeral readings, my mother or the publicist, but it was all very posh, and holy, and everything that was the opposite of my father. Go figure. A wobbly old voice crackles through the speaker system.

"And now Harold's daughter Elissa is going to say a few words." My stomach sinks and my mother and Riley each squeeze a hand. I look at Riley, and she gives me a reassuring smile. Her full lips mouth, *just give me a sign.* I squeeze her hand back, and when I stand, my hands smooth out my black cotton wrap dress and I tuck my hands underneath my ass to make sure that the skirt is still down. I edge past my mother in the pew, and my head feels hollow. My breathing echoes in my ears as I walk toward the podium.

Flashes and shutters click behind me, and I finally make it to the podium and turn. My hand sinks into the pocket of my dress and extracts the crumpled, folded eulogy the publicist wrote for me. I lay it on the podium, my hand running over the paper, smoothing out the bumpy wrinkles. I clear my throat and it rings through the speakers.

"Thank you all for coming. For some of you who may not know me, I am Elissa Black, Harold's daughter. My father, Harold Black, was generous, hardworking, and —" My voice breaks as my pulse throbs underneath my skin and my eyes prickle with static. My hands wrap around the edge of the stand and grip it tightly as I try to balance myself and concentrate on my breathing. Flashing lights obscure and blur my vision, only making my heart race faster. I take a few moments to pull myself together. When my heart calms down a little, my hands loosen, and I pick up the paper and fiddle with it between my fingers.

I don't dare to look up or into the crowd of nameless faces in front of me. They're probably looking at me with sympathy for being "heartbroken" over losing my father. But the truth is, I'm not sure what I feel, if I feel anything at all. I'm irritated, sure. Anxious, yes. But mostly I'm numb. My brain still hasn't quite processed the fact that he's gone.

It's like an elaborate prank he's playing on me, just to fuck with me and put me back in my place. Because that's just what Harold would do. My lips move, seemingly of their own accord, but the words coming out of my mouth don't match the words on the paper in front of me.

"My father, Harold, was a company man. Through and through. He loved his work, his company, and his employees, in that order." I take a deep breath and ground myself, as I'm going off script. My lips continue to move with a mind of their own. "Harold was rarely around when I was growing up. He was always at work, and on the occasions when he was home, he was in his study, working. I guess that's one useful thing I learned from him, how to work hard. Oh, and my love of whiskey." The church echoes with a polite chuckle from the crowd. "I always kept my head down growing up, and put in maximum effort to get good grades for him and my mother. To make them proud, to make them love me. To be the perfect daughter."

What in the fuck am I saying? Why isn't someone stopping me? The words just keep pouring out of my mouth, and I've never been more disgusted with myself. Who is this weak woman rambling into the microphone?

"What I'm trying to say, I guess, is that I should count myself lucky that I only have to strive for one parent's love and attention now. Takes a bit of the pressure off, doesn't it?" I'm cracked, I'm losing it. My eyes sting and my nose feels like I've inhaled a bucket of water as tears spring to my eyes. My laugh carries through the room, echoing and crackling on the speakers. My breathing, hard and erratic, echoes into the mic as I lose it in front of the congregation. Riley shoots to her feet and clambers over my mother, stomps up the stairs, and wraps an arm around my waist, pulling me from the podium. I stretch my neck, gripping the stand, my mouth still making noise into the microphone.

Bulbs are flashing, clicking, and snapping at my very public meltdown. Just another scene for the tabloids and papers. They must think I'm drunk. I wish I was. I don't know what the fuck is wrong with me.

"Rest in peace, *Dad*," I say, my words dripping with sarcasm. "Riley, let go, I'm coming…" My voice trails off as I'm pulled away from the podium. A shocked hush hangs over the church. No one dares to move, cough, or say anything. Riley's grip around my arm tightens, dragging me behind her, and I try to wrestle out of her grasp. "Riley, let go," I murmur, yanking back on my arm, but her grip doesn't waver, not until she's tugged me out of the side door of the church and into the hallway, and the massive arched doors slam closed behind me.

CHAPTER EIGHT

ELISSA

Riley's nails bite into my skin as she drags me out of the church, stomping her feet and tossing withering glares over her shoulder.

"Riley, stop. Please, you're hurting me." When we're finally far enough away from the main room in the church, her hands drop from around my bicep, the skin now raw and red, decorated with half-moon nail impressions. What the hell is her problem? What the hell is *my* problem? Riley's arms are folded across her chest, and her toes are tapping rapidly on the marble floor. Her lips are moving, but it's hard to hear what she's saying; she's just murmuring to herself. "What are you saying Riley?"

Her eyes dart to find mine, and when they do, they're hard and narrow, and I shrink to about three inches tall; so small I can see the miniscule specks of dust on the floor. Her eyes soften as she exhales, and her body relaxes. Her shoulders rise and she drops her head into her hands, rubbing her forehead like she has a headache.

"That did not go as planned," Riley finally says. My eyebrow twitches as I resist the urge to roll my eyes at her and say, *no shit*. "What the hell happened up there?"

My expression contorts, and my mouth opens and closes a few times without as much as a sound coming out. Finally, I throw my hands in the air and shake my head.

"Like fuck if I know, Riles. I started off reading the stupid page, and then something inside me broke. It's like my brain malfunctioned or something. I can't explain it. I was standing there, telling myself to shut the fuck up while I was talking, but my mouth wouldn't stop moving. Like my subconscious knew I finally didn't have to pretend anymore. And you know what? I think it kind of felt…liberating." Riley's eyes bulge out of their sockets. She's looking at me like I've lost my mind. And I kind of think I did lose my mind. But you know what? I don't care. I finally feel like I can be me. No more having to live my life for my father, no more worrying about his disappointment, no more trying to prove myself to him, to prove that I'm worthy.

No more trying to prove that I'm worthy…I never have to prove myself to him again. I don't have to try and earn his love, affection, and pride. I'll never get the chance… to prove to him that I'm *worthy* of his love, affection, and pride. My mind is muddled and jumbled with thoughts. I close my eyes, blocking out Riley's judgemental and concerning stare, and my head shakes slowly, trying to loosen these thoughts from my mind to no avail.

My heart sinks, and it finally hits me. Is there a reason to continue with everything I've worked so hard for if there's no Harold at the end, finally being proud of me? If I'm not chasing my father's attention, just who the hell am I?

A warm arm slides around my arms, pinning my hands to my side, and I stand there, cold and frozen, despite the radiating warmth of the body next to me. The charcoal grey of a sleeve in my peripheral and a familiar wintry scent does nothing to calm my mind.

I find my strength and push myself off Brandt's chest until we're a few feet apart. Both Riley and Brandt's eyes swim with worry, and I swear I see a tear roll down Riley's cheek. But I can't focus on that, or the growing sound of movement beyond the heavy doors, signalling that the service is over and people are preparing to leave. All I can hear is my panicked breathing, and all I can focus on is the prickle in my gut that's begging me to shatter. To collapse and hide from the world because the world only knows Elissa as her father's daughter, heiress to the Black media empire, an image of what her father *wanted* her to be. But who am I without my father's crushing disapproval?

I wish Lana was here, but her son Knox is sick with a fever, so she couldn't be here. I'm ever thankful my best friend is here right now. My eyes connect with Riley's and she gives a solemn nod. My best friend doesn't need words to know what I'm thinking. "Go. Take the driver and go," she whispers. My body responds, and without saying anything, I shove past Riley and Brandt and make my way to the front entrance, pulling my phone out of my clutch and texting Arthur.

I stop and lean against a railing on the way down the stairs and kick off my heels, holding them between my fingers so I can run the rest of the way to the car. I need to get out of here, fast, before the church empties and everyone sees me fleeing my father's funeral. Arthur pulls up just as I'm slipping my heels back on and hopping down the salted concrete stairs toward the car. The door slams as he gets out, walks around the side of the black sedan, and opens the door for me.

I slide in and he closes the door behind me, and when he gets back into the driver's seat, he doesn't ask where we're going, he just goes. I feel his eyes shift to the rearview mirror to check on me a few times as we drive through the chaos of downtown Toronto traffic. As my eyes swivel from one spot to the next, I shiver as I sympathize with those who have nowhere to go, sitting on the sidewalk, or huddling over the TTC subway grates for a small chance of warm air puffing through. I go to pull my coat around my neck to warm myself, and I realize I forgot it at St. Patrick's.

Without getting any directions of where to take me, Arthur glides to a stop and parks the car in front of a tall glass building. I peer out the window and look straight up. It feels like the building will never end. My shoulders are heavy as I press my forehead against the cool glass, creating a circle in the fogged-up window.

"Why are we here, Arthur?"

His deep, wise voice touches something inside me that calms me down.

"Because you need closure, Ms. Black. And I think it might be here." I look over to meet his gaze in the mirror. His amber eyes see me and his stare pierces my soul as my fingers wrap around the door handle. Arthur tips his head and tells me he'll be here when I'm finished.

"Thanks, Arthur." I climb out of the car, swing the door shut, and my keys jingle as I pull them out of my purse. My skin pebbles against the chilly wind as I twist my key in the lock and make my way inside. I nod my head at the security guard and make my way to the elevator, its muted humming the only noise in the lobby. When the doors slide closed, my finger hesitates over the button for my floor, but my finger seems to be magnetized to my father's floor.

I step into the dark corridor as the elevator closes behind me. It's eerily quiet, and only the natural light floods into the hallway from the windows. My heels echo in the open corridor as I walk to my father's office. His door is open, and everything looks normal. I half expect my father to turn around in his chair at any moment. I hear his hard, cold voice in my head from the last exchange we had, and a chill skates over my skin, raising the hair on my arms.

It's hard to focus when it feels like Harold is lurking around the corner, just waiting and biding his time to step out from the darkness and chuckle, like it's all some big joke. Even now, knowing he's gone, I still feel his presence.

Maybe he has unfinished business and is haunting his office right now. *Can you see me, Father?*

Pathetic. I'm talking to a ghost, a nonexistent ghost. I walk over to the large bookcase behind my father's desk and notice a picture of my parents and me at one of the obligatory family barbecues on Canada Day, years ago. I think I was around ten years old. My parents are standing on either side of me, and my father's black hair is short and slicked back, no noticeable greys. My mother's hair, very much like my own, is in a ponytail, with copper ringlets dangling down. She must have thought it would look more wholesome to have us matching, down to the white sundresses we're wearing, complemented by the khaki shorts and white linen shirt my father is wearing. My face is tight with a forced smile as my toes dig into the sand.

I remember that day clearly…

CHAPTER
NINE

ELISSA

Lana had to bribe me in order to get me to go to the company's Canada Day party. I am lounging on the couch, on my stomach, with one arm wrapped under my chin as the other dangled off the edge, flipping through a magazine in our downtown Toronto apartment when she sneaks up behind me. Her hands wrap around my shoulders and she yells, "Boo!"

I nearly jump out of my skin. My heart is racing and I struggle to catch my breath. I realize that I tore a page out of the magazine in fright. "Lana," I shriek. The sun is pouring in through the floor-to-ceiling windows of the penthouse, glittering off all the glass and shiny surfaces in the apartment. The cream couch I'm on is warm from the sun, and the heat prickles my skin.

"C'mon, kiddo. Time to go get ready for the barbecue."

I groan and scramble my legs, flailing and throwing a temper tantrum. "I'm not going, Mom. I don't want to, it's so boring." Lana clicks her tongue, her arms folding tightly and her foot tapping on the floor.

"Go get ready, Elissa. Your parents are expecting you. If you listen and get ready, I promise we'll leave early and go do something fun. What about if I take you to get our nails done afterward?" She piques my interest with that one. My mouth purses, considering this negotiation.

"Only if we can pick up Riley on the way."

"Deal," Lana says, sticking her hand out, waiting for me to take it. A grin twists on her face and when she shifts, the sun glints in her dark, almond-shaped eyes, and I can see the crinkles in the corners. I spring off the couch and sprint to my room to put on the clothes my mother had Lana lay out for me. Lana knocks on my door before entering, then walks in, turns on the curling iron, and gets to work on my hair. I sit in front of the vanity in my room as Lana brushes my hair, scraping it up into a high ponytail.

I stare at our reflection and wish that she was my mother. That it was just the two of us. And I know it's normally just the two of us anyway, but sometimes I wish there was no Harold or Collette, or Black & Wells Publishing and Press.

• • •

We arrive at the beach, the same one my father has used for his company celebration for years, and as soon as my feet touch the sand, I kick off my white flip-flops, the ones with tiny yellow sunflowers on the strap. I loop them through my fingers and my hand slips into Lana's as we walk the beach, looking for my parents. Along the way, I spot Riley and her parents, and I look to Lana, pleading silently if we can go over and say hi. She gives me a curt nod accompanied by a soft smile, and my heart leaps. I run over to where Riley and her parents are. Lana follows us and she chats with Mr. and Mrs. Jaimeson and I hear something about Riley coming with us after the party.

Riley's hand slips into mine as she pulls me toward the water, her other hand carrying two stacked buckets and some shovels. It's only been a few days since I've seen Riley at school, but it feels like a lifetime. As soon as school was over, my mother and father made me pack my things for another lonely summer in Toronto. We find a place close to the water so that we can haul the water and wet sand back and forth easily. She passes me a shovel and a bucket and I start digging as she takes another bucket and grabs some water.

An hour later, I'm being summoned. I hear a high-pitched voice calling me, the words dripping with elegance and fake parental love. "Elissa, baby. Come here, please." I see her French-manicured hand wave and some bangles slide down her thin wrist. My father is standing beside her, looking tense and impatient as I take my sweet time getting up out of the sand.

"I'll be right back, Riles," I groan. I push myself off the ground and stomp over to where my mother and father are.

"Jesus Christ, Collette. She's a fucking mess. Her dress is all dirty and she doesn't even have her sandals on."

"Calm down," she says to my father through gritted teeth. She waves her hand impatiently to Lana, who comes jogging over. "Clean this mess up and make her presentable. And where are your shoes, Elissa?" Lana's hands glide over my dress, swiping away the wrinkles and sand. I shrug my shoulders at my mother while Lana's hands tighten my ponytail. "Oh, forget it. Let's just get this over with so I can get a drink," my mother mumbles. Her hand wraps around my wrist, her nails digging into my skin as she pulls me toward my father and the photographer. She places me in the middle, in front of both of them, their hands weighing down my shoulders.

"Smile!" the photographer shouts, and the camera's shutter clicks as my mouth presses into a tight smile. My fingers curl into my sundress, making my knuckles white. Some of the other families pass by, murmuring things like "What a beautiful family," and "Aww, they look so lovely." My father smiles and waves to his subordinates and offers the photographer up for anyone who wants photos of their family. Ironic, huh? A man who has not one familial bone in his body makes a show of family for his company one day a year. And it's always mandatory. For his employees, whom he treats like family, and for his family, whom he treats like employees.

I wriggle out of my parents' grasp. "Are we done yet?" It comes out as more of a whine than I hoped. My father's warm, sunny face clouds over to a stormy grey, his eyes narrowing.

"We are done when I say we are done, you ungrateful child. Now, come along. We need to do the rounds and check in with everyone, and I need my *family* there." I throw a glance over my shoulder and see Riley with a few other employees' kids, and they're building a massive sandcastle. My heart sinks and tears well in my eyes when a warm hand is placed on my back and rubs in small circles. I look up and there's *Mom*. The only person I truly need. Lana's face stretches into a warm smile and she whispers, low enough so only I can hear.

"One hour, baby. Then we can go."

• • •

My fingers curl around the golden picture frame and I lift it off the shelf. My knuckles glow white as I grip the picture and the memories it represents. I crank my arm back and hurl the frame across the room, where it shatters against the wall, falling to the ground in glass shards and broken metal. My eyes roll shut. *Damn, that felt good.* I pick another item up off the shelf. It's a diamond-shaped glass trophy for "Best Media Outlet, 2000." I turn around and hurl it, hard. It flies across the room and smashes to the ground near his office door. Another swell of good rises in me. My hands wipe across my father's desk, causing his computer screen, keyboard, mouse, pens — everything on the surface — to scatter, crash, and tumble to the ground. I get a tingle in my body, feeling the adrenaline pumping.

I turn back to the bookshelf and start ripping things off. Binders, books, other knick knacks, and random trinkets. Everything goes soaring around the room, clashing and crashing. It's cathartic, euphoric, *freeing*. When I whip the last thing off the shelf, my chest is heaving. The blood in my veins is pumping, and I feel alive like never before. Until the guilt and something else settles in. Squeezing around me like a boa constrictor, snaking itself around my body. My throat feels like it's closing as I stumble around his desk, grabbing the edge for support. My legs give out under me and I fall to the ground. Little shards of glass cut into my knees as I settle to the floor, but I don't feel the sting.

My sinuses burn as I fight back the tears threatening to burst through. I'm heaving again, but this time panic is rising up in me. *What is wrong with me?* A tear breaks free from the dam and I'm undone. Sobbing for a father who was never there, sobbing for a life I never had, sobbing for the emptiness I feel inside. I sniffle, rubbing my tears away with the back of my hand before I take a deep breath and hold it, calming myself down. I jiggle the dainty Rolex on my wrist and check the time. It's been an hour. I stand up on unsteady legs and hobble over to find my clutch. I pull out my phone and there's a message from Riley.

Riley: *We took a cab back to the apartment. See you there when you're ready.*

God, I love her. I snort back some more tears and snot and brush myself off, picking the glass out of my knee-caps. Tossing my hair behind my back, I roll my shoulders and head toward the elevator and back to the car so Arthur can drive me home.

CHAPTER
TEN

BRANDT

It's been a few weeks since Harold's funeral, and I think Elissa has been holding up pretty well. I haven't seen her cry, and, other than the weird funeral eulogy, that's the only out-of-character thing she's done. She hasn't set foot on the twenty-second floor, where her father's office is, since the funeral, when she destroyed everything. That day is still so fresh in my mind.

Riley and I are waiting anxiously for Elissa to return when she walks in. Her shoes are in her hands and her knees are scraped, with a trickle of dried blood running down her leg. Riley rushes toward her, face white as a ghost, and her hands wrap around Elissa's wrists, dragging her to sit at the kitchen island.

Elissa slides onto the leather seat, her black polished toes wriggling as her feet dangle. Her shoes clatter to the ground where she drops them. She places her clutch on the counter beside her. Riley sprints back into the kitchen with a first-aid kit from the washroom. She places the white box on the counter and rummages through it, pulling out rubbing alcohol, some cotton balls, and bandages.

My hand finds Elissa's and I slide her cold hand into my warm one, giving it a squeeze. Elissa winces as Riley dabs the cotton ball soaked with alcohol on her cuts, cleaning them carefully before placing bandages on them.

"How did you do this?" Riley asks with concern. Elissa winces again as she answers.

"I went to my father's office on the way home, and I kind of lost it. I was throwing stuff around, broke some glass and accidentally fell and cut myself on the glass shards. I'm fine though," she says, wincing again. "Oooh."

Riley rolls her eyes at Elissa and mumbles something under her breath that's hard to catch. I study Elissa to make sure she's okay. Her eyes squeeze shut and her nose wrinkles as Riley pats the edge of the bandage on her knee.

"All done," Riley mumbles, standing and collecting the wrappers and cotton balls and tossing them into the garbage. Elissa relaxes into the chair as she sighs, her grip loosening on my hand. "So, want to tell me why you destroyed your father's office?" Riley's voice is stern and wary. Elissa looks away, her gaze lingering on somewhere in the living room. She shrugs absently and shakes her head.

"I don't know. Arthur drove me to the Black & Wells tower and my subconscious took me straight to his office. I was looking around, trying to feel something. And something inside me broke and then I started breaking stuff." Riley's face twitches with concern. "But seriously, I'm fine." Riley's body slumps in relief, but her eyes are still vigilant, like she doesn't quite believe what she's hearing.

"Collette and the publicist were telling everyone that you were just distraught that your father is gone," Riley says. Elissa bursts out laughing, rolling her eyes and shaking her head.

"Of course they did. They'll do whatever it takes to save face, even if it means I'm speaking the truth. My little outburst probably worked in their favour, and I'm mad at myself for that." Elissa shudders. Her hand slips from mine as she slides off the stool to stand, bending her knees one at a time to work in the bandages. "Thanks for taking care of me, Riles. You're going to be an excellent mom." Riley's face blooms red as she packs up the first-aid kit and returns it to the washroom. Elissa saunters closer to me, wraps her hand around mine, and pulls me closer to her bedroom.

• • •

Since that night, everything has been fine. She's been staying at my place more often now that we're official, and let me be the first to say — it's nice. I finally have her, and I can't screw up and lose her again. It's so nice having her lithe body next to mine when we wake up, and it feels good when my arm coils around her waist, tugging her in close so that her ass is snug against my cock. It feels nice being able to bury my face in her bronze hair and inhale the scent of her vanilla and coconut shampoo.

I was a little worried at first, when we found out her father died, that she would break, run away again. But she hasn't. I'd be lying if I said I wasn't a little apprehensive about her mental state — even knowing she wasn't close with her father, there's been little grieving. But honestly, she's been fine. Elissa has been perfect at work, like always. Always professional, always focused. She mentions little things like "when Riley takes over the apartment…" and "not sure where I'll end up…" it's almost like she's hinting at something. Hinting at moving in with me. But that couldn't be what she means, because really, we just started actually dating. I would say yes in a heartbeat, but I know she's just lamenting over having to find a new place. *Right*?

Regardless, for once, it feels like everything is clicking into place. Black & Wells' new division is operating well right now with Selena and Elissa at the helm, so well that I've been able to step back a little and make more time for my real company, Collins Global Collective. Elissa has even promoted Selena officially to her position as "Assistant Department Director."

A wad of crumpled paper swooshes through the air and bounces off my face.

"Earth to Collins," Rhys grumbles. I shake myself from my inner thoughts and focus on my best friend. Rhys Kessler and Liam West are sitting across from me in my office at CGC. They're slumped in the chairs, feet wide apart, and arms thrown over the back of the chairs, looking like bookends. Liam has been avoiding me after the whole thing with Elissa. They slept together one night, nine months ago, and he acted like they were soul mates. We've hung out a few times since then, mostly when we all get together to play basketball, but we haven't seen much of him since I started sleeping with Elissa.

My eyes dart to Rhys and I furrow my brows at him for throwing the paper.

"As I was saying…" Rhys continues, "Liam and I are going out tonight to have some drinks and hit on some girls. I *know* you're not available, but you can still come with us. We need to get laid, and you can help entertain the other women for us if there's a group of them." Before I can say anything, Rhys claps his hands. "Great, it's settled then. We'll all go out tonight." I huff, rolling my eyes.

"What about Riley?" I ask. Rhys' breath catches and his body tenses. His hands slowly curl into fists, then relax. His jaw pulses, then he takes a deep breath.

"Man, why do you have to bring her up?"

"I just don't see why you're going out, planning on getting laid, when you have a baby on the way."

"*Might* have a baby on the way," Rhys snipes. I grind my teeth as my eyes narrow and fold my arms across my chest.

"You really think Riley would lie about it being your baby? C'mon man, stop being a pussy and own up to your shit. Be the goddamn man we know you are, not this scared little boy running away from his problems." I glance at Liam and he just shrugs, as if he has no opinion on the matter.

"What?" Liam asks, when I stare at him expectantly, hoping he'll weigh in on the conversation. "I don't really know Riley like you two. I can't say if she'd lie about that or not." *No fucking help.* To be honest, I sometimes get the feeling that he doesn't actually like me. Even before the Elissa thing. We've known each other for years — since high school — and he's always been a bit closed off. Part of me wonders if it's because I upset the balance between him and Rhys when I moved to their school in freshman year. They were best friends before I came along, then we became a trio of sorts. I mean, I could care less about his problems with me and my being friends with Rhys, but it still grates on my nerves whenever he seems to take Rhys' side just because.

"Whatever. But I am not going with you two tonight, you're on your own. If Elissa found out, she'd be pissed at me."

"Be pissed at you? For what? Going out with your friends for some drinks? That's some bullshit, man. We both know how Elissa parties — partied." My teeth grit and my blood starts to boil from hearing him talk about her that way.

"First of all," I growl, "Do not talk about Elissa that way. And you know as well as I do it's not because of getting drinks with you two. She'd be pissed because I am enabling your fuckboy ways, even though you knocked up her best friend. And you know that I don't agree with what you're doing or how you're choosing to handle the situation."

My phone vibrates across my desk, tearing my attention away from the conversation.

Eli: *Are you coming over tonight?*

"Who's that? *Elissa?*" Rhys sneers. I flip him off and text her back.

Me: *Sure. The guys wanted me to go out tonight for drinks, but I'd rather pass anyway.*

Three dots bounce on my screen as I wait for her reply.

Eli: *Okay. If you want to come over tomorrow, that's okay too.*
Me: *No. I'll be there. I'll bring dinner for the three of us.*

"Sorry, Rhys. I've got plans tonight," I say, tossing my phone back on my desk.

CHAPTER ELEVEN

ELISSA

It's only a few days into February, but we finally got the call about my father's will. I guess it took a while for everything to be put in place and the lawyers to go over everything in detail. My mother called me this morning to let me know about the will reading on Friday. It was said that only my mother and I were bequeathed anything, other than the random charities he donated to. Ugh, that word. *Bequeathed.* The last thing I want is anything from my father.

But the thing I know is that my fate is tied to the will. My father made it very clear that I would inherit nothing unless I marry Brandt. I've resigned myself to the fact that

I'll either be exiled from the company I've worked so hard to be a part of, a company I never even wanted to be part of in the first place, or I'll be married to Brandt within a year — if I want anything to do with the company.

I groan as I roll my ass out of bed, just as a strong arm encircles my waist. As I place my feet on the chilly hardwood floor, Brandt's fingers dig into my hip, and he pulls me back into the bed.

"Not yet," he mumbles, pressing lazy kisses against my back. His lips warm my skin, stirring a heat in my groin. I wrestle out of Brandt's grip and toss my hair over my shoulder as I look at him.

"Got to shower and then head back to my place to get ready for work. It's going to be another long day. I decided to hire a new assistant for Selena, so we're meeting with applicants today." Brandt musses the bed as he sits up, the sheet cascading down his torso and collecting at his waist, showing off his rigid abs. He leans back against the headboard and his strong, corded forearms flex as he pushes himself up.

Knowing Brandt's eyes are on me, I sway my hips a bit more dramatically as I walk to the washroom, making sure my ass is taut and enticing. A few moments later, I hear the springs of the bed creak and footsteps fall into step behind me. I twist on the shower tap as Brandt's warm, hard body presses against my back and his arms drape around my waist as he nuzzles my neck. His tongue flicks out and licks my skin, causing a shiver to run through my body.

Steam billows, fogging up the glass walls of Brandt's shower. He moves us into his walk-in shower, kissing and sucking my neck as his hands palm and squeeze my breasts from behind. His cock throbs between my cheeks, growing harder as we stumble into the shower, the scorching water burning our skin. My nipples pucker as he presses me against the freezing tiled wall and his hands wrap around my hips, pulling my lower half away from the wall. His hand dives between my legs and strokes my clit with the rough pad of his middle finger.

His cock grows behind me, twitching against my ass. He swivels his hips, the tip of his cock popping between my folds as he circles his fingers on my clit faster. The thick tip is warm and slick against my opening as he teases me, and I arch my back higher to try and slide him into me. He pulls away, not allowing himself to enter me. He spins me around and my feet slip against the pebbled floor as he pushes me against the wall and falls to his knees.

My chest is heaving as I suck in every breath, anticipating his warm breath on my pussy. He kisses my pubic bone and trails his tongue down to the centre of my core, kissing it gently before devouring it. Brandt's teeth nip at my clit, and I throw a leg over his shoulder to allow him more access. A flick of his tongue on my clit sends sparks shooting to my toes, and I wrap my fists in his golden hair. He laps at my lips and clit, faster and faster. Alternating between licking and sucking until the stars start to shine behind my eyelids. I'm almost there when he...pulls away.

I'm panting, squirming, and writhing for him to bring me to the edge. He stands up and cups his hand over my mound and shoves two fingers deep into me. The heel of his hand is rubbing against my clit slowly as he drags his fingers in and out of me.

"Brandt, *please*. I *need* to come."

A dark chuckle rumbles from his throat as his lips claim mine, his tongue plunging into my mouth, and I taste myself. He's keeping me on the edge, speeding up his movements with his hand one minute, and the next minute slowing it down, pulling me back from the edge. Every time he does it, the smile on his lips grows the more I grow impatient and whimper.

"I want to be inside you," he mumbles. I'm gushing wet, my arousal dripping down my legs, mixing with the stream of water beating down on us.

"*Yes, please*," I whine. He grabs my leg and hooks it over his hip, lines himself up against my lips, and presses his thick head into me, and stops. "What now?" I groan. I'm panting and every nerve in my body is about to catch fire if I don't feel his dick inside me right now.

"No condom. Are you sure?" he growls. My hands reach down and clench around his ass, slamming his pelvis into mine and his cock into my pussy. We both moan and take a moment to catch our breaths. His hand grabs my wrists and pins them above my head while his other hand grabs onto my ass where my leg is hooked to him. Water runs between our bodies, making it all too easy for him to slide in and out of me. He rocks into me, one deep penetrating thrust at a time. He rolls his hips and squeezes my ass as he slams into me.

"Fuck, this feels too good," Brandt grumbles. I agree, and to feel Brandt unsheathed is overwhelmingly fantastic.

I feel his smooth skin and every vein pumping blood into his dick as it rubs inside me. I tilt my hips just enough and he's hitting me deep, bumping off my cervix. Feverish kisses crash against my lips as Brandt's breathing becomes ragged. "I don't know how much longer I can hold on. *Fuck!*" He recoils and pulls out of me, dropping his head to my shoulder, heaving every breath he takes. "One…second…" he says between breaths. I feel his forehead scrunch against my shoulder. He lets my hands fall, and he turns me around, pressing me against the wall again with my ass popping out. My hands press against the tile as I'm bent over.

He slides back into me, slowly, and takes another moment to adjust. His fingers dig into my hips as he starts to move. He gathers speed as he pistons into me, and his hand releases my hip and spreads my lips, rubbing my clit.

"Come for me, Eli," he grumbles, railing into me harder and rubbing my clit faster. It doesn't take long to rev me up again, and I'm speeding toward that climax. My toes curl, and the blood in my veins runs hot, bubbling underneath my skin. I feel him tense and suddenly my pussy is clenching around him, and fireworks are shooting off in my body. My pussy throbs as he pulls out, spilling hot liquid all over my ass and lower back. The sticky come runs down my cheeks to my legs. I finally notice all the water I'm breathing into my mouth, and the water that's pouring down my face.

After we've cleaned up, I'm back in his room, pulling on my clothes from yesterday. It's already 6:35 AM. *Shit. I'm going to be late if I don't hurry up.* I fling my wet hair over one shoulder as I tug my jeans on and button them up when soft lips tickle my shoulder, causing goosebumps to rise.

"You should leave some stuff here," Brandt rumbles in my ear, his voice low. My heart stutters in my chest, and I'm left breathless. *What did he just say?* When I don't respond, he walks around me, wrapping an arm around my waist and chucking a finger under my chin, tilting my head up to meet his eyes. His smooth, wintry-fresh scent rolls off his body and into my nose, and it dances with the mint of his breath. "Nothing crazy, but at least a few changes of clothes and a toothbrush. You've been spending more time here, and it only makes sense to have a few items just in case." I look into his eyes and see a slight tinge of red spreading across his cheeks. Something flutters and loops in my chest, and beads of sweat trickle down my spine. I give him a smile and raise up on my tiptoes to press a kiss to his lips.

"I'll think about it. See you at the office today?"

He nods, his shoulders sagging a little as I step out of his embrace and toward the door. I give him one last roaming look and take in his perfect body — the muscles, the abs, the "V" that has my eyes trailing down to the plush white towel that's wrapped around his waist. God, I wish I could rip that towel off him right now and take him in my mouth.

CHAPTER
TWELVE

ELISSA

Friday comes quickly, and I'm sitting in the lawyer's office with my mother, Brandt, and Riley. There's a trio of lawyers sitting around a long oval table with us on the other side. Both Riley and Brandt insisted on being here today to support me. My stomach roils and I feel like I'm going to be sick. What could my father possibly have left me? He made it clear that I was to get nothing unless I were to marry Brandt. But Brandt wasn't even asked to attend the reading, so he's not part of the will, which is curious.

My mother is wearing a black Chanel dress that's cinched at the waist with a belt that has a golden clasp.

Her brown Louis Vuitton bag clashes with her outfit, but I don't think my mother cares at this moment. Her ginger hair is scraped into a neat chignon, with a few curled strands framing her face. The pearl earrings match the rope of pearls draped around her neck. Everything about my mother screams elegance and class, but her face betrays that portrait. Her cheeks are hollow, eyes are sunken and worn, and her lips are chapped. Even the tastefully applied make-up does little to hide these imperfections on her face.

Riley is sitting between my mother and I, and every time Collette moves, I get a whiff of her Chanel No. 5 perfume, and it reminds me of loneliness. Her hands fiddle with her wedding band and engagement ring, which are soldered together, twirling them around her finger, which I notice are slim and bony. Something inside me stirs, and I feel for my mother, though I'm not quite sure why.

Brandt's hand gently rests on my thigh and squeezes, and I'm momentarily distracted from my mother. I give Brandt a reassuring smile as I place my hand on top of his and squeeze back. The lawyers continue shuffling papers while we wait for them to get organized. *Shouldn't they have been organized by now? My God, what kind of incompetent fools did my father hire?* One of the lawyers, a man with grey hair and large, aviator-style glasses, coughs, sits up straight, and folds his hands on top of a manila folder. The other two finally finish shuffling their papers and follow his lead. The man to the right is younger, maybe in the running for partner. He's fairly good-looking, with dark chestnut hair, bright, light eyes, and a chiselled jaw. He looks to be about thirty or so, and his eyes roam from Riley to me. I feel the heat in his eyes as he stares at me.

His mouth twitches as he suppresses a smile, and a shiver breaks over me as I feel an arctic chill coming from my right. Brandt is sitting up ramrod-straight, his jaw is tense, and eyes are cold and unyielding. His fingers press harder into my thigh, and if I didn't know better, I'd swear I heard him growl. My hand wraps around his again, prying his fingers from my leg, and I lace my fingers between his. He seems to relax a little and takes a deep breath. But his eyes remain cold. I think the good-looking lawyer notices, because the shadow of a smile creeps across his face as he clears his throat and returns his expression to more of a neutral state.

The older man in the middle clears his throat.

"I am Mr. Durphy, the lead lawyer on this case. I see we have a few extra people here for the reading of Harold Wallace Black's will." His voice is gruff, but shaky, as though his vocal cords want to collapse from exhaustion. "I need to ensure that the main two people present that are involved in the will are comfortable with the extra people witnessing the contents, for the record." He looks at my mother and then me over his glasses. My mother nods, giving a weak "yes."

"Yes," I say in a clear, loud voice. Mr. Durphy gives a quick nod as he flips open the file folder in front of him. The other two lawyers follow suit, the younger one making a note of our confirmation of extra people in the room. Mr. Durphy adjusts the glasses on his hooked nose and clears his throat again.

"The last will and testament of: Harold Wallace Black. I, Harold Wallace Black, of Toronto, Ontario, being of sound mind and body, do hereby declare that this document is my last will and testament..." He drones on and I drown him out for the next few minutes as he gets through all the legal mumbo jumbo, which literally means nothing to me. *Hell, being here and inheriting something literally means nothing to me.*

"...Article 3. I hereby give all personal property, including the houses and contents within, to my wife, Collette Liana (Morgen) Black. These properties include our investment properties in Chatham, Ontario, and our penthouse in Toronto, Ontario, on Richmond Street. My RRSPs and joint chequing and savings accounts will remain with Collette Liana (Morgen) Black. All vehicles will be sold, and the money returned to the savings account for Collette."

My mother lets out a sob, and Riley reaches across the table to pluck a tissue out of the box and passes it to her. My mother's hand grasps the tissue with one hand as the other hand braces around Riley's forearm, her eyes full of thanks. A cold sweat breaks out over me as I watch and listen to my mother cry. Part of me has a bubble waiting to burst with giggles at the ridiculous scene unfolding, but another part aches for her. I didn't realize my mother actually cared. I mean, they must have loved each other at one point in their lives. I see the pictures from their wedding day and they certainly looked in love, and you can't fake that kind of lightness in the eyes. But I'd only ever seen unhappy parents, who spent time together only when it was convenient for pictures and appearances.

Harold was always gone, doing who knows what, with who knows who, but claimed he was always working. Which, he must have been telling the truth at some point, because for all my father lacked, his work ethic certainly didn't. He did build a successful media empire, one which I am doomed to drown under in the shadow of his legacy — if I even inherit the damn company. Collette, on the other hand, was always sloshed, always a bottle of merlot deep by 11 AM, and with a new "pool boy" who was missing the pool.

"And to my daughter, Elissa Beatrice Black, I hereby hand over the Black & Wells Publishing and Press company and all its assets, along with the Black & Wells Tower property deeds…"

My heart fails to beat, my lungs fail to breathe. *What did Mr. Durphy just say?* My cheeks tingle as the blood drains from my face, leaving me cold and gasping for air. I can't hear Mr. Durphy speaking anymore, he sounds like an adult in a *Peanuts* cartoon. I get the company? Me?

"I'm sorry," I interrupt Mr. Durphy, "Did I hear that correctly?"

"S-s-sorry? Hear what correctly?" he asks haltingly.

"That I'm to inherit the company? *All* of it?"

Mr. Durphy adjusts the glasses on his face again, looks over the last part he read and nods his head. "Yes, I believe that you are inheriting everything to do with the company as per this wording."

"That would make me CEO?"

Mr. Durphy clears his throat. "Well, I suppose so. Not quite officially, but you'd be the major shareholder and chair*person* of the board. The board members would have to vote you in to make it official." I'm floored. If I wasn't sitting down already, I would have crashed to the floor. Seriously.

"I…I don't understand. I just get the company?"

"The company, the building, and the condo you're currently residing in. It's all yours."

"Just like that?" I'm not quite convinced it's that easy. There's that stipulation that's missing.

"Well, after you sign some papers, it's yours. But yes, just like that."

This has got to be a joke. I laugh out loud. My mother and Riley look at me with bewildered eyes. I don't even turn to see how Brandt is staring at me.

"No other stipulations? No clauses? Nothing?" Mr. Durphy's face twists in…disgust? Confusion? I don't know. But he shakes his head and remains silent. I feel Brandt tense beside me, and his hand grows rigid in mine, cold even. But I can't focus on him. I can only focus on the fact that everything is mine, even when it wasn't supposed to be. *Ha! What sick twist of fate is this?*

"Is this the most updated version of the will? When was it dated?" A deep, tense voice booms beside me, making the hair on my arms stand. My head darts to face Brandt and he's sitting like a statue, trying to keep measured breaths, his jaw ticking as he waits for a response. The good-looking lawyer is the one to flip through the pages and find the answer.

"It looks here to be signed and dated back in 2021. So, two years prior to his death, and this is the only will we have that is recent and notarized." Brandt's hand jerks out of my grasp and tightens into a fist in his lap. His eyes harden and it feels like the room has dropped thirty degrees. I reach out and place my hand on his and he pulls away, and I feel like I've been slapped. I shift my attention away, back to the lawyers, and try to finish listening to the rest of the will. Something just shifted between us, and it's making it really hard to focus on the rest of this meeting.

CHAPTER
THIRTEEN

ELISSA

We're all standing on the sidewalk outside the lawyers' building; my mother is standing off to the side texting her driver to come around to the front of the building.

"Did you want to go for lunch, Elissa?" my mother asks me. "Riley and Brandt are welcome to join as well." Riley's eyes light up at the mere mention of food, but Brandt still looks cold and distant.

"Sure, Mother," I say. I look at Brandt and he's rigid, busy messaging someone on his phone.

"Sorry," he says, not looking away from his phone. "But I have another meeting I need to get to." He slides his phone in his jacket pocket and takes a deep breath, the exhale fogging in the air. I step toward him, my heel squishing on the slushy sidewalk as his gloved hand raises up in the air to hail a cab. Stepping into his open chest, I wrap my arms around him and he's tense. Every muscle in his body is unmoving and I can feel the quickening of his heart pounding in his chest. His one arm slinks lazily around my waist. I tilt my head up to reach his, pressing a kiss to his mouth, but his lips don't move. My heart sinks in my chest, and a hot, sickening surge of anxiety courses through me.

Brandt steps around me when the car approaches. Without another word or look, he gets in, closes the door, and the car pulls away, leaving me standing there, stunned.

• • •

Riley's eyes haven't left me since Brandt drove away. Her eyes are swimming with concern, while my mother, on the other hand, is oblivious. Honestly, I'm a little worried about her. We're sitting in the new location of Griddle Cakes in Toronto, and she hasn't made one snide remark. She's staring at the menu, but her eyes are glazed, unseeing. The place is bustling with customers, and we had to wait in line for thirty minutes before we were seated. The new location looks like it's taken off, but also it's Friday — all-you-can-eat pancakes for $12.99. I'm so happy for Becca, and for her second location. I'm a little surprised she opened it in downtown Toronto; I would've thought that Kingston would have gotten another location first.

"Oh. My. God. Is that Riley and Elissa?" a familiar voice gushes from behind me. I turn around and there is

Becca, with her arms balancing steaming plates of pancakes. "One second, ladies." She bustles away, her long brunette hair swishing in a ponytail as she moves at a brisk pace, dropping off pancakes to five different tables. She brushes her hands off on her black mini apron that's tied around her hips. Her face brightens as she nears us, and Riley and I push ourselves away from the table, both opening our arms for hugs.

"What are you doing here?" Riley asks. I shoot her a disappointing look. "I mean, I'm glad you're here and doing so well, apparently. But, I mean, why are *you* here? What about Kingston?" Becca's smile doesn't falter, even though Riley's comment came off a little rude. On the contrary, Becca looks proud.

"I hired a store manager for that store and she's perfect, basically another me. So, I packed my things and came to Toronto to open this place." Her arms spread wide as she motions around her. "It's been non-stop since I opened a few weeks ago. Oh," her face falls, dampening the mood a bit. "I heard about your father. I'm sorry, Elissa." Her hands rub along my arms and I give her a forced, tight smile.

"Thanks, Becca. By the way, this is my mother, Collette. Mother, this is our friend from Kingston, Becca. She owns Griddle Cakes, both in Kingston and Toronto," I say with pride, and Becca glows, sticking her hand out to my mother. My mother grabs her hand and gives it a light shake.

"Nice to meet you, Collette."

"Yes, nice to meet you, too," Collette says in a strained voice. Becca doesn't seem to take offence to it; she's probably chalking it up to grief from losing my father.

"Well, I'll let you guys get back to lunch. Let me know if there's anything special I can get you. Your server will be over in a few minutes. It's so great seeing you two," Becca beams. She looks a lot healthier and happier than the last time we saw her. The bags under her eyes are less prominent and less dark, and she seems less frazzled.

My mother continues to look over her menu until the server comes over to take our order. My mother places an order for eggs Benedict, and Riley and I order the all-you-can-eat pancakes. My mother's eyes bulge out of her head.

"*Elissa*," she admonishes. "That's a little excessive, don't you think? All-you-can-eat should never be a thing. It's gluttonous, you need to be careful or it will catch up with you. Especially being *carbs*." I grind my teeth at her comment.

"Don't ruin it. I think this is the most time we've spent in each other's presence since I was born. Let's just have a good lunch, shall we? You can pick on my eating habits another day." I pick up the spoon sitting on the side of the upside-down mug on the table and clank the hilt of the spoon on the table. My mother's lips press together, thinning into a tight smile. She lifts her hand in the air and the rich scents of rose and jasmine float in the air as she flags down the server, impatient as ever. I roll my eyes and Riley's foot burrows into my shin. "Ouch, bitch," I mutter under my breath, and a smile breaks across Riley's face.

A few bites into our food, my mother places her cutlery down for a moment and studies me.

"Yes?" I ask. Her eyes narrow, but not in an aggressive way, more contemplative.

"So, have you given any thought as to what you're going to do with the company?" The thrumming in my body becomes erratic; I did *not* expect this conversation to happen right now.

"I'm not sure what you mean."

My mother scoffs, clasping her hands together, elbows digging into the table.

"Oh, don't play stupid with me. I'm not as dumb as I may have been portrayed or acted, but I do know what's going on and what Harold left to you. I was there in that meeting. We both know that is not what we expected." I swallow a painful mouthful of pancakes. My mother's eyes, which apparently I inherited from her, are sharp as daggers as they skewer me.

"I don't know," I say after washing my bite down with coffee. "I guess I'm going to see what the board wants to do and see if they appoint me as CEO and go from there. I mean, I've never wanted this company or wanted to work for it, so I could sell it. That would've really pissed Harold off." I chuckle to myself at the thought of him haunting me from beyond the grave because I sold his Black media empire out from the Black name. My mother's face turns solemn and drains of any playfulness. *Was there even any there to begin with?*

"You *know* that is not what I mean. We both know I am talking about the man that you were supposed to marry in order to inherit anything." My insides vibrate from just the mere mention of Brandt, and a lump forms in my throat, forcing me to bite back the tears, tears that are coming for reasons I don't understand.

"I'm not sure why anything has to be done? Things are fine." Riley's eyes are pinging back and forth from my mother to me, both with entertainment and worry. I shift in my chair, trying to get out of this hot seat.

"Elissa, we both know you don't do whatever the hell you're doing with him. You're seriously telling me you're not thinking about running for the hills right now? You're no longer obligated or tied to him. You're free."

"Collette, that wasn't necessary. Brandt is good for Elissa…" I hear Riley say.

Free. I'm not obligated or tied to Brandt, or *anyone*. I'm *free*. I knew this earlier, but I don't think it really hit me until now, until my mother confirmed it. I'm free from all expectations, obligations, and previous agreements. I'm free of my father and the crippling weight of his disappointment and expectations. Not like in university when I felt free, I am truly free. I can finally be me.

But…who am I without the expectations, obligations, and constant need for approval?

Who am I when I can finally *be* me?

CHAPTER
FOURTEEN

BRANDT

"Dude, you don't look so good," Rhys says, leaning against the doorway of my office. His ankles are crossed and his arms are folded over his chest.

"Thanks, jackass."

"So, I take it the will reading didn't go very well?" Rhys scrubs a hand in the new beard he's sporting and I clench my jaw.

"It went well. For Elissa and Collette."

Rhys pushes off the doorframe and stalks into my office, settling in a chair in front of me and crossing his ankle over his leg. "What does that mean?"

"It means Harold never updated his will or put in any stipulations about marriage, so she got the company anyway." Fuck. When I didn't hear the stipulations for Elissa inheriting the company, the world shifted under me. I acted like an asshole and pushed her away. It's not necessarily because the stipulations aren't there. I'd rather Elissa choose to be with me and marry me of her own accord, but without those conditions, I'm scared she's going to take off and leave me again, and I'll be fucking crushed. Again. Rhys sits up straight, his full focus on me and interest written on his face.

"She fucking left you again, didn't she?"

I grimace.

"Not yet. But who the fuck knows with her." I slump in my chair and swirl around to face the window behind me, with weak beams of sunlight poking through grey, snowy clouds. I sigh, dropping my head into my hands and rubbing the frustration away. "I never fucking know with her. She seemed fine at the reading, though. I was the jackass today. I was the one who pushed her away. But I couldn't fucking deal with the thought that she might break things off. God, I'm such a goddamn pussy." Rhys doesn't say anything, and I'm not sure if that's a good thing or bad.

"Speaking of pussies. How are you doing, *dad?*" I spin around in my chair and give Rhys a mocking smile. His eyes darken and ice over.

"Not funny, dude. I finally booked an appointment at a clinic for a blood draw to find out if I'm the father. Riley's still a bit pissy about it, but she agreed to meet me at the appointment in two weeks."

"Two weeks is a long time. Don't you think it'd be better to suck it up and just be a father to the kid that *is* yours? Deep down you know it's yours, and once it's confirmed and you get over this anger at Riley, you're going to regret missing all the time with her and the early stages of her pregnancy. To be quite honest, I'm not even sure why you're still mad at Riley for anything. You're the one who fucking dumped her when she was going through something hard. You're the one who screwed her without a condom and dropped her again right after. You're the one denying his responsibility in any of the wrongs in your relationship. It's not like you, man. I think you pushed her away because you got scared about how real things got so quickly for you. She's your first real relationship that's lasted more than a week."

Rhys' face hardens and turns a shade of scarlet, and his hands tighten into fists on his thighs.

"Fuck you, man. You're one to talk. You just admitted to pushing Elissa away and she's your first real relationship too," he spits back at me. I laugh and he looks at me like I've lost it. I laugh again, a bit harder this time, and his face cracks. A few seconds later and he's laughing along with me.

"We're both fucked," I say.

"Absolutely."

• • •

I return home later that night and I check my phone as I walk through the door, with a bag of tacos underneath my arm. I have a few ignored messages, about fifteen minutes apart from the last two hours.

Eli: *So, you ran out of the lawyers' office pretty fast today, and didn't come into Black & Wells. Everything okay?*
Eli: *Do you want me to come over tonight, or are you coming here?*
Eli: *Okay...good night then.*

Fuck. I'm such a dick. I just need time to process. *But she hasn't even given you any indication anything has changed.* Yeah, I fucking know that. *So, why are you still pushing her away?* Why *am* I still pushing her away? *Because you don't trust her.* No, that's not it. It can't be. I trust her. *Sure, just not with your heart.* Oh, shut up you fucking moron. Great...I'm arguing with myself.

I toss my keys and wallet onto the counter beside the food and shove my phone back in my pocket. I stalk over to the cupboards and pull down a plate and grab a beer from the fridge. The brown bag crinkles as I unroll it, and I lift out my paper-wrapped tacos as meaty and cheesy steam coils in the air, then place the tacos on the plate. Opening the fridge again, I grab the hot sauce and lace my tacos liberally. Sliding the plate across the island to the other side where the stools are, I grab my beer, twist off the cap and toss it into the sink, and round the counter to take a seat.

I shift my weight and drive my hand into my pocket to pull out my phone. Placing the phone on the counter, I side-eye it like it's a bomb, ready to explode at any moment. I fist a taco, eyes still trained on the phone as I bring the taco up to my mouth and sink my teeth into it. Carefully chewing and still staring at the phone, I try to contemplate what I should do. If I'm being honest, I love her. I've always loved her, even before I really knew her. But I don't know if I can go through the emotional rollercoaster of waiting for her to decide what she wants. My feelings are already all jumbled up in this messy arrangement — well, no ar-rangement now.

You're not going to get any answers avoiding her. Ugh, I know. But I can't deal with it right now; I can't be that guy whose feelings are used as a doormat. Now that I'm no longer convenient for her, I can't play fast and loose with my feelings. At least when she had to marry me, I had an end goal in sight. I had something akin to a promise that things would play out exactly that way. Now that she doesn't have to marry me, we could go back to only being business partners, and I'm not sure if I can handle that.

I take a swig of my beer and rip another bite out of my taco. Mashing the food between my teeth, I almost take a chunk out of my tongue. Irritation and anxiety grip me like a skeleton clawing its way out of the grave. I'm at a loss of what to do, if there's anything to do. Should I just let it play out and see what happens? Do I face this head on and ask her what's going to happen? Or do I cut my losses — which will still hurt like hell — and walk away from the only woman who's ever managed to wrangle herself into my heart? Sure, there was Lexi, but it just wasn't right. It wasn't the same as Elissa. Part of me is scared that if it's not Elissa, it'll be no one.

I toss my empty plate into the sink and rinse my beer bottle out before grabbing another one and tossing the lid into the recycling bin. I lean my back against the counter, crossing my ankles, and folding my arms with my beer in hand, staring off into the distance. This thing with Elissa, this…trying to have a real relationship thing…just start-ed — I'm scared it's not even going to have a chance to go anywhere before she bolts. And then what do I do? Go back to a miserable, Elissa-less existence? *Fuck.*

So, I don't know what I am going to do when she no longer wants to continue this thing we have. I'm going to be a broken shell of a man. There's one thing she can't deny and that's the chemistry we have. It's electric, mag-netic. It's almost all-consuming. She's practically all I think about, and I have a feeling I'm all she ever thinks about. Or at least, I hope.

Part of the problem is that I've had thoughts of Elissa walking down the aisle in a white silk dress. Decorated with floral lace, her cinnamon hair curled and loose like a red fountain flowing around her, with little sprigs of baby's breath twisted into her hair. Sure, it's not very manly of me to dream or think about these things, but I see them. I see *her* at the end of that aisle, walking toward me, carrying a bouquet of wildflowers and peonies, and her sapphire eyes sparkling and shimmering like jewels. I can see her in a few years from now, her belly swollen with my child. Her feet are puffy, so at night I rub her feet to keep the circulation moving. I can imagine being exhausted but excited to do those ridiculous midnight runs for food cravings. Holding her hair back when she gets sick, or listening to her stomach and feeling a kick on the side of my face for the first time. I see it all…with Elissa.

CHAPTER FIFTEEN

RILEY

Elissa's been a little lost lately. It's been a few weeks since the reading of the will, and she's been quiet. She's been home. I think she's only seen Brandt a handful of times, which is a bit unusual since they've been back together. I'm not sure what happened, but he's been acting strange since the reading. So has she, but in a different way. She's been kind of drifting along, not really reacting to much, keeping to herself more than normal, and won't open up about Brandt.

She's putting everything she has into her work, and I know she's focusing on that because the CEO vote is coming up soon. She and Brandt went out for Valentine's

Day, and normally she'd have a meltdown or mini panic attack about going on a real date, but there was nothing. She seemed unfazed. She didn't even tell me how the night went afterward. She hasn't even poured herself a glass of whiskey in a while. I think the conversation we had with her mother at the restaurant really fucked with her mind.

The day of the will reading wasn't so great for me either. Rhys messaged me to let me know he booked an appointment at one of the blood collection labs so we can do a non-invasive paternity test. Let me tell you, I've never been more humiliated in my life. To think that Rhys would think the baby is anyone's other than his? It breaks my fucking heart. So, here I am, sitting on my memory foam mattress, wrapped in a towel, and looking into my closet, wondering what the hell I am going to wear. Not necessarily to impress Rhys or anything — it's just that my belly is a bit swollen now, and I can't quite fit into any of my jeans. I'm left with a few pairs of Lululemon leggings and a handful of Fabletics leggings — the only things that fit right now.

I huff as I push myself off the bed and shuffle over to my closet to pick through the neatly folded and stacked colourful leggings on the shelf before selecting a sweater that will match. I've gone with some classic black Lululemons and a coral American Eagle hoodie with a white tank top layered underneath. Looking at myself in the mirror, I fluff my hair, which has grown significantly over the last couple of months (thanks to pregnancy hormones!) and is now much softer and glossier. I recently even got it trimmed to even out the lob that I once had, and it's grown more since then. A ding from my smartwatch warns me that it's now half an hour before the appointment, so I shove my feet into my tall black Hunter boots with the cream boot socks lining them and shrug on my winter coat, struggling to zip it over my bloated belly. *Breathe, Riley. You're growing a baby, you're not fat.*

* * *

When I arrive at the lab building, I thank the driver of the car service I ordered for the afternoon and ask him to wait until I text him that I'm done with my appointment.

"Will do, ma'am."

I shudder at the word "ma'am." It makes me feel old, and I'm only twenty-four. That, and now I'm going to be a mother? That only makes me feel older. As I slide out of the car, a cold breeze rushes past me, blowing my hair into my face. I accidentally inhale some into my mouth as well. I close the door to the car with a soft thump as my other hand tries to pull out the strands that ended up in my mouth when I walk into someone.

"Sorry!" I cry, still unable to see with the wind whipping my hair into my face. "Damn hair was stuck in my mouth and it's still blowing into my face." I give a self-deprecating chuckle as I finally manage to free my face from the chaotic black strands. My heart stills when I hear a familiar voice that makes my heart ache and my blood thrum.

"It's fine. Let's go and get this done."

My heart freezes over at his cold and distant tone, and I steel my nerves for having to deal with him for the next half-hour.

"You didn't have to come," I snip. "I'm perfectly capable of getting blood drawn on my own." I toss my hair over my shoulder and brush past him to enter the building. He's hot on my heels, and as he starts to speak, his voice is low, rumbling something inside me, making my pussy weep for him. No matter how shitty he treats me, it seems I'll always be attracted to him.

"Yeah, well, the least I could do is come with you and pay for the fucking test to see if the thing is mine."

I stop abruptly.

"*Thing?* It's a baby. And the least you could do? That's a joke, right? Fuck this, just leave. I don't even want you here, I can do this on my own. I can do it all on my own. You don't want anything to do with me or this baby? Fine. Here's your out. Paternity test or not, just fucking go, Rhys. I'm so sick of this. I'm not even sure what I did to incur this wrath you seem to have toward me. But I'm over it, and I'm done being punished for your own goddamn actions. I've done nothing to deserve the way you've been treating me." My cheeks flare with heat and I'm getting hot, so I unzip my jacket to release some of the heat building inside me before I really blow. Rhys' face looks pained. "This is hard enough as it is without the shit I get from you. I'm over this Rhys, so please just leave." My voice breaks as I hold back the tears. *I can't let him see me cry.*

I move my feet and start to head toward the room at the end of the hallway when his hand wraps gently around my elbow and pulls me to a halt. Even though his hand isn't directly touching my skin, I can feel his heat sear through my jacket, revving my heart. His face is worn, and his icy eyes have melted. He releases my elbow and I immediately grow cold, shivering from the loss of his touch.

"I'm sorry, Riles. I didn't mean to be such a dick right now."

The use of my nickname makes my heart leap and cry out for more. I need and want him more than I care to admit. And I should be a better woman, not just for me, but for the little kiwi growing inside of me. I should forget about him and try and move on. But I know in my heart that if he was sincere and wanted to try again, even for the sake of the baby, I'd do it in an instant, apology be damned. I miss his broad shoulders, his thick, black hair, and his long, thick cock. I miss the way his lips feel on my skin, the way his touch would leave me breathless, the way his dick fit me like it was made to fit me.

My watch vibrates, distracting me from my thoughts. A text notification from Elissa pops up.

Elissa: *Good luck! Let me know if I need to kick the asshole's ass.*

A wave of comfort swells in my heart at Elissa's message. To think that just a few months ago, when she left, I was a broken person who had relapsed because her best friend ghosted her. I'm so glad to have her back in my life. *In our lives. Auntie Elissa. Haha, I like that.* I glance up and Rhys' eyes are still on me, waiting for me to say something.

"Let's just go," I mumble, and before he can say anything, I turn on my heel and keep walking until I reach the lab's door.

• • •

I've always been afraid of needles. I'm a wimp when it comes to inflicting my body with unnecessary pain — this is why my skin is still unblemished, with zero tattoos and no bodily piercings, other than my ears (which I don't remember because I got them done when I was really young). So, when a cold sweat breaks out on my forehead, I start to tremble, and my leg starts jiggling uncontrollably, a warm hand slides into mine and squeezes as we're sitting in the waiting room. Every nerve in my body quiets down, as if Rhys' touch has magic soothing powers, and I hate the way that my body still responds to him. He lets go of my hand and places it on my thigh, pressing down and squeezing to get me to stop bouncing, and it works. But the floodgates open and now my pussy is seeping, wanting his hand to climb higher up my leg. To touch the fleshy mound of nerves between my legs.

"Riley Jaimeson," a flat voice hollers out. I jump, jolting me from my dirty thoughts. Rhys gives another squeeze to my leg, and I turn my head to look at him. I can hear the tapping foot of the impatient nurse waiting for me to follow her, but something about the look in his eyes makes me hesitate.

"Do you want me to come with you and hold your hand? I'll do mine after yours."

And just like that, my heart melts, and every bit of anger and resentment I've felt toward him is gone.

CHAPTER SIXTEEN

RILEY

Rhys walks me out of the building after the blood is drawn. We're both quiet, not quite sure what to say. When we're outside, I pull my phone out of my purse and text my driver, the crook of my elbow lightly throbbing. I shove the phone back in the pocket of my jacket and turn to look at Rhys.

"Well, the driver is coming to get me. I'll let you know the results. Thanks for holding my hand," I say, trying to leave emotion out of my words. A chilly breeze brushes past us and I can hear the car I called approach behind me, its tires crunching against the salted asphalt. There's a moment of charged awkwardness that leaves us standing in limbo, wondering what the hell to do. Rhys shuffles forward, his arms slightly opening at the same time that I step back, only increasing the level of awkwardness. My fingers tingle for him to hold my hand again, my body aches to feel his skin on mine.

"Uh, yeah, sure. I'll talk to you later, then," Rhys mumbles. I open the car door, slide inside, and Rhys' hand wraps around the top of the door and presses it closed. Rhys stands still, his black hair ruffling in the wind as the car drives away. I turn around to watch as we drive further away. He finally turns and walks in the opposite direction, digging his hands into his pockets, a puff of white steam trailing him from his hot breath.

• • •

When I get home, I slink into my bedroom and change into some Roots track pants, unclasp and remove my bra, and pull on a cozy off-the-shoulder sweater, along with some thick woollen reading socks. I twist my hair up into a messy bun and flick the light on in the washroom when I get there, then prep my face products to remove my make-up and wash my face.

In the middle of washing my face, I hear Elissa slam the front door. She comes stomping down the hallway, and a wet sound smacks on the floor with every step. Elissa appears in the doorway, her face red from the chilly air, but it looks as though smoke is rising off her head; she's mad.

"What's wrong with you?"

She grinds her teeth and her eye twitches.

"Fucking stepped in a slushy, ice-cold puddle on the walk home and I've been walking two blocks with a frozen fucking foot. FUCK! It hurts." She bends over, tugging off her sodden sock and it slops to the floor. She shudders. "I'll be right back. I'm just gonna change and warm up my fucking foot."

I chuckle and finish washing my face. Back in my bedroom, I walk over to my dresser and open my jewelry box. I take off my colourless one-carat diamond stud earrings, trimmed with platinum and gold, and my platinum and gold tennis bracelet, then place them inside the box, safe and sound. I hear Elissa grumble, and I head out to the kitchen and living area to find her rummaging around in the cupboards.

"Whatcha doin'?" I singsong. She slides cans and boxes along the shelves in the cupboards as bags crinkle.

"Trying to find something to eat. Something junky."

"We need to go get groceries. Wanna just order something in?"

Elissa's face twists, falls, and then she sighs.

"Nah. I'm not really hungry, just feeling blah. How was the appointment? How was *Rhys?*"

A flip of the stomach makes me nervous when I hear his name. *I shouldn't be stomach flipping for him.* I shrug my shoulders and lean against the counter. "I don't know. The appointment itself was fine. Rhys was a dick for the first little bit, but then he offered to hold my hand when I was getting my blood drawn, so there's that." Elissa nods briefly and chews the inside of her cheek. "What?"

She sighs. "He held your hand? That's it?" I nod, a blush blooming on my cheeks. "Oh, hun…just be careful, please. Don't let him get to you unless he's being sincere."

"I know," I mumble. "It was just nice having someone there again. I'm going to have to do this all alone."

"Ouch. All alone? I'm here for you, and I will be here for that little kiwi in your belly." I laugh.

"You're calling it a kiwi now too?" Elissa beams at me and winks.

"If it's a girl, you should totally name her like Kiana or something, so we can just call her Kiwi."

My eyes widen and I see hearts floating everywhere in the room.

"I *love* that name! Okay. Kiana is officially at the top of my girl name list," I say with resolve. "So, how are things with Brandt?" Elissa grumbles and turns away, going back to rummaging in the cupboards to avoid the question. "I'm not going anywhere, so you might as well tell me." Elissa huffs and turns back to face me.

"I don't know, Riles. When we're together he's distant. Like he's pulling away, and I don't know what I fucking did. I don't get it. I'm new to relationships, but I'm pretty sure you're not supposed to shut down and avoid each other. I almost wonder if he's bored of me, or maybe he thinks he made a mistake wanting to try a relationship with me. I don't know, I'm not really good at this kind of thing, but I'm trying. He texts me back one-word answers or emojis, and it's frustrating. When we get together it's always sex, which is fine, but he doesn't cuddle me like he was doing for a while there. Which, again, not such a big deal, but it is when it changes suddenly."

My heartstrings tug for Elissa and what she's going through. I can see she's trying really hard.

"Have you tried talking to him about it?"

"No. Of course not. If he's pulling away and I say something, it'll do one of two things. One, he'll get all defensive and dismissive and eventually dump me. Or two, he'll get all jumpy and freaked and dump me for pressuring him somehow." I furrow my brows at her and press my lips into a thin line.

"Yeah…I don't think he'd do either of those things," I say. "You just need to have a talk with him and get to the bottom of it. The longer you put it off, the harder it will get, and the more confusing it will be for both of you. Hell, he'll probably pull away even more if you don't say anything. You need to tell him how you feel, how his behaviour is making you feel." Elissa's shoulders drop, and she walks over to the couch and collapses to the cushions with a sigh. I follow her and plop down.

"Yeah, I know. It's just hard. I don't know how to do these things. He's the one who wanted the relationship."

"But you agreed, so you must have feelings for him, too." Elissa's face burns bright red. "Oh my God. You *really* have feelings for him. You love him, don't you?" Elissa tries to avoid my stare, and I see sweat beading on her forehead. I chuckle. "Why not tell him that then? Maybe that'll change things. I know he loves you; you destroyed him when you left in the summer." Her shoulders slump and her body sinks further into the couch like she's being pulled into a garburator.

"I…I can't say it. Those words."

"I know they can be scary, but it'll feel really good to share your feelings with him." She shakes her head, her copper strands floating across her face. Her shoulders roll and she straightens up on the couch, only to pull her legs up and tuck them under her ass. She leans forward, grabs the remote off the glass coffee table, and starts flicking through the channels, effectively shutting down this conversation. I sink into the couch and absentmindedly rub my belly and click my tongue. It kills me that she has this wonderful man, a man who we all know loves her, and she's terrified of opening her heart to him. Elissa flips through the channels, not staying on one too long — nothing is capturing her attention. She's clearly distracted with this shit going on between her and Brandt.

CHAPTER SEVENTEEN

ELISSA

The last few weeks have been strained, so I've been burying myself in work. My skin craves the way Brandt used to touch me. It seems like he's avoiding me, and I can't figure it out. He's pushing me away for some reason, and I'm too scared to bring it up. This is why I don't do relationships. This is why I stay away from attachments. One day everything is fine, and the next someone's done something to hurt the other. I like easy-breezy. The worst part of this is that I've finally allowed myself to be open to the possibility of more, of allowing myself to feel more.

I know Riley is right. I know I need to talk to him, but I'm terrified that if I put myself out there and lay it on the line, I'm going to get hurt. It's easier to just deny that something's even wrong. But truly, it's no longer the same. The passion is his eyes seems dimmed, the electric current that sparks between us is now more of a hum. We're seeing less and less of each other and I'm not sure what to do. I decide to take a week off work and relax, just to think about things. I schedule an appointment with my therapist and decide to go *home* for the week.

I roll my black suitcase into the spare bedroom in Lana's house, drop it on the plush double bed, and look around the familiar room. Soft yellow curtains with little daises on them frame the window in the centre of the wall, the brass bedframe shines from the light flowing into the room. There are two narrow white nightstands on either side of the bed, each with small colourful succulents on them, along with a lamp. Across from the foot of the bed is a closet, with those old particleboard doors with the brass circular finger hole. I let the familiar scent of lavender and honey from the linens fill my nose when little feet patter into the room. "'Lissa, do you wanna play dinosaurs with me?" I offer Knox a gentle smile as I ruffle his thick, dark hair.

"Not right now, buddy. I just need to get settled. I'll be down in a bit." Knox nods his head enthusiastically and runs out of the room, stomping down the stairs. I collapse on the bed next to my suitcase and my chest caves as I release a breath. I haven't talked to Brandt in a few days, so he doesn't know I'm here. I reach over to my purse and grab my iPhone 14 out and tap out a message to him, trying to keep the lines of communication open.

Me: *Hey...just wanted to let you know that I went to Chatham for the week to visit Lana, in case you're wondering where I am. I'll talk to you later.*

Three dots pop up on the screen, then disappear. I curl my hands around my phone, raising it above my head, hanging it in the air, waiting for him to respond. The dots appear and disappear a few times and then — nothing. I sigh, dropping my phone beside my head. *What the fuck is wrong with me? I've never been like this before. I need to figure some shit out and decide what to do and what's best for me, because clearly Brandt is having second thoughts.*

A light knock sounds on my door and I crook my neck to look over at the doorway. A pair of upside-down, soft, brown, almond-shaped eyes and downturned lips smile at me. Lana's sleek, straight black hair has strands of silver woven through it. "Dinner is ready, love." I push myself up onto my elbows and rest like that for a minute before heaving a breath and moving the rest of my body. When I reach the door, I almost tower over Lana's petite body. It's kind of funny to see the woman who raised me be half-a-foot shorter than me. Even though I'm taller than her, I will forever look up to her. She's the best person I know. She grabs my hand with both of hers and wraps her fingers around my fist tightly. She looks into my eyes, and it's like she can see into the depths of my mind. "It'll work itself out, don't worry." My heart skips as my face falls and

I nod my head. She jerks her head for me to follow her downstairs for dinner.

Steel clangs against ceramic as we finish eating dinner and Tiago clears the table and starts on the dishes. Knox runs off to his room to play, leaving Lana and me at the table. Her soft brown eyes melt with sadness as she looks at me.

"What's going on, baby girl?" My heart swoops.

"How do you do that? How do you just know?" She smiles and pops a shoulder up.

"A mother always knows." I've missed her.

"Things are strained between Brandt and I. And I'm not sure why. We decided at New Year's to give this relationship thing a try, and now he's pulling away, Mom. I don't get it." I prop my elbows on the table and bury my face in my hands. "I didn't want this, a relationship. I never did, but I was willing to try, for him, and he flipped his mind within a matter of weeks. I've always felt something was different or wrong with me, but the fact that he can't stand me for longer than a month of dating is just…frustrating. I thought I was doing a decent job at this girlfriend thing."

Lana looks at me with patient eyes as I pour my heart out to her. Her hands slide across the dark tabletop and clasp around my elbows, bracing me.

"So, what changed?" My eyes catch hers and I know mine are swimming with confusion.

"What do you mean?

"What happened when you noticed the change?" The will reading. I know that threw him off, and my mother even alluded to some things, but I didn't think that was an issue. I tell Lana as much. She's thoughtful for a minute, her eyes shifting as if she's mentally sorting something in her mind.

"A person usually has two reasons for doing something: a good reason and the real reason. Thomas Carlyle." I stare at Lana.

"I don't get it," I mumble.

"I just mean he's not doing it for no reason. Something happened to trigger this, and he has his reasons. If you want to know what they are, you have to ask. That's the only way, I'm afraid."

"Yeah, I'm afraid too. But it's the answer I'm going to get that really scares me." Lana's eyes shine and crinkle in the corner. Tiago comes out of the kitchen and places warm mugs with steam rising out of them in front of us, then leaves the room again. "What?" I ask.

"It's just nice seeing you being honest with yourself. I'm glad you're not closing yourself off this time."

"I...I'm trying. I don't want to lose him, but I don't want him if he doesn't want me."

She pulls my hands out from under my chin, gathers them in hers, and squeezes. "It'll be okay. And if it isn't, at least you tried. And no one can say you didn't try your best to give him what he needed." She always knows what to say. A lump forms in my throat and I bite back the tears.

My phone vibrates on the table and I look down at the illuminated screen to see Riley's name.

Riley: *I don't want you to see this, but I think you need to. But do NOT jump to any conclusions...*

My heart sinks as I open the text message from Riley and see the link to one of the newspapers that I own. It's an article on a charity gala for something or other in Toronto, from tonight. I don't pay attention to the words because all I see is a picture of Brandt wrapped around some brunette in a long black dress, her hand on his chest. Her perfectly sculpted nose and lips are tilted up and looking at him with a bright smile while he has a neutral face, staring at the camera. *Damn, does he look good. No, Elissa…stop that.* It looks like just another one of the photos he used to appear in all the time when I looked him up when we first met. Another ding sounds, and I see Riley's name pop up again.

Riley: *Do. Not. Freak. Out. I just wanted you to know. It looks innocent.*

My mind is dizzy, I can't think straight. I don't know if I'm mad, or sad, or what. I stare at the picture longer and my face must be white because Lana touches my face and when I look at her, her eyes are worried. I pass my phone to her and her shoulders sag.

"Honey, don't read into this. You know better than most how the media likes to spin things. Remember all those things they used to write about you in high school and university? Your father owned half those places, and they still wrote things and took pictures out of context." I sigh, my hands trembling as I clasp them together.

"Yeah, you're probably right. I should wait to see what he says. I guess I'm going back to Toronto tomorrow morning," I say weakly, a nervous chuckle puffing out of my mouth.

CHAPTER
EIGHTEEN

BRANDT

I scroll through the photos of myself at the gala last night for Autism Awareness. Every picture of me is from a different angle from the part of the night where I was talking to the gorgeous Ana Ruszi, a top fashion model in Toronto. The slit along the side of her long black dress showcases one long, tanned leg, her neon yellow toenails peek out of her black open-toed heels, and her long, luscious chestnut curls flow over her shoulders and down her back. There's no mistaking how gorgeous this woman is. Her eyes sparkle like diamonds in the flashes of the camera. My stomach grumbles, wondering what kind of fresh hell this is going to bring with Elissa.

I scroll through the articles on Google, each one stating my name in the headlines. I set up Google to alert me of any mentions of my name a long time ago. Once again, my name makes headlines being seen with another random "date" on my arm. There was no date, though. It just so happened we know each other from attending these functions over time and have chatted here and there. These photographers know how to take an innocent conversation and twist it.

A light rap on my door echoes down the hallway into my living room. I plant my feet on the ground and hoist myself off the black leather couch and make my way to the door. I shake my head, wondering why someone let a random person into the building without buzzing. Before I even look through the peephole or open the door, I feel a rush of electricity course through my veins. I know it's Elissa before I even make another move. My lashes brush against the metal peephole in the door, and sure enough, my vision is filled with wild bronze hair tucked behind her ears. I slide the locking mechanism across and unlock the deadbolt, swing the door open, and see bright, but unsure, oceanic eyes staring at me.

Elissa's lip rolls into her mouth, her teeth lightly scraping against the bottom lip, and I wish it was me sinking my teeth into her lip right now. My fingers itch to dig into her hair and hold onto those soft, copper locks, but I hold back. Things have been strained lately, and I know it's my fault, but it's my way of protecting my heart. I won't be able to handle it if she breaks things off. I need to distance myself so that when she inevitably does, I'm okay. What I went through last summer…I can't do that again.

She brushes past me, her vanilla scent overtaking my senses as a rush of blood runs south. I breathe her in, wishing I could bottle her scent up and keep it with me forever. My heart aches as the air in the apartment tenses and thickens, and my gut sinks at the vibrations in the atmosphere. This doesn't feel like a friendly visit. She slips her feet out of her shoes, drops her purse on the table in the entryway, and hangs up her jacket, making herself comfortable. I yearn to wrap her up in my arms, pressing feverish kisses into her perfect creamy skin. My tongue runs along the back of my teeth, fighting the urge to kiss her. She walks further into my condo, tossing her hair over her shoulder to look over and see if I'm following her. I shuffle my feet and follow her to the living room.

She perches herself on the edge of the couch and waits for me to join her. I sit at the opposite end, my hands curling into fists in my lap, hiding the trembling. Copper curls cascade over her chest and shoulder, and I fight the need to brush them out of the way so I can see her neck. The vein in my neck pulses with need, with want, but my heart is beating rapidly and my palms are sweating. I pushed her away for this reason, yet I'm still dreading the conversation that's coming.

"Hey," she murmurs, her tone soft and delicate. "So, I don't really know how to say this, so I'm just going to say it." I put my hand up and stop her from continuing.

"It's all right, no need to say it. I know why you're here. You should have been in Chatham visiting Lana, but you're here, twenty-four hours later. You don't need to explain. You said relationships weren't for you." Her face drains of blood, but shock is etched all over it.

"So, it's over? Just like that?" I nod, looking away from her face, because if I don't, I'll beg her not to do this, and I can't be that weak pussy. I can't pour my heart out for someone who doesn't want me the same. "Well, I guess the picture and headlines were right. You've decided to move on, without telling me." I stiffen at the accusation, but I can't find it in myself to deny anything. I'm breaking just listening to the lilt of her voice and what seems like…sadness.

She shifts on the couch, moving further to the edge, rubbing her forehead. "I don't understand," she says. "I know things were weird for a little bit, but…I didn't expect this."

"You didn't expect what?"

"This. You. Acting like this."

"Acting like what? Keeping my distance from someone who's bound to leave me again after she's already done it? And without warning, might I add." Her perfect fuck-me lips part, words lost on her tongue. She looks away, her eyes glimmering in the light, making me wonder if I saw tears. *Not likely.*

"I knew things were weird the last few weeks, but I didn't expect this. I thought it was just a…"

My face whips to face hers. "Thought it was just what?" Her eyes waver, looking between mine, and her lids flutter shut as she takes a deep breath.

"Never mind," she mumbles. "Well, if this is what you want…" My blood boils. *What I want? What I want is to throw this coffee table over, pull her to her feet, and shove my tongue down her throat. What I want is to throw her over my shoulder, take her to my room, toss her on the bed, crawl on top of her, and ram my dick into her, deep and hard. I want to rut into her like a voracious animal, starving from hunger, until I'm good and sated.*

"What I want…that's a joke," I mutter, my tone sharper than I hoped. She winces at my words, then smooths her jeans and adjusts her blouse. I feel a bead of sweat form on my brow and roll down my temple as I hold back every muscle in my body from grabbing her and doing exactly what I want to do. She sighs, and she looks…broken. But I don't know why. I'm the only one here who's broken because of this. She's the one who wants this. I knew it was only a matter of time, which is why I prepared myself.

She scrambles to her feet, pushing her hand across her cheeks and the hair out of her face.

"Well, then. I guess that's it. I will see you at the board meeting next Monday." She mutters something under her breath that sounds like "fuck." "See you around, Brandt." She bends down, pressing a light, chaste kiss to my cheek, and gives me one last look before collecting her things and walking out of my condo.

• • •

Rhys and I are at the gym, shoes squeaking on the court as we run toward the basket, dribbling the ball. Sweat is dripping down my face and pouring down my back as I push myself harder, sinking the next basket, dunking it over top of Rhys.

"Jesus, man. What is going on?"

"Elissa…broke up…with me," I say between panting breaths.

"Fuck man, I'm sorry." I nod my head, my hands locked on my hips as I force myself to take measured breaths. "What happened?" The muscles in my jaw and neck tense at the memories flashing through my mind of this morning's conversation.

"She asked if this strain was it. I mean, I know I've been pushing her away, but it was only to protect myself because I knew this was coming. If she truly wanted me, she would have fought for it."

"Did she ask about the photos from last night's gala?" Rhys dribbles the ball while we stand idly. I shrug my shoulders and give him a sneer.

"Possibly. She didn't really ask anything, but I didn't offer up any explanations. Not my fault if she gets something from nothing."

"Dude, what the fuck is wrong with you? Maybe she wanted you to say something. Maybe she was giving you space to say something so she didn't have to accuse you of anything. God, you really suck at this relationship thing."

My face grows red as my blood boils, prickling my skin. "Fuck off. Like you're one to talk. You suck just as bad as me," I growl. Rhys lets the ball drop and it gradually stops bouncing while he holds his hands up in the air, surrendering. "She did ask what I wanted, though. I guess I could have said something then."

"Why don't you go talk to her? But this time, actually talk? Get what you're feeling off your chest. Who knows, maybe she feels the same as you?" I stay silent, letting the conversation die.

I'm done talking about this. I've fought for her, for us, already. It's her turn, and she just walked away from us. I can't be the one constantly chasing her, asking her to stay. Rhys' eyes burn into me like a hot brand as I feel his concern burrow into my skin. I grab the basketball off the wooden floor and my shoes squeak as I run and dribble the ball. The ball is in her court, or was, and she let it drop.

CHAPTER
NINETEEN

RILEY

Another two weeks go by, and Elissa has retreated further into herself. She's burying herself in work and researching stuff for babies. I swear she's more prepared than I am for this baby. Elissa has really been supportive these last few weeks and I feel so grateful to have her back in my life. We plan on telling my parents about the pregnancy soon, when we go home for a visit. I'm terrified of their reaction. I'm also sweating the paternity test results coming back. I should hear any day now. I know the baby is Rhys', but it doesn't make me any less nervous. Nervous because of what his reaction will be. I'm preparing myself for the worst, that he wants nothing to do with me or the baby.

I'm hoping Rhys' softer demeanour two weeks ago was a changing point. Maybe he's coming around to the idea, and he'll be accepting of the situation.... *Are you kidding yourself, Riley?* I need to prepare myself even more for the possibility of raising this baby by myself. I know Elissa is here for me, and judging by the extensive research she's done, she wasn't just telling me that to make me feel better. But I can't ask her to help raise a kid that's not hers. I can't ask her to give up this place for me to raise a kid and have her move somewhere else. It's just not fair to her.

Elissa comes padding out of her room. Her blush blouse is half-tucked into her black leather pencil skirt, sheer black tights cover her slim, muscular legs, and her coral Coach heels click as she fastens an earring in her right lobe. The golden watch on her wrist sways and clinks as she shakes out the sleeves of her blouse. Her lips are stained red and her copper hair is sleek, the hair at her temples twisted into braids and tucked behind her ears. A shade of olive green is dusted across her lids and her lashes are thick and curled, thanks to black mascara. She looks so gorgeous, but her eyes reveal her soul, and it's shattered.

"Hun, are you sure you can go to work and face Brandt today? Last week he failed to show up at the board meeting, and he confirmed he's going to be there today. You don't have to go. Make up some excuse." Elissa's quiet and her lips part to suck in a breath, then blow it out.

"I'm fine, Riles," she says, clicking over to me. She bends down and talks to my swollen belly. "Good morning little Kiwi." Her thumb rubs my stomach, and my heart swells. "You're really starting to show now."

I groan. "I know…I can't hide it anymore. I'm going on four-and-a-half months. I'm almost halfway through my pregnancy. I guess it's time to tell my parents." Elissa walks over to the cupboard, pulls out the decanter of whiskey, and pours a couple of inches into a tumbler before slamming it back. "Er…you good?"

She beams a false smile. "Never better. Just a little liquid courage." She opens her mouth and stretches it wide, I assume from the burn of the amber liquid.

"Girl, if you need to take a drink right now, maybe you should just cancel the meeting altogether and wait until you're better equipped to handle it." Her copper hair whooshes and her vanilla shampoo clouds around me.

"No can do, Riles. I'm officially the CEO now and chair-*woman* of the board. Gotta suck it up and grow a pair of ovaries. I'm not going to let a man ruin things for me. The best way forward is to act professional," she says, packing up her oversized, pale green leather Kate Spade clutch. As she passes me, she presses a kiss to my cheek. "I'll see you later, Riles. I'll bring home some dinner. Let me know what you want. And keep me updated when the results come in! Any day now, right?" I groan and bob my head. She offers me a smile and gathers her jacket, slinging it over her arm, and heads out the door, calling Arthur, her driver, to meet her out front.

•••

I didn't feel like going anywhere today, so I asked my therapist if we could have a phone session instead. She was reluctant, but indulged my request.

"I really need you to come in for your sessions unless you're sick, Riley. It's good for you to get out of the house, especially since you're not currently taking on jobs."

"I know, Dr. Pierce. I've just been having a rough few days and needed to veg." Dr. Pierce clicks her tongue.

"All right, well. How do you feel about telling your parents about your pregnancy this weekend?" I sigh and nibble at my lips.

"A little nervous. Elissa said she'd be there with me when we broke the news." She *hmms*.

"And what about Rhys? Where does he fit into this reveal to your parents?"

"Well, the paternity test isn't back yet, so nowhere. I don't even know if he's going to be part of the baby's life, even if he has the proof he needs," I snipe. I can hear some faint scribbling on the line. I wait for her to talk again.

"I think it would do you and the baby some good if you get out this afternoon. Go for a walk around the block. It's only early March, but it's quite mild today. It might be nice to get some fresh air."

•••

I'm lacing up my shoes to go for a walk when my phone goes off.

Rhys: *Any news?*

Me: *Nope. Not yet.*

I stand there, waiting for his response like an idiot, and when those three annoying little dots disappear and nothing comes, I grind my teeth and push my phone into my jacket pocket. I grab my keys and wallet and shove them into my other pocket and leave my place. It's not until I'm in the elevator when my phone goes off again.

Rhys: *You busy? I'm outside, can we talk?*

Ha. God has a sense of humour.

Me: *I was actually on my way out to go for a walk...I suppose you can join me.*

When the elevator doors slide open, I see down the long hallway to the glass doors and window and there's a tall figure with black hair pacing, looking at his phone. My heart shakes inside my body and I need to catch my breath.

Rhys: *Okay. See you in a min.*

I smile to myself, biting the corner of my lip as I put my phone away and walk toward the door. When Rhys hears the doors shake, he turns around and his eyes soften and the corners of his mouth curl. I feel a sharp jolt in my chest and a flutter in my stomach. His hands grasp the metal handle and he opens the door for me. I whisper my thanks as I pass him. I breathe in his woodsy, citrusy scent and my panties are drenched. *Traitorous hormones.* He looks good. His hair is shorn tight around the sides, but the top is a perfect length to tangle my fingers in while he bucks into me. *Oh my God, get your head out of the gutter.* I start walking and he catches up, shoving his hands deep into his coat pockets.

"So, you wanted to talk?" I turn to face him as we walk, and he's chewing on the inside of his cheek, bobbing his head. I can almost hear the wheels turning in his head as he thinks of what to say.

"I just want to say…oh fuck, I feel so stupid." A small giggle bubbles out of my lips and he shoots me a glare, but his face quickly softens, and he chuckles too. His shoulders drop the tension he's holding. I take a deep breath as we continue walking, letting the March air clear my mind and my lungs as I wait for Rhys to continue. "What I'm trying to say is…if the baby is mine, I want to be there for it. For you." I stop and an ugly wave of red crashes through my body.

"*If* it's yours? God, Rhys. I can't believe that after all this, you still don't believe me." His face burns red as it screws up and twitches.

"Fuck, Riley. It's not about me believing you. I heard from Dante that you hooked up with him that night I ran into you at the hotel." I stop dead in my tracks and my mouth gapes open. I'm speechless. He clearly hasn't been paying attention to anything I've been saying.

"You're a moron," I say, and Rhys looks like I've just slapped him. "I can't believe you haven't heard a thing I've been saying. I was already about a month pregnant by then,

I just didn't know. I didn't start getting morning sickness until a week later. Fuck me, Rhys. I thought this whole paternity thing was just a way to hurt me, but it's more than that. You truly don't believe it could be yours. That day you ran into me on the street and came over to *talk*, you fucked me bareback, or did you forget? Fuck, fuck, fuck!" I shout out obscenities, and as people pass us on the busy Toronto sidewalk I get glares and wide-eyed looks of curiosity. Heat rises to my cheeks from my public outburst. I curl my hands into fists, count to ten, and release my breath, clenching my fingers. I hazard a glance at Rhys and his face is white. At that moment, my phone starts ringing. I shake my head at him and walk away a few steps to answer the phone.

"Yes, this is she." I feel the heat beside me, and I know that Rhys has caught up. "Yes, thank you. I'll check my email now. Thanks again," I say, hitting the red button and immediately opening my email app.

After a few clicks, I log into my health account and open the bloodwork that Rhys and I did. I scan the results, then shove my phone in his face. His eyes grow wide, and his face pales and twists with remorse. I rip my phone out of his face and stick it back in my pocket with a huff. I spin on my heel and start stomping away, calling over my shoulder, "Congrats, daddy. It's real now."

CHAPTER TWENTY

ELISSA

I'm a nervous wreck as I walk into the Black & Wells tower. I'm sweating through my blouse and it's below freezing outside. I haul ass past the security guard with a nod and make a quick jaunt up to my office before the meeting. My office is still on the twenty-first floor as I refuse to take up residence in my father's office on the twenty-second floor. I toss my jacket onto my desk and drop my clutch on my chair while I rummage through my desk to find my spare deodorant. I swipe the bar under my arms and pick up a file folder to fan and cool myself down. My heart is racing, and I'm feeling a little lightheaded as I try to control my breathing. *I should have taken the day off, like Riley said. For fuck's sake.*

I grab the folder, my oversized clutch with my laptop and phone inside, and walk toward the washroom. I fluff my hair in the mirror, reapply my lipstick, and shake out my blouse, trying to settle my nerves. Bracing myself against the counter, I stare at my reflection, trying to psyche myself up. *You can do it, Elissa. It's just Brandt. You can still work with him…I hope.*

Before I even reach the boardroom on the top level of the building, before I even leave the elevator, I feel the air humming with energy. My skin tingles and prickles with goosebumps as my limbs grow heavy. My tongue feels gritty, like the air is sucking all the moisture from my mouth. I roll my eyes shut, trying to brace myself for this interaction, but instead, all I smell is Brandt. His wintry, woodsy scent; like a burst of fresh air. My heaving lungs gulp air, bottling the scent inside, storing it for later. And when the doors slide open, I see his towering six-foot-one build and broad shoulders facing away from me, as he nods his head and chats with one of the board members, Donovan. I clench my insides, staving off the leaking that threatens just from looking at him. His strong, chiselled jaw and cheekbones are flawless as his perfect lips move, chuckling at whatever Donovan said.

It's like I'm walking in slow motion, wading through the thickest of currents as I approach them. Brandt's golden locks are styled to perfection. The sides are sheared close to his scalp, a new look for him. *Fuck, does he look good.* I notice my lips are parted, and I smash them shut before the drooling starts. With every step I take, the humming in my body turns to thrumming, and my heart is beating like a bass drum. I swear, if you were standing close enough to me, you would hear the rhythm pounding inside.

My skin prickles and burns as I near him, and my pussy and heart ache for the man that walked away. I shouldn't feel like this. I should be fine. I should have someone balls deep into me by now. But all I see is *him*. Brandt. Tingles erupt in my fingers, and I want to reach out and slide my hand into his, locking our fingers together. I want to push his broad, sturdy chest until his back smacks against the wall, my hands sliding down his chest, over the crest of his straining pants as I lower myself to my knees. I want to hear the metal grind of the zip as my nimble fingers pull it down. I want to hook my fingers in the waistband of his pants and pull them down, boxers too, allowing his cock to spring free, bobbing in front of my face.

Pressing my thighs together, I stop dead in my tracks. I shake off this incessant wanting and try to refocus my thoughts on work. As I get closer to Donovan and Brandt, the hairs on my nape stand, an icy shiver runs down my spine, and a pang ripples through my heart. *Fuck, I want him. I fucking need this man. Too bad he doesn't want me.* I offer the gentlemen a weak smile as I round the corner and head into the glass-walled conference room. Walking to the far side of the room, I place my stuff down at the head of the table and saunter over to the long, skinny table that holds pastries and coffee. I help myself to a cherry Danish and a large paper cup, filling it to the brim with coffee and heaps of sugar. The pulse under my skin thrums harder as I feel Brandt's presence enter the room. I take my pastry and coffee and hurry back to my spot to avoid unnecessary conversation.

Once everyone is situated, coffees and pastries sitting in front of them, I clear my throat, stand, and smooth out my leather skirt. I press a couple of buttons on my laptop and it mirrors onto the projector screen behind me. My hand grasps the presentation clicker as I run through the sales of the last month from all our newspapers and magazine outlets. Everyone seems to nod and hum as I explain the sales targets for next month, and a scorching burn rolls over my body. Every inch of my flesh singes and burns. I know Brandt's eyes are trained on me, and I don't need to look to know that his stare is hard and fuelled with anger. Rolling my shoulders back and tossing my hair, I boost myself. *Why the fuck is he furious? He's the one who wanted things to end.* When I finish with my portion of the meeting, I sit down and turn it over to Donovan to go over marketing strategies for boosting readership.

Still feeling the heated gaze on me, I refuse to acknowledge it. *Like fuck if I'm going to willingly give him the satisfaction of knowing how badly this is fucking me up right now.* But the thought of his eyes still focused on me does something to my stomach, as it flips and flops around inside me. My panties grow moist, knowing that I'm his sole focus right now, knowing that he isn't paying attention to this meeting as much as I am. A fire ignites in my belly, and it takes all my willpower to continue this meeting and not adjourn early so I can take care of this burning fire that's growing inside me. Thankfully, my phone distracts me from my thoughts.

Mother Dearest: *Are you available for lunch today?*

Weird, my mother never wants to get a meal together. I flip my phone over and ignore her message, trying to focus on the meeting, when my phone beeps again. I look around the room, but no one seems bothered by the interruption.

Mother Dearest: *We can meet at that café by your work. Is noon okay?*

I'm floored. I really don't know how else to describe it. My mother wanting to get together for a meal. I can only imagine what horrors this meal will bring me. I tap out a quick reply.

Me: *Fine. I'll see you at noon. In a meeting.*

• • •

The rest of the meeting was uneventful. I tried my hardest to keep my eyes focused on the screen, but caught myself glancing at Brandt a few times. His strong jaw seemed to clench every time my gaze landed on him. God, what I'd do to press my mouth against his jaw, feel his scruff against my lips. My lips tingle with the memory of him, and I absentmindedly brush my thumb against the bottom edge of my lip.

The bell rings above me as I walk into the café across the street, and I spot the familiar sleek copper hair twisted into a tight bun. My mother's back is facing me, and I let my shoulders drop momentarily as I brace myself for this interaction. Taking a deep breath, I roll my posture and my heels click as I make my way over to her.

"Hi, Mother," I mumble as I take the seat across from her, the chair scraping along the tiled floor. The scent of freshly baked pastries and bread mixed with the rich notes of coffee lingers in the air, causing a pang of hunger in my stomach. My mother's lips purse in a tight smile.

"Hi, honey," she says in a soft tone, her eyes focused on the menu in front of her. I stall for a minute, letting the term of endearment douse me in ice water. She only uses those words in front of other people, when she needs to hold up the appearance of being a loving and attentive mother. My fingers clack on the table as I wait for my mother to fully acknowledge me. She flags down the server to place her order. "Oh, great. I'll have a Greek salad and an ice water with lemon." Her eyes finally rest on me, and I blink and turn to the server.

"My regular, please. Thank you, Devin." He nods as he scribbles down the order and then walks away. My mother is staring at me, eyes wide, like a deer caught in headlights. "What?" I ask her.

"You come here often enough that you have a *regular* order?"

"Please don't sound disgusted, Mother. It's not like I'm at a greasy spoon asking for the sloppy joe. It's a turkey sandwich." I try to brush my mother's comment off, but I feel the blood starting to simmer under my skin. She rolls her eyes and raises her hands in surrender. "So, why did you want to meet?"

Her eyes dart around the cafe, avoiding eye contact with me. Her body tenses and the vein in her neck throbs. Her perfectly French manicured hands rest on top of the table, twiddling her fingers in a rapid movement. She's nervous.

"C'mon, Mother. What's going on?" Her eyes meet mine and there's moisture rimming the corners. She looks fragile, and I recognize the loneliness in her eyes. Collette lets out a careful breath.

"I just wanted to have lunch."

CHAPTER TWENTY-ONE

BRANDT

That meeting was one of the harder things I've had to endure lately.

Being in the same room as Elissa and not being able to reach out and touch her killed me. My fingers twitched to feel how soft her bronze curls were, to feel if her skin is still as silky as I remember, to feel the plush curves of her breasts and ass. I've been sporting a semi-hard-on all day since walking into that boardroom this morning. I was not properly prepared to encounter her again so soon after she dropped me…again. But, let's be real — I don't think I'll ever be properly prepared to deal with Elissa and how she affects my body, my heart. I just wish I affected her the same way she does me.

Throughout the meeting, there was this annoying little burning sensation prickling the side of my face, and without looking, I knew it was Elissa stealing glances my way. It took everything I had not to look at her and give her a moment of my attention, but the truth is, she had all of my attention. Not a single ounce of my attention was spent on the meeting. Every nerve, cell, and atom in my body was hyper-focused on Elissa. My lungs felt like they were screaming for air, for the chance to touch her.

And god-fucking-dammit if she didn't look like a fucking goddess. She shone so brightly you'd swear there was a halo glowing around her entire body. Her creamy skin glowed, her hair was perfectly curled, her makeup was flawless and elegant. Her lips were stained with a dark rouge that would look fucking amazing ringed around my cock. Her hips were wide, perfect for holding onto. And her ass was round and plump in that tight leather skirt, making me want to hike it up and fuck her from behind. I want to slide my cock into her slowly and watch her take every fucking inch of me.

Fuck. I'm rock hard.

I adjust my cock, tucking it into the waistband of my slacks before heading out of the washroom and down the corridor to the elevator so I can head out for lunch. I catch a glimpse of Elissa walking across the road to the café across the street, disappearing behind the door as it closes. The urge to follow her is too strong, and before I comprehend what I'm doing, my feet carry me across the road and into the café.

A warm, rich aroma of coffee and fresh baked goods laces the air and I breathe deep, letting it fill my lungs, saliva pooling in my mouth. My eyes roam around the room, searching for someone I shouldn't look for. And then I see her, with her mother of all people. Curiosity stirs inside me, wondering why they're meeting. I don't think Elissa has noticed me yet, and I find a spot behind them that's divided by a half wall, a planter box on top with a bush, so she can't see me. Tingles and sparks ignite all over my skin; just being within her proximity sets my soul on fire.

Her mother's smooth and sophisticated voice is just above a hush, but it's clear, and I can hear what she's saying until the waiter comes over to take my order. I place it rather hastily so he can take off and I can get back to eavesdropping. My ears prick at my name being spoken.

"So, what's going on with Brandt? Are you still together?" Collette's words are low and cold, almost disapproving. Elissa is silent a beat too long. She must be avoiding the question. *But why?*

"No." Her tone is clipped. "He broke it off with me." My brain doesn't believe what it's hearing right now. A gradual warm simmer starts in my stomach, slowly percolating. I turn my head as if it will help me hear the conversation better, and my ears flex like I'm a dog.

"*Brandt* broke it off with *you?* My, my. Here I thought that man was in love with you, but for him to walk away first is rather surprising. What did you do?"

Elissa sighs. And, although I can't see her, I know that sigh. It's defeatism; her shoulders are drooped, she's slumped in her chair, and she's probably picking at the cuticles on her nails.

"I didn't *do* anything. At least, not that I know of. He all of a sudden started pulling away."

Yeah, for good damn reason. I knew she was going to walk away again. I had to protect myself.

"I went over to confront him about how he was acting, and he broke it off. I couldn't even really say what I wanted. He cut me off several times, then he cut me out." Her voice sounds little and broken, and I want to walk around this wall, scoop her up in my arms and press her to my chest, smooth her hair and tell her everything will be okay. *Wait. Did she say I broke it off? No, I didn't. She did.*

My mind races back to the conversation we had a few weeks ago, desperately trying to remember. But then Collette says something that has me swallowing the vomit burning in my throat.

"Well, if you want, I know of a nice young gentleman looking for something serious. And before you say anything, please keep in mind that you're now in a position of power, and sleeping around is going to get you nowhere but in the board's bad graces. You need to be thinking about your future." Elissa groans and I fight back the snarl rumbling in my throat. *Who the fuck does Collette think she is? Elissa. Is. Mine.* My knuckles turn white as they curl around the edge of the table, and with any more pressure it'd crack in my hands.

"Mother, I'm not looking for anything right now. I'm thinking of just being on my own for a while. This thing with Brandt, I was taking it seriously. I thought we were on the same page…I thought. I don't know. Can we drop this, please, and just eat our lunch?"

Thought what…thought what? My mind is racing, trying to figure out what she was going to say. The waiter comes back and places my sandwich in front of me. Fingers clack against the table for a few seconds and then stop abruptly.

"Fine. As long as you think about it. Theo is a beautiful, kind man and his mother is on a charity committee with me. He would be thrilled to meet you…" Collette continues to chat for the next few minutes, but I can't hear any more because the blood is pounding in my ears. I feel like I'm burning from the inside out. There's an invisible set of claws scratching its way out of my body, gripping my throat, choking me. Bile and acid churn in my stomach. *What the fuck is Collette thinking, setting Elissa up with someone else? She knew the deal, that Elissa was supposed to marry me. She's supposed to be my wife. Fuck!*

As my thoughts run wild, I suddenly hear some shuffling from behind me. I hazard a glance over my shoulder and roughly see through the plants that the two women are standing and slipping their coats back on. My thighs and feet tense. They're wanting to stand up and call Collette out and tell her to fuck off. That Elissa is mine. But something stops me; a nagging voice in the back of my head, compelling me to stay where I am, because revealing I've heard their conversation would only make things worse.

I grind my teeth together as I wait for their footsteps to fade and when the bell over the door sounds, I can finally relax, but my body doesn't get the message. Every fibre inside my body is rigid. The thought of Elissa in someone else's arms leaves me in a white, fiery rage. And the fact that she thinks I walked away from our relationship fucking kills me. She's the one who walked away. I may have kept my distance, but she was the one who instigated this breakup. *Right?*

I wolf down my food, throw some bills down, and push myself away from the table. I stalk out of the café and force myself to not cross the street and go back into the Black & Wells tower. I have to stop myself from following Elissa back to her office, slamming the door, bending her over the desk, hiking up her skirt, and fucking her from behind.

I curl my fists and shove them deep into my pockets as I walk a block, cooling off before ordering a car to take me back to Collins Global Collective. I'm all fucking confused about what happened the other week between Elissa and I, and after hearing the conversation between her and her mother? I don't know what to think anymore.

A pang ricochets in my chest, and it hurts to breathe. *Did I just fuck up immensely?*

CHAPTER
TWENTY-TWO

ELISSA

Collette and I are standing outside the Black & Wells tower. The murky March sun streams through the clouds, warming up the slight chill in the air. I linger, feeling incredibly awkward as I wait for my mother to dismiss me, or say goodbye, or something. But she just stands there, staring at me. It's almost like she doesn't know what to say or do either.

"Well…thanks for lunch, Mother." My tone is stiff, only increasing the awkwardness. I shift my weight, bite the inside of my cheek, and look away. My mother clears her throat and tucks a wisp of hair behind her ear, then looks down to tap on her phone, presumably to call her driver.

"Yes, it was nice." She steps forward and wraps her arms around me, plastering my arms to my sides. I'm unsure of what I should do. She presses a light kiss on the side of my cheek, and a part of my hard exterior cracks. *What the hell is going on? Collette never gives affection unless there's someone watching.* I glance around, trying to find a camera, a board member, someone. But there's nothing, no one. *What the hell...*

"Let's do it again soon, darling. Maybe next week you can come for dinner, and I'll have Alessandra whip something up for us." My brows furrow as my eyes grow concerned, but my mother says it without flinching or sarcasm. I'm so confused as to what's going on with her right now. "And please think about Theo. I think you two would make a wonderful couple."

"Thanks Mother, but I don't think that's going to happen."

"Just keep an open mind and think about it, please."

"Sure," I say, just to appease her. With a small but warm smile, she dips her body into the black sedan that's pulled up beside us. I watch her car pull away, and I stand there, feeling a whole lot of confusion. This lunch was clearly meant to be used to set me up with someone, but it was different. It was the most pleasant meal I've had with her, and she didn't push the issue of me meeting Theo. Just then, the sky tears open with a rumble and rain starts pouring down on me. Risking looking like a drenched rat, I stand under the chilly rain anyway and let the droplets wash away the feeling of this weird lunch.

I decide to duck out of work early because of my drenched outfit, and the fact that my mascara was running down my face, leaving me looking like a really ugly trash panda. I squish through the door of my apartment and I hear a muffled crash, then Riley's bedroom door clicks open. A flustered Riley, her hair wild and eyes wide, pokes her head outside of the door. Her head turns toward the living room first, then finds me at the foyer. Her eyes widen even more as she sucks in her lip and a nervous smile twitches on her face. She looks rather guilty, and I can't understand why, until another bump comes from behind her as she maneuvers herself out of the door and closes it behind her. Riley's face is now burning red.

"Oh. My. God. Rhys is here, isn't he?"

Her face drains of all colour and tears rim her eyes as her breath catches in her throat. She gives me a shy, curt nod. And that's when I really take her in — her clothes are mussed and her lips are swollen and red. The hair would have been an identifier, but she tends to nap hard, so messy hair doesn't always mean *this*.

"You're hooking up with Rhys right now? After how he treated you and denied the baby was his? Guilt molds her face, her brows furrowing and eyes quivering as she searches my gaze for some sort of acceptance. Something to tell her it's okay. When she doesn't get it, she sighs.

"'Lissa, I'm sorry. I know how you feel about it. But he…he called and seemed apologetic. He asked to talk —"

"Isn't that what happened last time?! Isn't that how he got you fucking knocked up in the first place?!" I'm fuming. Rhys is here, taking advantage of a broken Riley, again. "Get the fuck out of here, Rhys!" I shout, anger seeping into every syllable of my words. My eyes cloud red, my blood is boiling.

The door clicks again, and Rhys pops his head out of the door, looking drained and scared. He's buckling up his belt as he shimmies himself around Riley. His eyes are avoiding mine, his shoulders are slumped, and his mussed black hair matches Riley's. For fuck's sake. He pushes past me, grabs his coat, and whispers a goodbye before disappearing out our front door.

"Seriously, 'Lissa? You really had to do *that*?"

"You're fucking right I did. Especially before you made another mistake." Riley's face reddens as she grits her teeth; her jaw pulses.

"Who the fuck are you to tell me about mistakes? Who let Brandt fucking slip through her fingers because she couldn't own up to her feelings? Huh? Who always keeps people at arm's length so she doesn't get hurt? At least I try. At least I give myself a chance to find something I'm looking for. Sure, maybe I was about to make a mistake. But that's my choice to make! Fuck, Elissa. And you know the worst thing? You didn't even let me explain anything before throwing Rhys out. It should surprise me, but it doesn't."

My heart aches as I stand here, letting my best friend yell at me. But there's nothing I can do or want to do. She's right. Everything she said. When she finally finishes her rant, her face and eyes are red, she's got tears streaming down her face, and her hands are balled into tight fists. I raise my hands in surrender and hang my head.

"I…I'm sorry, Riles. I didn't mean to spin out like that. He just gets under my skin. He uses you and then throws you away like garbage when he's finished with you. I just didn't want to see you hurting again after another hookup. Especially now that you're pregnant. You don't need all that extra stress."

My eyes plead with hers, begging for her forgiveness. Her arms cross, locking into position like she's bracing herself for impact, but a moment later, she drops her arms. She lets them fall to her sides, her fingers wiggling nervously. She looks away, and the hair that's not all tangled swishes in her face. After a few more seconds, her shoulders fall, curling inward, as she wraps her hands around her small belly bump. Another long sigh slips from her lips and her eyes meet mine. She gives me a weak smirk and I rush forward and pull her in for a hug.

"I'm sorry, Riles. I'm just protective of you. You *and* little Kiwi, now." My hands slide down her arms and I lock our fingers together as I wait for her response. Her eyes glimmer with sadness and happiness, two conflicting emotions, and I don't know which one I've caused. Probably both. Fuck.

"I know, 'Liss," she says, her voice a weak, wobbly whisper. She clears her throat, rolls her shoulders back, and nudges her head toward the living room. I kick off my shoes, my feet squishing as they land on the tile, and Riley giggles, tugging me along until we both plop onto the couch. The moisture from my wet pants seeps into the couch, I groan, hoping that it doesn't make the couch smell like mildew.

"Look, Riles. Let's do this in a minute. Let me change first, pretty please." She playfully rolls her eyes and sticks out her tongue. I hop off the couch and make a quick exit to my room. I peel off my clothes, letting them slide to the floor in a puddle, and unclasp my drenched bra and hang it over the door to the en suite washroom to dry out. Digging through my dresser, I find a ratty, oversized sweater and a pair of cozy black leggings and put them on. I cross the room over to my bed and crouch to the floor to reach under my bed and find my slippers. My feet push into the soft, fuzzy slippers and I feel immensely warmer. I pad back to the living room and Riley has laid down a towel on the couch from where my ass left some water.

"So…" Riley starts. Her eyes shift as she chews on the inside of her cheek.

"So." I confirm. She wriggles in her spot and releases a heavy breath.

"I don't want to hear what you think. I know what you're thinking, but I love him. I can't help it."

My lips tighten into a thin line.

"I know you do, but I just don't want to see you hurt when he freaks out and leaves again. Who knows? He might freak out when the baby is born and disappear on you, leaving you to raise it alone, anyway. I think you just need to be careful, and tread lightly. I just don't want to see you hurt. You know I always have your back and am here for whatever you need." Her posture and face soften. Her hand slides off her lap and into mine, grasping my hand.

"I know you do, E. I love ya."

"Love you too, Riles."

CHAPTER TWENTY-THREE

RILEY

After Elissa and I talked out our heated argument about Rhys, I retreated to my room. It's not that I'm mad at her or anything, but I felt she was a little hostile about the whole situation. Yes, I know Rhys and I were in my bedroom, but we weren't doing anything but laying there and talking. His hand was gently grazing my shoulder as we laid facing each other, his soft fingertips tickling my skin. It was honestly quite nice for a change. For a moment, it felt like the days when we were in love and happy. A sharp pang rips through my chest at the thought.

I sink into my bed, letting Elissa's comments during our fight ping back and forth in my mind. I slide my phone out of the side pocket of my black leggings and tap out a quick message to Rhys.

Me: *Hey, sorry about E. She's been a bit overprotective since I got pregnant. It was nice hanging like that again.*

A few moments later, Rhys replies.

Rhys: **Thumbs-up emoji**

Huh…that's rather weird. No. Don't do that. Do not read too much into one tiny emoji response.
Easier said than done.

• • •

Four days go by, and I can't blame this sinking feeling in my gut on the baby. Nope. Rhys hasn't reached out at all except for that one thumbs-up. I'm a bundle of nerves and anxiety; a live wire that's wriggling around on the ground, sparking at every little jostle.

"Morning," Elissa says as she walks into the kitchen behind me. I jump about a foot in the air, and my heart is racing as I spin around to face her.

"Fuck, Elissa. Don't just scare people like that," I snap. Elissa's eyebrows crease and her eyes narrow as she stares me down.

"What the hell is wrong with you?" She folds her arms, and her eyes shift past me and to the toaster that's smoking behind me.

"Shit," I mumble as I rush toward the toaster and press the circular blue "cancel" button, popping up my charred toast. Groaning, I pluck the blackened slices up and toss them between my hands until I reach the garbage, dumping them in. I stalk over to the vent fan above the stove and turn it on, trying to air out some of the burnt toast smell before Elissa or I think we're having a stroke.

When I turn to face Elissa again, her arms are still cemented across her chest and she's tapping her shoe on the floor, clearly growing increasingly irritated. My shoulders drop as I release a breath, then lean my hips against the counter and brace my hands behind me on the edge of the cool marble countertop.

"Rhys hasn't reached out to me since you so *kindly* threw him out."

Elissa scoffs, rolls her eyes, and shrugs. "See? I told you he would do this. Fucking retreat when things get hard. These men are all the same."

"I'm not getting into this with you again, E. You're just as bad as the men. You push people away on purpose or avoid anything altogether if it's not platonic. I really need you to be supportive right now. Just listen to me whine right now and tell me he'll come to his senses. I know you may not believe that, but it's what I need to hear right now." I take a deep breath and sigh. "I need a bit more positivity before we go home to Chatham to tell my parents about… this." I point to my stomach.

Elissa's features soften and her arms drop to her sides as she walks toward me, her heels clicking against the hardwood floors. Her arms wrap around my shoulders and she pulls me in, one hand rubbing my back.

"It'll be fine, Riles. He'll come around, eventually."

I snort out a laugh. "Well, you could have said something original, ya know." We both burst into giggles. Elissa steps back, her hands clasping my upper arms and rubbing them reassuringly. Her eyes search mine to make sure I'm really okay. I give her a curt nod and a weak smile. She returns my smile and rolls her shoulders back.

"'Kay. Well, I've got to get to the office…I'll see you tonight for dinner? Let me know if you hear any updates." I tell her I will and we say goodbye. When the door to the apartment clicks, I saunter back over to where the toaster sits on the counter and fish out two fresh pieces of bread, praying that I don't burn these pieces too.

• • •

The morning seems to drag on as I lie around on the couch, flipping through the channels on the television mindlessly. It's almost noon when the email alert goes off on my phone. Still laying on the couch, I shimmy my body so I can reach for my phone on the coffee table. Once I grab it, I shimmy myself back into a comfy position and open my email app. Nothing but junk mail. I was really hoping it was going to be Rhys messaging me or something since I haven't heard from him. My heart sinks in my chest and an overwhelming sense of dread creeps in.

• • •

Not quite sure what else to do, I push myself off the couch and pace the living room for a few minutes until my hands start twitching. I close the distance between me and the kitchen and pull out the cleaning supplies to start scrubbing everything in sight. The coarse, scrubby part of the sponge grates away at my smooth skin, and my hands prune from being dunked in water over and over. Once the entire kitchen is clean, even the cupboards and shelves, I move on to the bathrooms.

A few hours later, the entire apartment is wiped, vacuumed, mopped, and smelling like the inside of a Pine-Sol bottle. I'm physically exhausted and frustrated that Rhys still hasn't mentioned anything. I hear the front door open and Elissa's shoes click down the hallway.

"Hey 'Liss. How was work?" I mumble, too tired to even move my lips. My chest heaves as I swallow deep breaths. Elissa's eyes roll over me with concern.

"Is everything okay?" she asks. A second later she sniffs the air in a dramatic fashion, using her hands to waft the scent into her nose. "Were you stress cleaning today?"

I roll my eyes.

"I don't know why you'd ask that when you can clearly smell that I was stress cleaning." Elissa's eyes narrow at me, and anger flickers behind them.

"You need to be careful with cleaning products and stuff. It's probably not healthy for the baby. And neither is working yourself until exhaustion."

"Okay, *Mom*," I tease, sticking my tongue out at her. She swats at me playfully, then plops down on the couch beside me. Her head falls back onto the top of the couch as she closes her eyes and releases a heavy sigh. "How was work?"

Elissa shudders and that tells me *almost* everything I need to know. "I'm assuming it was another meeting and Brandt was there again."

"Yeah, and he acts like I don't even exist. Which I think is way worse. He avoids me at all costs. I just don't get it…I don't even know what I did to get this kind of reaction from him. I thought things were going well." Her posture deflates, and she lets her body slip down until her head is laying in my lap, her loose bronze curls cascading over my legs. My hands automatically find her hair and stroke it.

"It'll work itself out. Don't worry."

"No, someone just needs to give him a kick in the ass."

We both chuckle, and I reach forward, my belly pressing into Elissa's head slightly as I grab the remote and turn the television on. We lounge in comfortable silence together until it's bedtime.

CHAPTER
TWENTY-FOUR

BRANDT

The last few meetings that I've attended at Black & Wells Publishing and Press…to say they've been weird is an understatement. It takes everything I have not to reach out and touch her. Pull her into my arms and bury my face in her neck. To breathe her in so deep, I choke on her scent. To tangle my fingers in that unruly cloud of hair. To press my mouth against hers and kiss her until her lips are chapped and swollen.

But I can't.

I need to protect myself. I need to protect my heart. Now that there's no clause, who knows how long it would have been until she wanted to be free of me again? Free of her father's demands? I need her to come to me. I need her to want me. I need her to fight for me. To fight for us. I can't be the only one who holds us together. But it's killing me, staying away, keeping my distance. It kills me that I need to act cold and distant when all I want to do is melt into a puddle at her feet and beg for her to take me back.

"Yo, Brandt…" Rhys' voice pulls me from my anguish. I blink the thoughts of the beautiful redhead from my mind and refocus on Rhys.

"Sorry," I say. "I was lost in thought."

"That's been happening a lot lately," Rhys says. I nod my head. There's nothing else to say about it. I feel lost when she's not there, now that I know what it's like to have her beside me. I struggle daily with how I handled things between us, but it's always been me chasing her.

"What's going on with you?" I ask Rhys, wondering why he wanted to meet up at 7 AM on a Saturday. The diner, Griddle Cakes, is filled with the early morning crowd, and the sound of clinking dishes, chatter, and the bustle of the kitchen fills the air. My stomach grumbles, begging for food. Rhys looks white as a ghost, and his face is sunken and gaunt. Dark circles rim his eyes.

"So, the baby is definitely mine," Rhys grumbles. I try, and fail, to hide my look of "I told you so." "Yeah, yeah. I know. I'm an idiot for thinking otherwise. I get it."

"What's the problem then? Why do you look like shit?" I fold my arms across my chest as I wait for his response, but the server comes over first.

"What will you two have?" she asks, her voice flat and uninterested. Midge, as per her name tag, looks haggard and worn down, and deep crow's feet line her eyes. She scratches Rhys' order down on her pad of paper, then turns to me and puts her weight on her back foot.

"Uh, I'll have a coffee, black. And French toast for me, please." Midge nods her head, and a stray strand of silver hair flies free of her ponytail. She swivels on her heel and scurries away, smacking the gum in her mouth as she goes. "Have you spoken to Riley at all?" Rhys' face contorts guiltily. Any colour that had returned drains again, but this time it's replaced with a green tinge, like he's going to be sick. "C'mon, Rhys. When did she tell you?"

"About a week ago," he says. "And…I've kind of been avoiding her ever since." My eyes narrow at him, questioning why he would ignore her. As if reading my mind, he explains. "I've just been a little nervous about reaching out, I guess. It's been a lot to process. I mean, yes, the possibility it was always mine was clearly there, but I didn't want to believe it. I've also been feeling a little guilty, pushing her away so hard after everything. I know I've been a dick. But this relationship stuff is all new to me."

We both sit in silence for a few moments, letting his revelation settle. "I guess I was just being a chickenshit." I give a lighthearted hum at his statement. His hands reach into his black hair, tousling it.

"What are you gonna do, man?" I ask. Rhys runs his hands through his hair again, tugging at the roots a little. Tufts of black hair stand up once he's done. He's a mess, and a nervous one at that.

"I don't know…I'm not ready to be a father." His knee bounces underneath the table, connecting with the underside at random intervals, shaking the table.

"And you think Riley is ready to be a mother? Grow up." Rhys rolls his eyes at me, leans forward, and grabs the ketchup as Midge approaches with our plates. He douses his hash browns in it once our food is in front of us.

"Back off. I just need more time to digest this." I sit there, staring at Rhys as he actively avoids looking at me. He's running away from what could be the best thing in his life, because he's scared. I get it, I do. But I'm also envious as hell. I've pictured Elissa's belly swollen with my baby, a ring on her finger…she'd be all mine. Maybe it was all because of a business deal, but I still had her. Now, I don't.

Who are you to judge Rhys? Didn't you break things off with Elissa because you feared getting hurt first? Well, fuck. I grab the syrup bottle off the table and drizzle my French toast before I grab my knife and fork and tuck in.

• • •

After breakfast, Rhys and I head over to the gym to meet up with Liam and shoot some hoops. Once we finish getting changed in the locker rooms, we head toward the basketball court and stop by the fountain to fill our water bottles. We place the bottles on the benches at the side of the court and lightly stretch before doing some warm-up line drills. Our shoes squeak on the court as we run back and forth. And as I run, I race away from this feeling of dread that crashes over me any time I think about Elissa. One mention of her and I'm sent hurtling head first into this spiral of fear that I may have just fucked up enough to make it never work again.

Something round and orange comes flying at me, and I stumble trying to avoid it. Rhys is off at the sideline giggling like a schoolgirl.

"You're supposed to catch it, Brandt," he snickers. I roll my eyes and run over to retrieve the ball that went soaring by me. I pick it up and dribble it over to where Liam and Rhys are standing.

"Wait, wait, wait," Liam says. "You're telling me he fucking broke it off with Elissa?" His eyes are wide and his pupils dilate. I swear, if I see a tent in his shorts, I'm gonna kill him. "What is wrong with you? She's like…perfect. Fuck, does that mean I have another shot at her?" He says it mockingly, but my burning glare quickly wipes the goofy smile off his face as he turns away and grabs another ball off the rack, dribbling it quickly.

"Jesus, if looks could kill," Rhys laughs. "If you didn't want another guy going after her, you shouldn't have walked away from her. Besides, Liam *did* have her first." This sets off a growl in my throat, rumbling throughout my body.

"Don't need to remind me of that," I snap, and I launch the ball from my chest into his. He grunts as it collides with him. The knowledge that she was with Liam before me sits very close to the surface of my mind, grating on my nerves. I wish I could wipe her slate clean and know it's only been me who's been inside her.

"Shit, Collins. We're only joking with you. Fucking relax. If you still want her, then go and get her." I ignore his remark and run onto the court, swiping the ball away from Liam and setting myself for a lay-up. He has no idea how badly I want to *go and get her*. To grab her and twist my hands into her gorgeous, thick, copper hair and tug until her head tips back and her lips part. So I can slide my tongue into her mouth and taste her. Drink up every last ounce of air she breathes until she's nothing but a husk in my arms. To have her give herself to me completely, in a way she'll never give to anyone else. That's what I want. But until she's ready to fight for us, I need to stay away. She needs to reach out first.

I'm scared I'll be waiting forever for her.

CHAPTER
TWENTY-FIVE

ELISSA

Suddenly it's almost April, and Riley can't hide the baby any longer. Her cute little bump has grown into a cute little ball. I keep pressing Riley to tell her parents, but she keeps putting it off. I don't understand why. Her parents are nothing like mine. They're caring, loving, wholesome. They'll probably be excited at the news of a grandbaby. A small twinge plays at my heartstrings, wanting the family she has.

"Okay, enough is enough, Riles," I say. Her mouth is wide open and the spoon hangs in midair outside of her mouth while her gaze slides across the island to meet mine. Her mouth takes a full minute to close as she slowly drops her spoon back into her bowl of cereal. She rolls her hunched shoulders back, sitting straight up on the stool with a worried look etched on her face. Her lips quiver and tears well up in her eyes. *Fuck.*

"I…I know. I have to tell them, my parents. I'm just scared," she says. A heavy tear drops from her eyes, like a swimmer from a diveboard, and lands in her bowl of cereal, followed by another, then another. The room grows silent until the hum of the refrigerator kicks on. I round the corner of the island and walk over to her, cradling her into my chest and hugging her head.

"You're not going to do it alone. It'll be you and me, so don't forget that." My voice is soft and comes out in more of a hush, trying to calm her down. She snorts back some tears and snot, and, using the sleeve of her shirt, she dries her cheeks.

"Aww," she groans. "I have tears in my cereal. Now it's going to be too salty. And I was *really* craving that bowl of Cinnamon Toast Crunch." My cheeks puff from trying to stifle a laugh when her shoulders start to shake, and we both burst into hysterical laughter. Tears start running down Riley's cheeks from laughing so hard.

"Let's just go out for breakfast. Let's go see if Becca is working today." Riley rolls her eyes at me.

"Dude, you know she's always working." She shakes her head and laughs. "But yeah, let's go and get something to eat. I'm still starving. Mmmm…real cinnamon French toast," she says dreamily, practically drooling.

• • •

Griddle Cakes is packed, to no one's surprise. The Toronto location has practically become our regular spot, so much so that Becca keeps a lone table in the corner of the restaurant open just for us at all times of day. God, I love that woman. Sure enough, as we push through the doors and snake past the line-up, a chorus of groans and grunts following us, there's the small two-person booth in the corner. Becca's head pops up as she looks over in our direction and a big smile stretches across her face.

"Over here, ladies!" she shouts. Riley gives the line an apologetic look. I roll my eyes.

"We have a reservation," I say to them, which seems to shut them up. Under my breath I mutter, "A standing reservation." I chuckle. As we take our seats, Becca comes over carrying two mugs and a pot of coffee, placing all three down on the table. The restaurant is buzzing and humming with chatter from the other customers. The sweet scent of syrup and pancakes fills the air while the rich steam from the pot of coffee teases my taste buds.

"Oh. My. Goodness. Look at you, Riley! You're getting so big!" Becca squeals. Riley pushes away from the table and stands up, proudly showing off her baby bump. Her hands rub her swollen little bump and tug at her shirt, tightening it so it makes her tummy more protruded. Becca's eyes are full of wonder and happiness. "May I?" she asks. Riley nods her head, and that's all the permission Becca needs before her hands are wrapped around Riley's belly and rubbing. "Have you felt any kicks yet?" Riley's eyes light up as she nods her head.

"Mhm, I have! It's such a weird feeling. Like something is trying to claw its way out of you." She chuckles. "Well, I guess in a way, it will be soon enough!"

"How far along are you now?"

"Um, almost five months. Wow, yeah…five months. That's crazy," Riley responds, her expression growing thoughtful. The bell over the door sounds, and the crunching of the till rings in the background as customers scrape and scratch their plates. The noise momentarily fills the silence.

"Well, I'll just leave the pot with you gals, and be back to take your orders. Although, I'm pretty sure I know what they'll be."

"Thanks Becks!" I call after her. Riley absentmindedly sits down in the chair, teetering on the edge of a breakdown it looks like. "What's up, Riles?" Her eyes dart around the room before finding mine.

"I only have four months left…a-a-a-and I have nothing done. Nothing! I don't have a room for the baby. Hell, I don't have a crib-thingy that they first sleep in. I don't even know if I want to breastfeed, or how the hell I'm gonna push this thing out of my vagina!" Her chest is rising and falling rapidly as she gulps air.

"Take a deep breath, Riley. It's fine. Four months is more than enough time, it's called a bassinet, you don't need to decide if you're breastfeeding right now, and many women have done it, and you can too." Her eyes quiver as they look into mine and her shoulders relax as she draws in a big breath. "That's good. Now, let's get some breakfast, drink this delicious coffee, and…" I reach into my purse to grab a pen and rip a napkin from the holder on the table.

"Let's make a list while we eat, of all the things we need to do, and all the things you're worried about. Then we'll spend the rest of today researching things and planning our trip to see your parents. And, before you have a chance to interrupt me, we're doing it in two weeks. Just before the end of the month. It's your mom's birthday, it would be a nice surprise, and I'm sure she'll love the fact that you're giving her a grandchild. Now you may speak," I say. My hand extends, giving her the floor to speak. Her mouth is open and gaping, but instead of saying anything, she closes it and gives me a heartfelt smile as her eyes well with tears.

"Thanks 'Lissa. I don't know what I'd do without you." I reach over and grab her hands, which are wrapped around her warm mug of coffee.

"Well, you'll never have to find out. I'm always going to be here for you, babe. You *and* the little Kiwi."

After a moment of staring into each other's eyes and holding hands, Becca returns. "What can I get you gals?"

I smile, turning my head towards her and order for the both of us.

"She wants French toast with cinnamon on it, please. And give it to her deep fried. Baby loves the carbs. And I'll take a stack of flaps, please." Becca smiles, winks, and turns away. As she walks back behind the counter to place our order, I take a good look around, taking in the atmosphere of the restaurant. If we thought the Kingston location was busy, put an already-great restaurant in downtown Toronto and you'll see what busy really is. The line is out the door, and people have been waiting longer than before we even got here. I *almost* feel bad for them, but Becca's made the choice to leave a booth open for us, and we're her loyal customers. We come back here almost every day, especially since Riley's cravings have been strong.

Riley and I chat away, creating the list of things we need to do, research, and should probably start shopping for as we wait for our food. By the time Becca returns with our food, we've written four napkins of things to do, some of which we are going to do after we eat breakfast. Going shopping, obviously. The easiest of all of them.

Becca sets our plates down in front of us. Stacks of fluffy, scrumptious pancakes and French toast sit in heaping piles in front of us; my mouth starts salivating.

"Oh, I forgot to tell you. Midge said these two ridiculously handsome guys were in earlier. I was so upset when she told me, because I was like, I would have totally gotten their numbers or something, ya know? Apparently, the one guy looked like he got kicked in the stomach and was about to be sick, though. Something about him being a dad… too bad the good-looking ones are always taken." My eyes wander to Riley and she's sitting looking dazed.

"What did they look like?" she asks weakly. Becca thinks for a moment, but then turns and calls Midge over. Midge, a silver-haired fox in her day, walks over, smacking some gum between her teeth.

"Tell them about the cuties you saw earlier…she was even saying she wished she got their numbers for us girls," Becca says, wiggling her brows. Midge rolls her eyes and then wiggles her eyebrows as well.

"One was tall, broad shoulders, with golden-brown hair. The other one looked like hell, but still handsome. He had black hair…" Midge keeps talking animatedly while I zone out, looking over at Riley to make sure she's okay. These pregnancy hormones are awful, because her eyes are constantly misty and brimming with tears.

"Uh, thanks Midge," I say. "Maybe next time you'll get numbers for us." I chuckle halfheartedly, and she shrugs and walks away.

Becca's expression is full of concern as she glances between me and Riley. "I'll just let you two eat and come back in a minute," she says before walking away. I cut into my pancakes, keeping a watchful eye on Riley as she picks at her plate, pushing around the pieces of French toast she cut up.

"Eat up, Riles. We're going shopping after this, and you need your strength." She nods her head in a slow, sad bob.

CHAPTER TWENTY-SIX

ELISSA

Arthur, my driver, helps haul all the stuff we bought upstairs. There are piles of bags with baby clothes, toys, and other random things babies need, like nail clippers and booger suckers. We even picked out the crib, which is being delivered in a few weeks. Riley seems to have calmed down a little bit, but she's still upset from hearing about Rhys being all devastated about having a baby. I'm sure it's not what she thinks. He's probably just feeling guilty over the fact that he's been acting like a dick for the last few weeks.

"Where do you want to put all this stuff?" I ask Riley. She's standing in the middle of the living room with bags lined up on the couches, coffee table, and floor surrounding her. Her face is devoid of emotion. She looks like a shell of herself. It crumbles my heart knowing that there's little I can do for her in this moment, other than be there for her, in whatever way she needs. "Why don't you go lie down and have a nap? You're probably exhausted. We can deal with this stuff later," I say. She nods her head once and shuffles off to her room, the door closing behind her with a soft click.

A wave of anger pummels me and I have to struggle not to take my phone out and message Brandt about his friend being a fucking moron. What good will it do? Not a fucking lot. Can't make a man be a father when he doesn't want to be. I know that very well from experience. I just pray that everything we heard is a big misunderstanding, and Rhys comes around to make things better. Riley deserves so much more than an absent baby daddy. But even if that's how this turns out, Riley will have me by her side, no matter what. I push away the rest of my thoughts of Brandt for now and focus on what I'm doing.

• • •

Approximately two hours later, Riley emerges from her room looking worse than she did when she went to lie down. I can only imagine how she feels, because if it's even a fraction of how I feel about how Brandt left things between us, I know she's going through hell.

I honestly didn't think I'd see the day where I'd be the person in a relationship, and who's upset over losing one. If anyone were to run, I'd have thought it would be me, not Brandt. I can't explain this sense of abandonment I feel. It's worse than what I've ever felt with my parents being absent in my life. He *wanted* me. He *wanted* a relationship, with all the little things, like cuddling, and whatever else you fucking do in relationships. I just *wanted* him. But he went and walked away from me. *He walked away from me…*and what does that say about me? Clearly, my parents aren't the only ones who think I'm unlovable. Brandt probably realized his mistake and ran for the hills. Who would want to be with someone as unlovable as me? I'm just lucky I have Riley and Lana.

"Where is everything?" Riley asks, pulling me out of my spiral.

"Oh, I started putting everything away while you were napping. The random baby stuff, like toiletries, is in the washroom, I've started a load of laundry, and the other random things I put in the storage closet until you're ready to figure everything out."

She gives me a single nod, not saying much of anything. Right at this moment, I am so worried for her. She seems off-kilter, and I'm worried that she's not recovered enough to handle this disappointment and sadness. I shuffle over to her and wrap my arms around her thin frame, pulling her in close for a crushing embrace. "Rhys will come around, Riles." And that's all I can say, because I can't promise her that he will, but I also can't leave her with no hope.

"Yeah…you're probably right," she whispers. She steps out of my arms and walks over to the fridge, rummaging around but coming out empty-handed. She's so disconnected right now.

"Do you want to go out and grab something to eat?" I ask her. She shrugs her shoulders and sighs.

"Sure, I guess. Doesn't matter to me." Her tone is nonchalant and monotonous. I clear my throat and shoot daggers with my eyes at her.

"You're eating. I'm not arguing with you about this. That baby needs nutrition."

She rolls her eyes at me.

"Yes, Mom," she says playfully. "I didn't mean it like that. I just meant I was fine having something here if we didn't go out." I fold my arms across my chest and kick out a leg.

"Go get dressed. We'll go somewhere nice for dinner. Maybe grab a juicy steak or something."

"Mmm…steak," she says, and I can practically hear the saliva pooling in her mouth. I giggle to myself as she walks past me toward her room.

"And we still need to plan our trip to tell your parents!" I holler as she disappears behind her door.

• • •

When we get to the steakhouse, I let Arthur know that we'll text him when we're almost finished eating. That way, he doesn't need to park and wait right in downtown Toronto, and he can go have dinner or something himself. Inside, the restaurant is swanky and upscale. There's grey marble flooring, expensive-looking chandeliers that glitter across the vaulted ceiling, lots of rich mahogany wood throughout the place, and a massive waterfall fountain that stands in the centre of the entryway, dividing the waiting area from the dining area. The hostess counter is right in front of the fountain.

"Do you have a reservation?" the hostess says condescendingly, without looking up from her book.

"Uh, technically no," I respond. "But I believe the Blacks have a standing reservation?"

The hostess' eyes snap up and her body becomes ramrod straight as her lips curl into a cheshire smile. Porcelain-white teeth, impeccably straight, gleam behind her plump rouge lips. "Oh, Ms. Black. So sorry, I didn't see you there. For two?" Her eyes flick between me and Riley. "Right this way." She extends her arm and grabs two menus, then leads us to the VIP area in the restaurant. As we pass the other tables, there's a shift in the air within the restaurant, but I can't quite put my finger on it. Every nerve in my body feels awakened, on high alert.

We take the stairs up to the platform in the middle of the restaurant and the hostess sets the menus down on a table, dips her head, and saunters off. The chairs make no noise as they glide across the smooth marble floor with ease. The place is pulsing with energy as people drink, eat, and converse, and I feel myself drown in the background noise, letting my thoughts disappear. I mellow and relax into the soft jazz that flows all around us.

A sharp pain stabs my shin and when I look up from my menu, Riley's face is drained of all colour, staring straight ahead at the bar. I stiffen a little as I turn, wondering what the hell has made her look like she's seen a ghost. The world slows down as I turn around and my eyes settle on what, or who, she is looking at. What are the odds of being at the same restaurant as them on the same day? My heart skips a beat before it starts racing, and everything inside me begs to go over there. For Riley, but also, selfishly, for me.

There, at the long, sleek wooden bar, with its marble top, are Brandt and Rhys.

I want to scream. I want to laugh. I want to cry.

I want to go over there and place myself in between his legs, press my lips firmly against his, and drink in everything he can possibly give me. I want to kiss him so deeply I will never forget what he tastes like, and then I want to slap him across the face for putting my heart in this irreparable state of loneliness. One that I thought could never outshadow the loneliness my parents left me with.

I squeeze my eyes shut, barricading the opening for my eyes to cry, and tell my mind that he's not here. That he means nothing to me, even if it takes lying to myself. When I open my eyes, I find Riley. She's still staring over at them and she looks broken. My hand drapes over hers before I grip her hand tightly and she breaks her stare to make eye contact with me. She gives me a grateful look and I can see the emotions swimming in her eyes, holding back the same tears that I just forced back.

CHAPTER TWENTY-SEVEN

BRANDT

Rhys still wasn't himself after breakfast this morning. So, I spent the day with him to try to get his mind off everything. I think it helped, but not by much. After a game of basketball at the gym, he was still feeling down, so I suggested we spend the day at his place and play video games. Shooting things, killing things, that kind of stuff. The shit we used to do in high school and in the early years of college, before I dropped out.

It's hard to console him when I'm not sure why he's upset. Is it the fact that he's actually going to be a father? Or is it that he treated Riley so fucking badly that he's now filled with regret? I hope it's the latter, honestly. Rhys can be a douche, but this is the worst he's ever been.

"Okay, I'm fucking sick of shooting people," I finally say. Rhys pauses the game and tosses the controller onto the coffee table, then drops his feet to the floor from where they were propped on the table.

"Let's go grab some drinks," he says. I hope he's not talking about going out to the bar, because one, I am not in the mood for it, and two, he's just found out he's going to be a father. He doesn't need any more drama.

"Sure," I say hesitantly. "Let's go to The Prime Cut for drinks, and we can have the full menu at the bar as well." Rhys nods his head, jumps off the couch, and retreats to his room to change into something nicer. Luckily, I always dress in some sort of casual business attire. Some dark slacks and a nice button-down shirt are my signature go-to for every day. Yeah, it might be a bit overboard for a Saturday or Sunday, but I'm busy running two fucking companies. I never know when I'm going to get pulled into a meeting.

I let my head loll back onto the couch and close my eyes. My hands run through my golden hair as I take a deep breath, and my mind wanders to where it always goes when I have a moment to myself: Elissa. It's been weeks since Elissa and I have been together, and I'm slowly losing it. Each day, there's another crack in my resolve to stay away from her and have her fight for us. Some days, I don't even know why I'm staying away, why I'm torturing myself with this need for her to choose me for once, instead of me always choosing her. But I have to. *Right?*

If I'm being honest with myself, it's more than that. It's more like the point of no return. I was an idiot, and now I need to stick to my guns. I can't crawl back like a little bitch and beg her to love me, even if that's exactly what I want to do. I want to run to her, fall to my knees, wrap my arms around her perfect legs, and cry, begging her to take me back. I miss the way she feels in my hands, my arms. She fit me so perfectly. And the way she kisses. *Fuck.* I miss her gorgeous, full, heart-shaped lips and the way they felt pressed against mine, and when they wrapped around my cock. Mmm. *Fuck. You need to get her out of your fucking head. Easier said than done, motherfucker.*

• • •

The Prime Cut is a posh, exclusive joint that I used to dream of being able to get into on a moment's notice when I was first starting up Collins Global Collective. The decor is a little over the top for my taste, but I never grew up in the atmosphere that it takes to impress the rich. This place screams opulence. Giant crystals drape off the light fixtures and sparkle brightly, the shiny marble floors gleam, and the ridiculous fountain waterfall at the hostess stand is just pretentious. *Really, who needs a waterfall fountain in their restaurant?*

The hostess walks us to the bar where Rhys and I sidle up against the reddish wood bar, with its sleek marble countertops. The restaurant is buzzing with life and laughter. Over here at the bar, it's more low-key. Mostly us businessmen talking shop, having a drink or two to unwind. The bartender comes over and I order a round of beers for me and Rhys. When the bartender walks away to get our drinks, I turn to Rhys.

"Any better?"

He shrugs. "Meh. I just need a few drinks and then we can talk about it. I really don't want to talk about it right this minute." I get that more than anyone — not wanting to talk about things, that is. But it's hard when you see your friend going through something and you just want to support them. He's my brother, and I'd do anything for him. Lord knows he's been a rock for me over the months that Elissa and I split for the first time. I nod at the bartender as he slides the beers over to us and I toss my black card down on the bartop.

"Open a tab for us, please."

● ● ●

We're pretty quiet over the first few beers, sometimes sitting in complete silence, punctuated with brief chatting about CGC. Things are finally running smoothly now that I'm back in the office more. Rhys has had his hands full these last few months and has done a great job with what he could, but there was too much on his plate. It was too much for anyone. No wonder this stuff with Riley is really weighing on him. Hopefully now he can get back to his regular self and step up, be a man.

"So...Riley," I say. Rhys shoots me a deadly look.

"So, Elissa."

"We're not here because of me and Elissa. It's you and this Riley situation that's got you all messed up."

Rhys sighs, his shoulders drooping as his head bows over his hands, which are clasping his beer on the counter. "Yeah, what about Riley?"

"Well, what are you going to do? You're going to step up and be there for her, right?" He side-eyes me and shakes his head in a noncommittal way. "What the fuck does that mean?" I grumble, my tone a bit threatening. Rhys straightens and his head falls back as he lets out an exasperated sigh.

"I don't know. It means I've fucked up and I don't really deserve to be part of this. She's better off without me." A wave of anger rumbles through me and my words taste bitter as I speak them.

"No, you don't deserve her. But she deserves to have a man beside her raising the child you two made together. And if it's not going to be you, it's going to be some other fucker, someone who realizes just how amazing Riley is, and he'll be the one raising *your* baby. Is that something you want?"

Rhys looks stricken with grief but gives nothing away. He's quiet and stewing over my words when something inside me hums. Something in the atmosphere shifts and it's like I can feel her here. *You're crazy. Yeah, crazy for Elissa.* I squirm on the stool, trying to refocus my thoughts on Rhys and his impending doom, but there's something nagging at the back of my mind telling me to look around and find her. *She's here; she's got to be.* Shut the fuck up, brain. I cautiously turn around in my chair and I see Elissa and Riley walking behind the hostess to the VIP section of the restaurant.

My heart pangs, and I'm overwhelmed with the need to run over there, scoop her up in my arms, and kiss her until she can't breathe anymore. Of all the places to run into her, she's here. With Riley, no less. I resolve to try to avoid Rhys running into Riley or seeing her, as I'm sure it'll only make things worse right now. I glance over again and Riley is cute in a black sweater dress, clearly trying to minimize her baby bump, but it's still noticeable. But Elissa...Elissa looks more radiant than I remember. Her luscious bronze curls flow down her back, her tight thighs and ass look amazing in a black pencil skirt that has a slit halfway up the front, and a burgundy chiffon top with a black tank underneath shows just the perfect amount of cleavage.

I'm straining so hard against my zipper that my cock throbs in pain.

Fuck, I need her.

It takes all my willpower to keep the distance, so I turn my attention back to Rhys and engage him in more work talk, avoiding the Riley issue because it triggers thoughts of Elissa — knowing they're here right now, it won't take long for my resolve to crack and I'll rush over there and plead for her to take me back. The conversation between Rhys and I flows a little easier when we're talking about work. But my mind keeps a tab on Elissa. It's like I can feel her presence everywhere. Everything inside me feels so much for her. It's hard to breathe when she's this close and I can't touch her. I love her, and I just need her to love me. Then, everything will be all right. We can fix things if she just admits she loves me and fights for us. That's all I need…

•••

The rest of the night is fine. Rhys seems to be in better spirits. As we're getting up to leave, I glance over and take one more look at Elissa before we leave. My eyes must be radiating with intensity at what I see, because Rhys follows my gaze and shuts up immediately. We're both standing here, brooding over *our* women, and there's some tall schmuck laughing and flirting with our women. Did I fail to mention they're *ours*? *No, they're not yours. You both were idiots and screwed it up*. It's hard to tell which one he's truly interested in, Riley or Elissa, but my heart sinks anyway. Just as we're about to walk away, Elissa stands up and this fucker pulls my woman into his arms, a rather cozy embrace, and she kisses him on the cheek.

What.

The.

Fuck.

Has she moved on while I'm here pining for her? I know I was the idiot who pulled away first, but could she really move on that quickly? After everything we've been through?

Rhys' elbow nudges my ribs, breaking my stare at Elissa and her new fuck buddy. Because that's all they can be. Fuck buddies. She doesn't do relationships. She was only going to "try" with me. *Fuck*. My head is spinning and I can't get a grip on any rational emotions. My skin is on fire and sweat is trickling down my back as I burn with rage. Rhys shoves the back of my shoulder, making me stumble slightly. It takes everything I have, all my strength, to turn away from her and walk out of the restaurant. And even when we step outside, with an abundance of fresh air surrounding us, I still feel like I can't breathe.

CHAPTER TWENTY-EIGHT

ELISSA

I've never been more thankful to have my back facing away from everything in a room as I am right now. The anxiety that sparks through me, knowing that Brandt is a handful of feet away…I feel like every piece of me is chipping and breaking away. I swear I can smell his wintry evergreen scent from here, filling my nostrils and giving me air to breathe. *Fuck, I miss him so much.*

Riley has done an impeccable job of ignoring the fact that Rhys is across from her. I can't tell if she's using her peripheral vision or what, but I haven't noticed her glance over there once. The fact that she's remaining strong in this moment spreads warmth all over my body, and it triggers the fighter in me to be stronger.

The waitress finally comes over and takes our order, both of us ordering the prime rib with a twice-baked potato and seasonal veggies. I strike up a conversation first, trying to fill the tense silence we have going on between us.

"So, next weekend?"

"Hmm?" Riley's absent eyes find mine as she rids herself of her thoughts and comes back to reality. Her amber-laced chocolate eyes blink the haze from them and she brightens. "What's up?"

"Next weekend. I was thinking we should take that weekend to go down and tell your parents about the baby."

Riley groans.

"Do we have to? I can wait a little longer before I need to tell them. Better yet, let's just send them a text, or a photo of the ultrasound picture," she says, full of optimism. My expression flattens as I stare at her, giving her my best "Are you kidding?" face. Her chuckle comes out whiny. "Yeah, I know. I need to tell them. I guess we can do it next weekend." With that settled and out of the way, I make a mental note to let Lana know that I'm coming down for the weekend and see if she wants to catch up.

"But honestly, E, do you think my parents are going to be pissed?"

I'm quiet and thoughtful for a moment, and her face drains of colour.

"I don't think they'll be pissed. Will they be upset? Maybe, but only because you're still recovering from your last episode. But you're an adult, and they love you, so I think they'll genuinely support you." Relief washes over Riley's face and she settles into her chair, letting her posture relax. "It's not like your parents are mine," I mutter under my breath.

Honestly, if I were to have gotten pregnant out of marriage, I think my father would have actually disowned me on the spot, the image of throwing his daughter out be damned. Because embarrassing him like that would have been one hundred times worse. It's hard to believe a man like him was so likeable across the company and in the public. He really knew how to put on a show. *Well, look at me now, Father. I know how to put on a show just like you. Never letting my mask slip. Always hiding my feelings, never letting the cracks show. Even when I'm broken inside from you, Mother, and Brandt.*

"'Lissa?" Riley murmurs. The worry in her tone breaks me out of my internal turmoil and the one-sided conversation with the ghost of my father.

"Sorry. My thoughts drifted for a moment," I say apologetically. Her eyes fill with concern and she nods empathetically.

"I know. It's hard being in the same room as Brandt and Rhys, isn't it?" Again, I can't let this false strength break, or we'll both be broken together.

"Uh, no. I was off thinking about work."

"Oh," she says in a small voice.

The server comes back, placing our food in front of us and filling my glass with more white wine. She places a bottle of sparkling water on the table for Riley. Riley rubs her stomach now without even realizing it, and she's doing it now as she fills her water goblet. A small breathy sigh escapes me as I pick up my wine and drink half the glass. The bright, fruity taste leaves a lingering note of hope on my tongue.

• • •

When we're almost finished eating, I realize I've spent the entire night fretting over whether Brandt and Rhys have noticed us, or if they've left yet. But I've not allowed myself a single peek to see if they're here. Truthfully, I don't need to turn around and look, because my skin still tingles with his presence. My body vibrates on the same frequency as his, and when we're in the same room, our bodies charge the air, like rubbing your socked feet on the carpet, causing static electricity. The tension between us is so thick that it suffocates everyone in the room until we're the only two standing.

So, no, I definitely don't need to look. I know he is still here. I feel him all around me.

"Elissa?" A deep, resonant voice fills the air. My eyes slide to my right and up, and there's one of the most handsome men I've ever seen. He has dark chocolate hair, clear, wide, light eyes, and stubble that covers a firm jaw. He looks familiar, but I can't quite place where I know him from. "It's Theo," he says with a wry smile. And then it clicks. He's the guy my mother wanted to set me up with the other week. Now it all makes sense. Theo Greenbelt is the son of the philanthropists in my parents' circle. His wide shoulders are a stark comparison to the tapered torso I can make out from his form-fitting charcoal Armani suit.

"Oh, Theo!" I push my chair back and give him a quick, friendly hug. "It's been years since I've seen you," I say. The last time I remember seeing him, he was a geeky fourteen-year-old with thick-rimmed glasses and braces. He was adorable then, but not like the man he is now. He certainly had a glow-up.

"Yeah, I know," he chuckles, and it's a sweet, robust sound. "It's been a while since I've seen you in the news, to be honest." A slight flush creeps across my face. "I heard about your father. I'm sorry. I know you weren't very close, but I'm sorry anyhow." He's still the sweet little kid at heart I knew back then. I give him a soft smile.

"Thanks, Theo. And regarding those headlines you're talking about, I'm not sure what you mean. I was, *am*, an angel," I joke, fluffing my hair over my shoulder. Riley is still sitting down when she clears her throat. "Oh, meet Riley, my best friend." Theo takes Riley's hand in his and presses a kiss to the back of it like she's a princess, and I swear she swoons. Her cheeks flush and her eyes shine.

"Nice to meet you, Riley." His voice is friendly and warm before he shifts his attention back to me. Riley quirks her brow and gives me a knowing smile, chuckling to herself. "Elissa and I used to be forced to hang out together whenever her parents made her come to Toronto in the summers," he says, and I notice something shifts in his eyes. His pupils dilate and his gaze fills with hunger. My heart patters, and it feels like I'm getting kicked in the chest by a horse. I can't even stand another guy looking at me this way anymore. I just wish it was the man behind me across the room.

"Well, Riley and I should get back to our dinner," I say softly. I try to break the goodbye to him gently so I hear nothing back from my mother about my rudeness.

"Oh, sure. Of course. Maybe we can meet up one night and really catch up." It's not a question he asks, it's more like a promise. One that I'm going to have to eventually break because I'm nowhere near ready to date anyone, even as a favour to my mother. The only man I want is over there. All this brooding over Brandt has the song *Issues* by Julia Michaels echoing in my head. Yeah, I've got issues. But I need him. *Fuck*.

"Yeah. That would be lovely," I say, just like other women do when they insincerely mean it. Part of me is disgusted at employing the same tricks I've seen my parents use time and time again. I move to Theo to say a polite goodbye just as his hand wraps around my lower back, tugging me in close. I circle my arms around his shoulders in the most platonic way possible, and kiss him on the cheek like my mother does with me. A quick brush of the lips against the cheek and a "mwah" noise. I feel his body stiffen slightly at the clear line I've drawn, but it's for the best. Besides, I really don't want to give him false hope. I can't do that to him. He really is a great guy, but I know he's just not for me. "I'll see you around, Theo. Give your mother my love," I say. His handsome head nods, a small, regrettable smile on his face.

"See you around, Elissa."

He walks off, and I suddenly feel this searing, burning pain burrowing into my back. Like a drill bit spinning around, sparking, growing hot from metal grinding on metal. I know immediately that Brandt just saw our exchange, and my heart sinks like a boulder in my chest. Now I definitely refuse to look in that direction. I stand frozen in place until Riley calls my name.

"What the fuck is wrong with you?" she asks. Her head turns slightly and I'm sure she sees the anger that I feel. "Oh…" That's all she says. I slowly sit down, pull the napkin off the table, let it rest in my lap, and pick up my fork and knife to continue eating.

CHAPTER
TWENTY-NINE

BRANDT

What the fuck have I done?

Has she moved on?

No, she couldn't have. She doesn't do relationships.

But then why was that guy mauling her with his eyes? Like he *knew* her. My heart feels like it's being ripped out of my chest, and I wonder — how many times can someone's heart withstand this type of pain and torture? She's supposed to be mine.

I've been avoiding going to Black & Wells over this past week, sending one of my assistants in my stead. I can't bear to look at her right now. Just thinking of that other guy, with his hands on her body, makes me see red. I don't even know if they're anything, but I just can't look at her without being consumed with wondering if she's moved on. It's better if she's out of sight, then she's out of mind. Except, my mind is always on her. *What the fuck did I do?*

My fingers curl into tight fists, crinkling the paper on the table in front of me. A sharp blow to my ribs shakes me from my spiralling thoughts. Shifting my eyes, I see Rhys giving me a stern look. His eyes narrow in an angry glare, spearing me on the spot. Suddenly, I feel eight pairs of eyes trained on me, waiting expectantly. Shit.

"I'm sorry. Continue," I grumble, my heart rate speeding up from my stupidity. The men and women gathered around the table shift uncomfortably in their seats and look at each other with eyes that say, "Is he okay?" *Fuck no, I'm not okay.* Rhys clears his throat.

"They want to know what you want to do with the stock that's been dropping in the tech sector. Specifically, Harrington Tech. With the CEO gone, it's dropping significantly," Rhys explains in a low voice out of the side of his mouth. I straighten my posture, adjust my suit jacket, and fiddle with the platinum Rolex on my wrist.

"Buy up to thirty percent more," I say resolutely. Murmurs and whispers break out across the table, and the suits look at me as if I've gone insane. "Take advantage of the dip in the market. They'll go up again. They're the leading tech company and we're second. Let's take advantage of this opportunity. And I doubt it'll be down for long. It's just the initial shock." My tone comes off more irritated than I hoped, but I am irritated. With them, for looking at me like I've lost my mind. With myself, for losing my mind over Elissa *again*. The meeting continues, and it takes everything in me to focus on the agenda at hand.

Leslie, a fantastic, kick-ass lawyer, makes some brilliant suggestions regarding some policies that could be revamped to not only make our workflow more efficient, but also give our employees a bit more autonomy. One thing I pride myself on when it comes to CGC is giving my employees increased time to be with their families and do things outside of work. No one wants to spend their lives living to work, so I've made it part of my company's ethos to adapt to the newest technologies, have four-day work weeks, the ability to work from home two days of the week, and other smart moves that make the employees feel valued and in control of their lives. If they're still making me money and doing their work, what the fuck do I care? Hell, I even have an open vacation policy, and as long as people don't take advantage of it, they technically have unlimited days off. And let me tell you, the productivity of my employees is amazing.

When the meeting adjourns, Rhys swivels in his chair to face me and waits until everyone files out of the room. I'm waiting for his formal reprimand of my behaviour in the meeting. Three, two, one. Here it comes…

"What the fuck was that today?" Yep, I knew it.

"I'm not sure what you mean. I think that meeting went really well," I snort.

"Like fuck it did. You were spaced out for the first half and were barely present for the second half. If you don't care, then don't be here. Fuck's sakes, man." His tone is pissing me off, like he hasn't had an off day. He's had plenty, and many of them recently.

"Holy fuck, it was one day."

"Uh, days," Rhys says, stressing the "s" and drawing it out. I roll my shoulders, stretching my neck until it pops.

"Whatever. What do you want from me?" Rhys doesn't like my answer and scoffs.

"Well, for one, being present in the meetings would be nice. You're the CEO. Second, you need to get over this whole Elissa thing. It was your choice this time to walk away. If she moved on, well, then that's too bad. Go out and find some other chick to bang. You need to start moving on too."

I don't like his suggestion. I feel like I'm grinding my teeth to dust, and my jaw throbs. My hand reaches up to rub at the aching joint.

"Coming from the guy who can't make up his mind about Riley and the baby," I snipe back. Rhys' eye twitches and he cracks his knuckles.

"Fuck you, man. It's not the same."

"How is it not the same? You're sitting here, just as miserable as I am, and you're doing nothing about it. You were the one who walked away from her." He scoffs at my remark, shaking his head, and his inky hair falls across his eyes.

"Not. Even. Close," he says through clenched teeth. "My situation is a little more delicate. If I go back to Riley, I am *back* with Riley. I have to be in, one hundred percent. With her, the baby, everything." I roll my eyes.

"How is that any different from if I choose to be with Elissa? If I go back to her, it's got to be one hundred percent as well. There is no half-assing this stuff. And if you go back to Riley, I'm sure she'd willingly take you back. You're the father of her baby, and I know she still loves you. Eli, on the other hand, who knows where her head is at? She's a fucking enigma. And it's completely my fault. I pushed her away before she had a chance to do that to me. After I convinced her to give us a shot. A real shot. And I completely fucked it up." I scrub at my face.

"Man, I can't even talk about this anymore. It gets me so fucking angry, and I already think about it way too much. But you need to fuck off and stop telling me what I need to do or not do. You have problems, just like mine, that you need to figure out. So stop wasting your breath on me. I already know how badly I've fucked up. Figure out your own shit, man." I've completely snapped. I'm losing it. Losing it on my best friend, losing it at work, losing it over a woman.

My hands anchor against the conference table and I push off. My chair glides along the granite flooring and I plant two feet firmly on the ground. Deft hands button my suit jacket as I stand.

"If that's all," I say, clearing my throat. "Let's get back to work." I leave Rhys sitting there, staring after me as I walk around him and out of the room. I head to the elevator to go back up to my office. My heart aches just thinking about Elissa, and I wonder just how she's doing, and if she's seeing that guy from the restaurant. My heart needs to know, but doesn't want to find out. It would crush me if she's moved on. *But just how far has she moved on?* It's been almost a month without touching her, kissing her, fucking her. My body craves her creamy skin, the way her mouth opens and moans my name as she's coming apart, and the way her pussy clenches around me as I thrust into her.

Shoving the door to my office open, I quickly slam it shut behind me, pressing my back up against the thick oak door. My hand slides into my pants to adjust the raging hard-on I'm sporting so that it tucks neatly into my waistband. This woman is going to be the death of me and I'm not even with her.

CHAPTER
THIRTY

ELISSA

Riley has been a wreck over this last week. She's been frantically packing for our trip back home. She's even making me nervous to tell her parents, and I'm not the one who's pregnant.

"Riley, settle down." She whips her head around and her eyes narrow on me.

"Don't fucking tell me to settle down. You're not the one who's telling her parents she's pregnant and unmarried!" she yells, throwing her hands in the air. "Hell, I'm not even with the guy that fathered this child! Fuck, just make me sixteen again and I'll be the perfect example of an accidental pregnancy." I slide off her bed, placing my feet firmly on the floor before moving over to her and bringing her in for a hug.

"It'll be okay, Riles. Your family is everything mine isn't. They're warm, understanding, loving, and caring. Like I said the other day. They might be upset, but they'll be supportive no matter what." Riley's body melts into mine as she takes a deep breath. Her hands wrap around my waist and she snuggles her head into me.

"Thanks, E. I know I can be a spaz sometimes."

"Just sometimes?" I say playfully. She smacks my back lightly and steps out of the hug.

"Smartass," she snorts.

"You know you love me." I give her a wink and pucker my lips at her.

"Yeah, yeah," Riley drawls, shooting me the middle finger. "Are ya gonna help me pack now, or what? I need clothes, so I need you to help me pick out the most flattering maternity clothing I have. Things that hide my bump."

My brows furrow as I frown.

"Why do you want to hide your bump?" Riley's shoulders fall and her back slouches, her hand rests on her forehead and rubs.

"I just don't want to flaunt my mistake, especially around my parents. Don't get me wrong, I love the little Kiwi already. I do. I just…wish I was more ready for this. I didn't think I'd be twenty-four, unmarried, and pregnant."

Not that it really matters, but I understand where she's coming from. If I were to be pregnant right now, I'd be lost. How could I be a parent when I don't know what it's like to have parents? The closest thing I have is Lana, and she was our housekeeper. She loved me the best she could, but it's not the same. I crave my parents' love and affection, and every time I'm left with nothing, a little piece of me chips away. Now that my father's gone, I don't know if I'll ever be able to heal, but at least I can't break any more because of him.

But now, instead of my father breaking me, it's Brandt. One man for another, I suppose. Is that how it's supposed to be? I thought there was one man a little girl could trust and that was her father. Boy, were they wrong. Not only did my father not protect me from men, he threw me to the one who hurt me the most. These last few weeks I've really come to terms with how I feel about Brandt. And I love him. No, I'm in love with him. And it hurts so bad I can barely breathe some days. But I get up, put on my face, and make it through the day. Luckily, he doesn't hang around much at Black & Wells. He only shows his face for the shareholder meetings and leaves quickly after they're done.

He's distant, cold, and when he does look my way, he seems angry. Almost uncomfortable with being in the same room as me. The disdain I see on his face breaks off another little piece inside of me. Soon, I'll be nothing but a shell of who I once was, and that person was already a shell. So, what do you get when there's a shell of a shell of a person? I miss the warmth that used to be in his eyes when he looked at me. I still feel the heat and the electricity between us, but it's different from what his demeanour says about him. Us.

Shaking the thoughts from my head, I move from Riley's room to mine to finish packing. I don't pack anything fancy, since we're only going to our hometown and don't plan on going out at all. So, I shove a couple pairs of American Eagle jeans into my suitcase along with some t-shirts and blouses, and a couple of oversized sweaters. I plan to be comfortable this weekend. I add a few pairs of Lululemon leggings to the suitcase and a pair of running shoes and a sports bra. Who knows when the need to run will be triggered? Although lately, I haven't been itching to run as much. Is it a coincidence now that my father is gone? I don't know. But I'm not about to look a gift horse in the mouth.

Riley calls from her room that she's finished packing, so I toss in my makeup bag and zip the suitcase up. Grabbing my computer, chargers, and iPhone, I make sure they're snug and secure in my large black Kate Spade tote. I toss the keys for my Corvette in my purse, grab my suitcase off the bed, and wheel it out to the living area. Once out there, I'm met with Riley, who is scrolling through her phone, perched on the edge of the couch. She has one leg slung overtop of the other one, but it's slipping because of the baby bump already getting in the way. I smile to myself. She's going to be so beautiful when she's big and fully fucking pregnant.

When she notices me standing in front of her, she drops her phone into her purse. She stands up, sighing dramatically while shaking out her sleek raven hair.

"Are we ready to head out?" she whines. My lips tug into a smirk. "Stop fucking smiling at me. I so don't want to do this, ya bitch. You better be nice to me this weekend." I burst into laughter, and my reaction to her makes her crack a smile.

"Let's go, Riles. We've got a four-hour drive ahead of us."

• • •

It took longer than four hours to get to Chatham. The traffic leaving Toronto was horrible. Bumper-to-bumper traffic across all six lanes of the 401. We finally pass the reflective population sign for Chatham-Kent at 9:01 PM. We're both exhausted after five-and-a-half hours of driving, and we only stopped to pee once for Ms. Pregnant-Pants.

My nerves turn to high alert as we get closer and closer to the highway exit. Knowing we're back in town makes me feel…uneasy? Sentimental? Both? I don't know, but it's a mix of emotions I can't explain. Riley is shaking like a leaf beside me, and I turn on the heat to try to help, but I know it's all nerves. She's terrified of facing her parents, and I still don't know why. I know Brianne and Connor are amazing people and are extremely supportive. And I'm with her. She has nothing to worry about.

"You ready?" I ask, downshifting the Corvette as I take the exit ramp. Riley stares straight ahead and I can barely make out the shake of her head in the dark. "Riles?"

"No, Elissa. I'm not ready." My heart goes out to her, it really does.

"Well, you really don't have a choice. Ready or not, the baby is coming, and that means you need to tell your parents as well." She falls back into the seat and buries her head in her hands.

"I know," she mumbles through her hands.

We drive on a long stretch of country road, passing farms and an old antique store on the way into town. It always amazes me that my parents chose to live in such a small town. But then again, they didn't really live here. I did. They mostly spent their time in Toronto during the week and left Lana to raise me, then would only come back on weekends. They still have the house I grew up in, but I never visit it. It was one of the properties my mother received in the will. But I have no intentions of going back there.

It's about a fifteen-minute drive from the highway into town, unlike getting off at exits along the 401 in the Greater Toronto Area. But it's a nice, calm drive. It gives you a chance to unwind, for your mind to think without having to worry about highway traffic. I look over at Riley and the glow from the entertainment screen on the dashboard lights up her face, illuminating the worry in her expression. I move my right hand off the gearshift and wrap my fingers around her hands where they rest in her lap.

"I'm here with you. There's nothing to be nervous about."

Her eyes find mine briefly before she looks away.

"I know. Thanks, E."

We're only a few minutes away from her parents' house. They recently moved into one of the new subdivisions in the south area of town. Their old house was massive before, and when Riley moved out, you would think they'd have downsized. But no, when they moved this time, they moved into a five-bedroom house with a three-car garage, a fully finished basement, a kitchen that could host an army, and a gorgeous in-ground pool in the backyard.

As we pull into the driveway, a gravelly crunching groan escapes Riley. She really doesn't want to do this. I give her hand another squeeze, then I push open the door and step out of my car. Riley's door clicks open and thuds shut a second later, and we meet in the middle around the back of the car at the trunk.

"Can we please just go back home?" I give her a pointed look, pop the trunk, and point to her suitcase.

"Let's go. Grow some ovaries."

"Pfft. Ovaries are what got me into this mess," she mumbles under her breath.

"No, unprotected sex got you into this mess." Riley whines and groans as she lifts the suitcase out of the trunk, then sets it down on the driveway. She extends the handle with a metallic click and rolls it with her as she goes to the front door. I do the same with mine and haul my massive purse over my shoulder. The trunk rattles the car as it closes, and I stand there, staring up at the massive house as a spark of joy settles in me, knowing I'm about to get a weekend of parental love.

I hear high-pitched squeals coming from the front door, and I know it's Brianne. She hasn't seen Riley since her relapse and she's probably happy Riley is home for a visit. I step up the stairs to the porch and Riley has her butt sticking out, pulling the lower half of her body away from her mother's embrace so that Brianne can't feel the baby bump. I chuckle to myself. *This is going to be an interesting weekend.*

CHAPTER
THIRTY-ONE

RILEY

I can't stop fumbling with the hem of my soft Abercrombie & Fitch sweater, praying it hides the baby bump well enough until I'm ready to tell my parents about the pregnancy. Which, I mean…there's never going to be a great time to do it this weekend, but I can at least wait until tomorrow morning. I don't need to spring this on them the moment we walk through the door.

"Well, come on in girls," my mom beams at me and Elissa. My father is chuckling behind her, waiting for me to get inside, and after I slip my shoes off my feet, he tugs me in for one of his best bear hugs. I panic at the close contact, and try sucking in my stomach to avoid my stomach pressing against the small beer belly he's growing.

"It's good to see you, honey." His warm, sturdy voice braces my core and I feel like anything is possible. He's so warm and inviting, and his tone has a touch of calm to it. No wonder his patients love him.

"It's good to see you too, Daddy." I squeeze him back and melt into his hug before he releases me.

"'Lissa!" My dad exclaims, strutting over to her and pulling her into a big bear hug as well. My heart swells. I know how much Elissa loves seeing my parents because it's like she gets a piece of that familial bond she needs, and my parents typically go overboard with showing their affection to her. Although they're best friends with Collette and Harold, they know how neglected Elissa was, so they tend to overdo it, to make up for their friends' failures.

When we were little, maybe like ten or so, I was jealous they would pay attention to her so much when she was over. My mom pulled me aside one day to explain it to me.

"Riley," she said. "You'll always be our favourite. But sometimes being an adult means knowing when someone needs something more. Elissa tends to need more attention from us when she's around. Her mom and dad are constantly gone for work and who knows what else. So, your dad and I try to make Elissa feel like she's part of the family. We'll always love you most, but sometimes we need to show Elissa a little more love and kindness."

I was probably still too young to know exactly what that meant, but as I grew up, it slowly made more and more sense. I'm incredibly proud to be their daughter, and their capacity for compassion is infinite. I only hope it'll still extend to me when I tell them the news.

"Come in, come in!" My mom says as she ushers us in, gesturing at my dad to grab our bags from us. Elissa is polite as she thanks my dad. She kicks off her pale pink Chelsea Hunter boots and tosses her jacket onto the foyer bench, making herself at home. My jacket is draped over my arm, another evasive maneuver to hide my baby bump from my parents. Both Mom and Dad follow Elissa further into the house as she gushes over their new home, complimenting my mother's decor and taste. And I'm thankful she's taking the pressure off me by indulging them in conversation so I can collect my wits. I place my jacket over Elissa's and follow them down the hallway, past the rounded staircase, to the open kitchen and living area.

• • •

Elissa sits herself on a stool at the island as my mom asks if she wants a coffee. I shuffle over and the stool grinds against the floor as I tug it out from under the counter.

"Riley Mikayla!" my mom shouts. "Be careful! You're going to scratch our floors." My cheeks heat.

"Sorry mom," I mutter. My Mom waves her hands in the air, telling me it's already forgotten. Her back turns to face away from us and she makes her way to her Starbucks-quality espresso and coffee machine.

"Want one as well, Riles?" my mom asks. I tell her sure. "Have you ladies eaten? I have leftovers from our dinner earlier."

"Sure, Brianne. We didn't get a chance to eat on the road," Elissa answers for us. My mom tugs on the fridge door and it hums. Elissa pushes away from the counter and hops off the stool, striding over to my mom to help her take stuff out of the fridge. "You make the coffees, Bri. I'll grab the leftovers." Elissa smiles sweetly at my mom and she returns the kind gesture.

"Thanks, darling," she says, stretching her hand out and placing it on Elissa's cheek. Her thumb brushes lightly against Elissa's skin before she steps away and turns her attention back to the coffee as Elissa opens a bunch of cupboards, trying to find the dishes. "Far left, hon," my mom says. Elissa opens the right cupboard and grabs two porcelain plates out of the cupboard, then starts opening drawers until she finds the utensils. She brings everything to the island facing me and dishes out the leftovers of chicken, potatoes, and broccoli, covering it with waxed paper and popping it into the microwave under the island.

Elissa places the steaming plates on the white granite counter, slides my plate over to me, and passes me a fork and butter knife. I shift so my foot comes up and I tuck it under my butt, letting the other leg hang down. I grab my fork and push my food around on my plate until I feel the heat of my mom's eyes on me, so I stab a piece of chicken and take a massive bite to sate her curiosity. "Mm, the chicken is fantastic," I say, with bits of chicken flying out of my mouth as I speak.

"Riley," my mom chides. "Don't speak with your mouth full. But thank you, sweetie." From behind us, my dad hollers from the couch, watching the highlights from the hockey game that was on earlier.

"Your mother is a damn good cook, that's for sure. Don't know where she finds the time to be that good and a skilled surgeon at the same time." The love between my parents is unreal. It's everything I ever wanted as a kid growing up. They're so supportive of each other and their dreams. There was a time back in high school where they were going through a rough period because their schedules were always opposite shifts and they never saw each other. I can only imagine how hard that is on a marriage. They're both in demanding jobs; surgeons at the C-K Hospital. Dad is in general, while my mother is a cardiothoracic surgeon.

"Speaking of work," I say, before swallowing another bite. "How is work going for you guys? Any plans of retiring?" There's a pregnant pause, and both my parents are staring intensely at each other, and my heart rate spikes and tingles erupt over my body. "Uh, guys?"

My mom sighs. "Well," she starts. She takes a moment, and it looks like she's carefully contemplating what to say. "Your dad and I are actually retiring soon." I'm stunned, so much so that my jaw drops.

"What?" I ask, shocked.

"Oh my!" Elissa quips. "That's fantastic. Good for you two." My mind shuts off and goes blank. They're retiring already?

"Thanks sweetie," my mom says softly. Her eyes grow worried when I don't speak. I'm just confused. They've never really talked about retiring before. I'm so confused. They love their jobs, so much.

"When is this happening? I mean, congratulations, I guess. I'm just shocked. You've never talked about it before."

My mom's face relaxes and a serene smile touches her lips. She leans against the island, stretching her body across the countertop and grabbing my hands in hers. Her warmth radiates over me and makes me feel *home*.

"Well," she looks cautiously at Elissa. "When Harold died, things changed. We realized we didn't need to be working ourselves to the point of exhaustion. Yes, we're young and healthy. So there's nothing to worry about there. We just want to enjoy our time." My head shakes. I'm a little confused still.

"You two just bought this massive house. Don't you think you should have downsized instead if you're retiring?" My mom giggles.

"The house has nothing to do with our retiring. We wanted a new place and loved this one. That's all. I don't know why this is part of your argument."

"But the bills must be astronomical!" I retort.

"Well, we have savings and our retirement," she shrugs. "And we're still going to be working at the hospital." My head quirks, and I close my eyes, trying to concentrate on what she's saying.

"So…you're not quitting?"

"No. We're retiring."

"Same difference. How are you still working if you're retiring?"

"We're going to be working on-call only; help out when they need an extra hand." My dad gets up off the couch, circles the counter, and opens the fridge to grab a beer.

"What about you ladies? Anything new happening for you two?" Elissa turns to look at me, giving me stern eyes, and then they shift. I know what she's mentally saying: "Now's your chance, tell them." Well, shit. My dad places the beer on the counter and circles his arms around my mom's waist from behind, tugging her in close as he whispers something into her ear, making her smile wide. They sway together and then they both turn their attention back to us, waiting with eager eyes and ears. My heart pangs in my chest as I think about how Rhys and I could've been like that. The two of us, growing old together, raising a family together, retiring and spending time together. Elissa's foot nudges mine and I take a deep breath and sigh. *No time like the present.* I brace myself against the counter.

"Well, there is something new…" I say, my hands fumbling and fiddling as I pick away at the edge of the granite. "I'm…pregnant." My dad chuckles like it's a joke, but my mom's mouth drops open.

CHAPTER THIRTY-TWO

RILEY

My dad finally clues in that this isn't a joke. His arms drop from my mom's waist and he steps beside her. His face is ashen. My heart sinks like the Titanic. I can't tell if they're in shock, disappointed, or both. Probably both, if I had to guess. The room is silent and only the announcers from the hockey channel are chatting away in the background. A warm hand wraps around mine and squeezes, and I turn to look at Elissa gratefully.

"Mom? Dad?" I say weakly. My mom shakes her head in confusion. Her eyes are squinting and her nose is wrinkled.

"You're…pregnant?" she says, not quite believing what I'm saying.

"Um…yep." I stand and walk around the counter so they can see me clearly. I lift the soft blue Abercrombie & Fitch sweater up, revealing my tiny swollen belly. It looks more like I'm housing a taco baby in there, but it really is a baby. I look at my mom and dad with worried eyes and I hold my breath, waiting for them to say something. My dad is just standing there, stunned. My mom clasps her hands over her mouth and tears spring to her eyes. Chills wash over me and anxiety prickles at my skin while my heart stutters a few times in my chest.

"Please say something," I say weakly, my voice breaking. I'm so scared. I knew this was going to happen. I knew they were going to be upset. My mom sidesteps my dad, heading straight for me. She falls to her knees in front of me, places her hand on my stomach, and I freeze. *What the hell is going on?* Her smooth hands caress my baby bump, and she rubs the entire surface of where the baby is growing, then sidles her head up against my stomach, and says in a low, soft tone, "Hi baby. I'm your Gramma."

Tears form in my eyes and are seconds away from streaming down my face as I am doused in relief. Elissa was right. *Elissa is always right.* My mom is on her knees, talking to my belly and saying all kinds of cute, wonderful things about how much she already loves it. My lip quivers as I hold back my tears, and I look to my dad. His eyes are misty and his lips are pressed together in a tight line. His brows are furrowed, and he looks mad, but his face is otherwise soft and mushy. My dad looks so fragile right now. If anything else were to happen, he might just break.

"Daddy?" My voice is small, but it carries throughout the quiet room. He inhales a deep breath, and it stutters like he's hyperventilating. His cheeks puff out and he's holding his breath, and once he can't hold it any longer, he lets it out as tears start rolling down his cheeks. He strides over to me, pulls my mom up to her feet, and encloses us both in a crushing embrace. I've never felt so loved and accepted as I do in this moment.

Elissa and I head to our rooms for the night shortly after my confession, because that long drive was tiring and I'm incredibly tired all the time. Growing a human is exhausting. And I know everyone says that, but holy fuck, is it ever true. The door clicks shut behind me and I drag my exhausted feet across the carpeted room to my suitcase, which my father has generously brought up to my room and set down on the bed. I extract some of my comfiest Roots heathered sweatpants and a soft, buttery sweater, then slip between the sheets of the bed, snuggling in deep.

•••

Sunlight streams into my room, warming my face. I groan, rolling over to look at the clock on the nightstand. It's 10 AM already, and I still feel like a zombie. A light knock sounds on my door and my mother's voice floats through the door.

"Riley, we have breakfast ready downstairs."

"'Kay, Mom. Be down in a sec," I respond groggily. My hands swipe the sleep from my eyes and I reach over and grab my phone off the nightstand. There's a new message waiting from Rhys.

Rhys: *Hey, can we meet up today and talk?*

Another groan escapes my lips. Thankfully, we're not in Toronto, and I don't have to deal with him right now.

Me: *I'm visiting my parents this weekend. Won't be back for a few days. I guess we can talk then.*

I chuck my phone back onto my nightstand and slide my ass out of bed, my socked feet planting firmly on the carpeted floor. I shuffle my way to the washroom, and I'm overwhelmed with the clean scent — it smells like waterfalls and chlorine. My feet make no noise as I glide across the tiled floor of the washroom and make use of the new en suite in my bedroom at my parents' new house.

I wriggle into a bra and finger-comb my hair to detangle it before heading downstairs for breakfast. As I descend the stairs, I am met with the mouthwatering smells of bacon, scones, eggs, toast, and coffee. My parents are chatting away with Elissa and her bronze hair is tumbling down her back in loose, tangled, flat curls. Her legs are crossed at the ankle, hanging off the stool at the counter, one foot looping through the footrest. The room is dim, with only a few lights on overhead of the counter. I look to my left and the giant windows exhibit a gloomy, rainy day. *That wasn't part of the forecast.*

"Ah, good morning sleepyhead! Look who's finally up!" my mom chimes, rounding the island to pull me into an embrace. Elissa swivels on her stool to look over and offers me a sweet smile. "Come, sit. Let's load up a plate of food for you and that growing grandbaby of mine," my Mom gushes as she presses a light kiss into my hairline. She guides me to a stool beside Elissa and I take my seat. Elissa and I mumble "Good morning" to each other as my mom piles heaps of food onto a plate for me and slides it across the island.

"So," my dad breaks the silence. "I am assuming Rhys is the father. Why isn't he here with you?"

Shit. My dad just gets right to the point, doesn't he?

"Er, well…you see, Rhys and I aren't together anymore." My mom's expression drops and she generally looks sad for me. My dad, on the other hand, looks outraged.

"You mean to tell me that meathead broke up with you when he found out?"

"Well, no. Not exactly. See, we weren't together when I got pregnant," I say. Confusion washes over my parents' faces.

"Who's the father?" my dad grumbles haughtily. His face morphs from confusion, to anger, to disappointment. I can only imagine what's running through his head when I tell him his unmarried child is having a baby and I haven't been quite clear with the details.

"What she means," Elissa interrupts. "Is that her and Rhys broke up before she got pregnant, but they hooked up one night and that's when it happened."

"Gee, thanks, E," I mumble under my breath. She nudges me with her elbow and ignores my comment.

"Rhys is the father. They're just not together."

A hush fills the room and the scraping of my fork on my plate as I push my food around is the only noise. My mom's face is drained of colour, her eyes are soft around the corners, and she looks like she's about to cry. And my dad? Well, he looks like he's about to have a heart attack. His face is red, strained, and all his features, like his lips and eyes, are tight, sharp lines.

"I suppose you don't need to be together to raise a child," my mom says cautiously. Elissa chuckles sardonically.

"If only," she says. My dad's eyes dart to her, his jaw clicking.

"What the hell does that mean, Elissa?"

Elissa's shoulders sag. She draws a breath and explains.

"It *means* he's being a douche about the whole thing. Didn't think it was his at first. Riley had to get a paternity test to prove it was his, and when it was proven, he's been MIA and seems to be shirking his responsibilities."

My dad grows beet red first, like someone is grabbing hold of his throat and squeezing, then he slowly turns purple. I shoot Elissa a death glare, kicking her under the island, but instead of getting her, I kick the stool and yelp. My dad's eyes bore into me as he tries to keep control over his emotions.

"It's not what it seems, Dad. Honestly. I think he's just coming to terms with it. I kind of sprung everything on him."

"And that makes it okay for him to act like this?!" my dad bellows. "It was just sprung on you too! Why do you have to be the only mature one about a baby coming into this world? I'm very disappointed in him. I genuinely liked him, too." My dad humphs and mutters something unintelligible under his breath, and I can only imagine it's something not very nice. My mom rests her hand on my dad's forearm and whispers something in his ear, and Elissa and I share a glance. Whatever she says has my dad calming down and his complexion returns to normal.

We finish the rest of breakfast in hushed silence, keeping what brief conversation there is to neutral territory. My mom makes idle chatter about a local nursery she wants to go to out in Essex, to grab some plants for the solarium until the weather is nice enough to plant them. She asks if we want to spend the day with her, shopping at a few of the clothing stores downtown on King Street. They're nothing like the fancy, ritzy stores we shop at in downtown Toronto or online, like Coach, Tiffany's, or Louis Vuitton, but they carry higher-end items. When Mom comes to Toronto for the weekend, we spend all day shopping at the Eaton Centre and the outlet malls in the area. Elissa and I agree to accompany my mom and go shopping for the day, but I have a feeling we're going to be stopping by the kid's store downtown and spend most of our time there. My mom has that glint in her eye that only grandmothers get when they think about their grandkids.

CHAPTER
THIRTY-THREE

ELISSA

We end up back at Riley's parents' house with a car full of shopping bags. Her mom only dragged us into the kid and baby stores, buying up everything she could. This baby is going to want for nothing for the next five years.

"Mom, you really went overboard. I don't even know how Elissa and I are going to be able to bring this all back. She's only got a tiny two-seater Corvette." Brianne waves her tiny hand in the air, dismissing her daughter.

"Don't worry. Your dad and I will come up to help you settle everything in a few weeks. I'm assuming you'll be finding a new place to live for when the baby is born?"

Riley shifts uncomfortably and doesn't dare to look at her mom. "Er…I'm not sure yet," she mumbles. Brianne pauses in the driveway a few paces behind us, her hands heavy with bags. And as her salt-and-pepper hair ruffles in the wind, I catch a whiff of Chanel No. 5. *What is it with rich, white, middle-aged women and Chanel No. 5?* My hand laces around the crook of Riley's elbow and I pull her to a stop with my free hand. She turns and her eyes spring open with confusion. "What's wrong, Mom?"

"What do you mean, you're not sure? Where's my grandbaby going to live? You can't possibly be thinking of staying with Elissa; you can't do that to her and inconvenience her with a newborn," Brianne huffs. Riley groans, and I jump in to save her.

"Actually, I offered for Riley and the little kiwi to stay with me. I really don't mind. Besides, I know she's going to need all the help she can get." Her mother looks unfazed but perturbed. She clicks her tongue.

"How sweet of you, Elissa. And yes, she is going to need all the help she can get, and if that's the case, she can move home, where her family will help her. Especially if Rhys isn't going to be in the picture." Riley's eyes nearly pop out of her head at her mom's words. Her face blooms into a deep shade of red.

"I will not be moving back home," Riley sputters. "I can't believe you'd possibly think that's even an option at this point. I have a life in Toronto; I have a job, friends…a baby daddy. I can't just leave everything behind because you don't approve of how my life is shaking up right now." Her mom's face softens, and a small, apologetic smile stretches across her face.

"Oh, honey," she whispers. "I didn't mean it like that. I'm sorry. I just want the best for you and the baby, and moving home might be the simplest thing to do. Staying with Elissa, which is an incredible offer by her, is fine, but it'll get cramped. Especially once the baby starts moving around."

"Then we'll find something bigger. I can afford it," I break into the conversation. "Or Riley can have my apartment, and I'll find another place to live. Either way, I'm not letting Riley suffer alone." Brianne's amber eyes fix on mine and they glimmer with gratitude and love.

"Thank you for looking out for my babies," she says warmly. We all continue into the house, unloading bags upon bags of stuff. As if we didn't already have enough stuff at our apartment from our last shopping trip, we now have piles more to add to the mess at home. I hope Riley kicks into the nesting phase soon, because we're going to need the organizing skills.

As we're in the living room, gathered around the couch, Brianne is showing Connor all the stuff "they" bought for Riley and the baby. Maternity clothing, baby clothes, toys, and other minor items. Connor seems detached, but he maintains an interested expression. I catch his eyes slide over Brianne's shoulder to the muted TV behind her, and he nods along with what she's saying. Her hands are waving frantically in the air, pulling stuff out of bags and holding it up for Connor, happiness shining in her eyes. I chuckle to myself at the dynamics between her and Connor's enthusiasm levels in this current situation when my phone bleeps in my purse.

I rummage through my purse and find my iPhone and check the notification. My heart sinks. Another board meeting on Monday, and I wonder if Brandt is going to send his assistant in his stead again. A wistfulness aches in my chest knowing that Brandt is actively avoiding me for some reason. I thought we could have been mature about everything, but I suppose we can't. After the whole falling-out, I thought we could work together amicably — we were for a while there. Then, suddenly, he started sending someone else to take notes on his behalf. Part of me wonders if he's moved on and couldn't care less about this part of the company now that he's no longer entangled with me and my father. Maybe he's transitioning to being more of a silent partner.

My heart aches for him and my body craves his touch. It's only been a handful of weeks since we've been together, but it feels like years. *What has this man done to me?* I've never been one to pine over a man, to care enough to have him be part of my world, or want him to be part of my world. But every fibre in my body calls out to him like a siren in the night, begging for him to come to me. Can he hear the song? Will his boat crash into me?

"Elissa?" Riley whispers, nudging me. I shake the thoughts from my head and turn to face Riley. Her eyes are worried, and I see my reflection in her eyes. There's a distant look in my eyes and a soft, sad smile touching my lips. I'm not sitting as tall as I usually do. I'm slumped, and I feel closed off. I feel...*broken*. Her hand laces through mine and she squeezes, as if she can read my mind and knows I'm thinking about Brandt again. "It'll work out," she whispers again. I send a thank-you with my eyes, gently squeezing her warm hand back before pushing myself off the couch.

"Well, I'm going to go get ready for a run," I say, picking my purse up off the ground and tossing my cell back into it, trying to ignore reality for a little longer. I still have tomorrow before I have to worry about whether I'll be seeing Brandt at the office. I vault up the stairs, taking them two at a time, and dump my purse on the bed when I get to my room.

The room is decorated in calming seafoam greens and corals. There are little gold accents placed around the room, giving the atmosphere a relaxing, beachy vibe. I walk over to the corner of the room by the closet where I've set my suitcase and haul it over to the bed. I grab some running clothes and a puffer vest because it's still chilly outside. After I'm changed, I lace on my runners and twist my earbuds in.

When my feet strike the pavement of the subdivision, the tension of the last few weeks drains from me, emptying me enough to hold in all my emotions again. A light drizzle pings off the waterproof material of my puffer vest, and my nose fills with that fresh rain scent, mixed with wet asphalt. It invigorates me, propelling my legs a little faster, while *Body Bag* by Machine Gun Kelly, YUNGBLUD, and Bert McCracken pounds in my ears, making my blood pump. The air rushes out of my mouth in clouds as I huff, pushing my body further, and pushing the thoughts of a golden-brown-haired god of a man who makes my body feel electric out of my mind.

• • •

Two hours later, I'm sopping wet with sweat, heaving heaps of air into my lungs as I walk the rest of the last few kilometres back to the Jaimesons' place, my hands planted on my hips, cooling down to *Headlock* by Imogen Heap. I walk the last bit of trail around the creek and down Tweedsmuir Avenue West. I pull the headphone case out of the pocket of my jogging tights and pop the earbuds in, allowing myself to enjoy the sounds of the late afternoon outdoors. It's been a while since I've jogged around Chatham. Across the road there's a small park with two baseball diamonds, and bundled-up kids are playing on the equipment. Their laughter and screams ring through the air, and the early spring birds chirp, making their presence known.

My breathing has finally regulated and I'm almost back at the Jaimesons' house when I pass by a house that has a black Dodge truck with the words "Collins Construction" in orange, and a little house logo. My heart rate spikes again as I think about Brandt, and I tell myself that it's just a coincidence that there's a construction company with his last name. But there's a nagging voice at the back of my head that's telling me his parents did something with construction, and it's not a coincidence. *No, that can't be it. There's no way. I've got to be mistaken.* I resolve not to look up the information when I get back because I don't want this revelation to eat me alive, but also I don't want to find out I'm wrong.

It's still bugging me as I continue down the street and finally make it back to the Jaimesons' front porch. I peer over my shoulder and the house is still in view. I pray it is just a coincidence. Pushing open the door to the foyer, I toe off my running shoes, shout a greeting into the house, and jog upstairs to my room. A wave of heat crests over my body at the lingering thoughts of Brandt. I strip off my wet clothes and throw them in the laundry basket in the corner, then strut to the en suite washroom, butt naked. My skin is flushed and warm, and I can't tell if it's the effects of the run or my thoughts.

I step under the steaming hot water, allowing it to wash over me. My hope is that it will cleanse me of these thoughts, but I only get revved up more. My hands travel across my body, tickling, dancing, and caressing my curves. I cup my breasts and close my eyes, pretending it's Brandt's big, muscular hands touching me, him taking my pebbled nipple between his thick fingers, rolling and pinching it. My mouth falls open and a soft groan rings through the washroom. I clamp my lips shut and bite down on them to stop more sounds from escaping.

Daring further, my hands slide down my stomach, and a middle finger slips between my lips and strokes softly. The water cascading down my body makes the swipe smooth and pleasurable. Using two fingers, I stroke my clit again and again, building faster and faster. I hitch my leg on the piece of stone that juts out from the wall as a shaving platform, and turn to face the water, allowing the pulse from the shower head to massage my clit while I rub. I imagine that Brandt is tongue-deep inside me; his scratchy stubble brushing against my thighs as his tongue slips in and out of me.

I press two fingers in deep, bending and angling them so I reach the spot where my toes start to curl. I groan in frustration because it's not as good as having him do it to me. My body craves his touch, his tongue, his pleasure. I'm slowly building to the crescendo, to the point where I shatter. But I'm growing impatient. With him, it's so easy. With him, it takes no time at all. I squeeze my eyes closed tighter and brace myself against the wall with my free hand as I inch closer to the finish. Keeping Brandt at the fore-front of my mind, I picture the last time we were together. I think about how good it felt having him slide in and out of me, filling me to the brim. How it felt when he came inside me, and when my pussy clenched around his thickness. And I'm there. I'm tipping over the edge, and it's a pleasant little release, but leaves me more frustrated than satisfied.

CHAPTER
THIRTY-FOUR

ELISSA

Sunday rolls around and I'm utterly exhausted. I had a fitful sleep last night, wondering about Brandt and if he misses me; if he still craves me the way I crave him. *Seriously though, what has happened to me?* My mind hasn't stopped racing since I saw that damn truck down the road, making me think about Brandt and how badly I miss him. And now my heart feels ripped open all over again, wondering how he could just finish things like that. Wondering how he could turn his back so easily after fighting for us so hard. After convincing me to give us a chance, even after he broke my trust by making a deal with my father.

The room is dim, and I feel as dreary and gloomy as it is outside. I roll over in bed, wishing I could go back to sleep, but a soft knock on the door lets me know it's time to get up.

"Good morning, dear." Brianne's chipper words are muffled through the door. I groan, roll over, and stuff my pillow over my head, then hear a chuckle from the other side of the door and the sound of footsteps fading away. After a few moments, I toss the pillow off my face and across the room and rip the coral and green duvet off me. I quickly get ready, swiping on a quick pass of mascara and brushing my teeth before pulling on some cozy travelling clothes.

My hand palms the top of the banister as I take the stairs down, and I round the corner toward the kitchen.

"Morning," I mumble, and Riley snickers. I shoot her my middle finger and it earns me a disappointed *"Elissa,"* and a tongue click. Riley snickers more and I glare at her, silently cursing her.

"Come sit and have some coffee and something to eat," Connor offers. When I approach the island, his arm snakes around my shoulder and tugs me into a side hug for a minute. I rest my head on his shoulder, reciprocating the gesture. He squeezes my shoulder before letting go and passing me a plate. "What time are you ladies leaving?" he asks.

"Not sure," I say, though it sounds a lot more like "Nut shurr," because I'm stuffing my mouth full of Brianne's delicious, freshly baked croissants. "Most likely soon," I continue when my mouth is empty. "I want to try and get back before it gets dark, especially since this rain likely isn't letting up anytime soon." Brianne's eyes are sad, but she nods approvingly. After breakfast, we stuff the trunk of my car as full as we can get it with all the shopping we did and our suitcases. We pile back into the house, chatting and making and eating lunch before we leave.

When Riley and I are getting ready to head out, Mrs. Jaimeson's eyes are misty as she says her goodbyes, clearly not wanting Riley to be so far away while she's pregnant.

"Oh, Mom…stop!" Riley complains, but her eyes are tearful as well. "You're going to make me cry, and that's not fair because my hormones are all over the place." They giggle through the tears, and I hear Riley mumble, "Thanks for being so understanding" into her mother's neck. Mr. Jaimeson and I stand there chuckling, and he gives me a quick hug.

"Drive safe, you hear?" I give him my best confident smile.

"I always do," I confirm. His eyebrows lift in disbelief at me, and my stomach sinks as I laugh nervously.

"I seem to remember two teenagers stealing my Audi before they were supposed to drive and side-swiping another car," he grumbles. I smile innocently at him and shrug my shoulders.

"I always do, *now*. Is that better?" He grumbles some more, but drops the conversation and gives me a wink.

Riley and I leave the house and climb into the car, the rain still pouring down outside. We slam the doors closed and sit there for a moment, shivering. I press the ignition of the car and it rumbles to life. I click the buttons for the seat heaters to warm us up from the bone-chilling rain. I flick the windshield wipers on and they spring up, swiping the windshield quickly to compete against the rain.

Riley twists the knob to the radio and turns the volume up as I back out of the Jaimesons' driveway. Throwing the car into drive, I slowly speed up, giving us time to look around the neighbourhood when we pass the house on my left that had me up all night thinking about a certain something, or someone. I clear my throat.

"Riles?"

"Hmm?" she responds, looking forlornly out the window, her elbow propped up on the window ledge and her head being held up by her hand.

"Do you remember what Brandt's parents did? Or where he was from?" She turns to me and cocks her head to the side in confusion.

"Um, no. I don't...why?" Huh. I bite my lip, thinking for a moment before responding.

"Uh...no reason. Just thinking." Riley nods her head and turns her attention back to the passing scenery as we drive down the road, heading out of town.

• • •

It's been one hell of a long drive. The long stretch of the 401 seems to never end. The rain turned into freezing rain as we approached the city outskirts, and we've been crawling along the highway to get back to Toronto. So far, we've been on the highway for six hours, including two breaks for the pregnant lady to pee. It's been a boring drive as well. We've both barely spoken, and we're both gloomy. It's like this weather has put a damper on our mood.

"What are you going to do about Rhys?" I ask her. She sighs, fumbling with the black Canada Goose coat draped across her legs.

"I don't know, E…I'm dreading the talk he's wanting to have. Part of me hopes he'll say that he's going to be in the baby's life and that he'll help. But I have this sinking feeling that he's going to tell me to screw myself and that he's out."

"Aw, Riles. I don't think he'll do that."

"Doesn't matter what you think, E. It matters what he's going to do. And there's just something telling me something bad is going to happen. I don't know how to explain it, but I can't get rid of this feeling," she says, looking down and rubbing her belly as tears brim in her eyes. "I don't know what I'm going to do if he chooses not to be in our lives. I think…I think I might actually have to move home, E, because I don't know how I am going to raise a baby by myself, and I *cannot* ask you to help or support me. I know that's the last thing that matters to you, but what kind of person would I be if I did that to you? No, I can't do it. I need to do what's best for all of us, and that would be moving home. Hell, I wouldn't even have to live with my parents. I could buy a small place for just me and the baby, since it's much cheaper back in Chatham."

I say nothing and let Riley get everything off her chest. She rambles on nervously about what she plans on saying or not saying to Rhys. I nod along, but I get lost in my own thoughts. My heart aches. I don't know what I'll do if I lose Riley at this point. If she moves home, it won't be the same.

We've always been together, and if I lose her after losing Brandt…I just don't know.

We're nearing Toronto as we take the exit to the Don Valley Parkway and continue heading toward the Gardiner Expressway. Itching to get off the highway as we're so close to being home, I press the gas a little harder, and the sound of Riley snoring as she's just drifting off makes for competition with my engine revving. I chuckle to myself at her little snores. Up ahead, I see a car swerve a little, but I think nothing of it. They're probably just avoiding something.

I think back to Brandt and how tomorrow is the bi-weekly board meeting, and he personally confirmed his attendance. The beating of my heart picks up, racing as fast as my car on the highway. *I'm going to see him tomorrow.* Part of me is dreading it because it'll be so hard keeping my distance, keeping myself restrained from running over to him, jumping into his arms, wrapping my legs around his waist, and devouring him with hungry lips. But another part of me is nervous and excited to see him. It's been a little over a month, and I'm craving him. Even just a glance of him will help fix part of this ache…I hope.

The car in front of me swerves again, but bigger now. I tap my brakes, slowing my speed and trying to prepare for anything. The other car straightens out and keeps going. I don't even realize I'm holding my breath until I let out an enormous sigh. With shaking hands, I grip the steering wheel tightly and transfer to the other lane, trying to avoid the car in front of me as much as possible. My heart is racing, but it's only a few clicks until our exit, and then

I can relax. I glance at the radio and turn the volume up a bit more to help me settle my nerves when bright red lights flash into my eyes and the car. My eyes snap ahead and the car in the next lane is swerving again, all over the road. I slam on my brakes to avoid the car that comes skidding toward us, but my car glides and the brakes lock up. I throw my hand out to brace Riley, and she jolts awake. She screams as we spin around and around toward our exit ramp. I turn the wheel opposite to our direction, trying to straighten us out, and lightly tap the brakes to slow down and try to regain control of the car. Riley is screaming loudly and crying, and it doesn't help my nerves or focus.

"Riley, please," I plead with her. One of her hands wraps around the door's handle and the other wraps around her stomach, bracing herself for impact. The car finally stops spinning and I get us straight, but we're still sliding until we crash into the exit wall ramp head first. Time slows, and my head smashes off the steering wheel, then bounces off the window, and when the airbag deploys, my head is thrown backward into the headrest. My vision bursts with stars and Riley is screaming hysterically. I try to tell her it'll be okay, but my mouth won't move, and everything fades to black.

CHAPTER
THIRTY-FIVE

RILEY

A hand smashes into my chest, waking me abruptly from my nap. When my eyes pop open, we're spinning around in circles on the Gardiner Expressway, and another car has crashed further down the highway in front of us. My head spins as well, making me motion sick as I scream my lungs out.

"Riley, please," Elissa pleads with me, but my logic isn't listening right now. Piercing screams that could shatter the windows keep ripping out of me as Elissa tries to get ahold of the car again. I dig my heels into the floor of the car and squeeze my fingers around the door handle until my knuckles turn white. My throat is sore and ragged, but I can't stop screaming. My eyes widen as we slide closer to the exit ramp, then slam straight into the wall.

The front end of the car hits the cement wall with a loud bang and there's a thump to my side as another car from behind us taps into my side of the car. To my left, I see Elissa's head bob like a rag doll. The air bags deploy, and then suddenly she goes limp.

"Elissa! Elissa!" I scream, but she's not moving or waking. A visceral, bloodcurdling scream rips out of me; I'm losing it. Tears start streaming down my face, and my screaming turns to sobbing. "Please wake up," I plead.

"Elissa…Elissa…" I bend forward to grab my phone from my purse and a sharp pain streaks through my stomach, causing me to scream again. Clutching my stomach with my one hand, I reach forward, breathing through the pain to grab my cell phone and call 911. The phone rings twice before being answered.

"911, where is your emergency?" a calm voice on the other end answers. Another scream breaks from my mouth and I try to breathe.

"We're on the Gardiner Expressway in Toronto. Near the Yonge Street exit. We crashed into the wall. My friend is out cold, she was driving —" a scream breaks my words as another sharp pang ricochets through my body. "…and now she's…she's…passed out. I'm five months pregnant and something is wrong. Another car slammed into us as well."

"Okay, ma'am. Please stay with me. I have a few questions to ask you. Can I please get your name?"

"Riley Jaimeson."

"And your friend's name?"

"Elissa Black."

"And how did the accident happen?"

"Ahhhhh." A groan rumbles from my lips. "I-I-I think we hit a patch of black ice. I-I'm not s-sure." *Breathe, Riley. Breathe through the pain.* "I was asleep in the car when we started spinning, but it's so icy outside and we just kept sliding."

"Okay, Riley," the 911 operator says calmly. "The ambulance is on its way now. I'm going to stay connected to you while we wait. They're only one minute out. Why don't you tell me what's going on with you?"

I grunt before answering as I breathe through another sharp pain. It feels like it's radiating through my middle to my back. "I...I don't know. My stomach hurts. I think something is wrong with the baby."

"And why do you think that?"

"Are you joking me? The pain is horrendous. It hurts to even —" Another pain comes shooting across my midsection. "— breathe." In the distance, I can hear multiple sirens, and they slowly grow louder until I can finally see the glowing lights flashing. The sirens are deafening as the ambulance pulls up beside us and I say goodbye to the operator and hang up the phone. The driver's door is being pried open, and a paramedic sticks his head in.

"We're going to extract the driver right now. We're working on moving the other car out of the way of your side of the car so we can get you out. It'll be a few minutes." I thank them and breathe patiently through the aches.

When they've finally moved the other car, I open my door and the paramedic hollers at me to stay still until they remove me from the car. I'm in so much pain, I'm clutching my stomach and just trying to focus on my breathing. A hand stretches out in front of me, and I grab it and allow the paramedic to hoist me out of the car. His powerful arms wrap around my back and behind my knees as he sets me on a stretcher, buckling me in. When we get into the back, he starts pulling my shirt up and strapping all kinds of wires and bands across my stomach and chest.

"I'm just putting a few things on you to monitor yours and the baby's heart rates," he explains, his voice velvety calm. I nod solemnly and pluck up some courage.

"Where's my friend? Is she okay?" His face is blank, giving nothing away.

"She's in excellent hands. They left a few minutes ago, and we'll be following them in a second. Just try to stay calm and relaxed." *Well, thanks for that. A lot of information that was.* The ambulance jerks as it pulls away and I can see the wreckage as we drive off. Elissa's poor car is damaged beyond repair, and the front end looks crumpled like a piece of paper.

I still feel my heart racing in my chest and my breathing becomes a little more ragged. As the crash site gets smaller as we drive away, my anxiety increases. "Are you okay?" the paramedic asks. But I can't reply. My breathing is rapid, and I feel like I can't suck in enough air. There's too much pain ripping through my stomach.

"Ahhhhhhhh…" I scream. The paramedic focuses on the screen hooked up to me, and then turns around, rummaging through the cupboards in the rig, finally extracting a needle and a vial. "Wh-wh-what are you d-d-d-oing?" I say through stuttering breaths.

"Don't worry. This is just something to help you calm down," he says gently. He pushes the needle into the IV port that he's hooked me up to and presses the syringe down. A gradual calm overtakes me, lulling my senses to sleep. Lulling me to sleep. I feel every muscle in my body relax, and even though there's pain, I'm finding it easy to let everything go. Slowly, I drift off to sleep.

•••

I wake up and am surrounded by bright white, even though the lights are dim in the room. The last thing I remember was being in the ambulance.

I bolt upright.

Where's Elissa?

I look around the room and notice I'm at the hospital, still hooked up to a bunch of machines and this big, bulky belt is wrapped around my midsection. I'm in a private suite and Elissa is nowhere to be seen. I press the call button on the side of the bed, and moments later a nurse rushes into the room.

"Oh, Ms. Jaimeson, you're finally awake! How are you feeling?" I rub my eyes and think about her question. Things are coming to me foggy, and jumbled.

"Uh, a little groggy. I'm not quite sure what happened. But where's my friend?" I look to the nurse and her pinched nose, crinkled eyes, and pursed lips give nothing away. She's a middle-aged woman with fine lines rimming her mouth and eyes. She looks a bit crotchety, but sounds pleasant.

"I'm sorry, sweetie. I'm not sure right at this moment, but let me see what I can find out for you. Okay? You're in the maternity ward and she's in another part of the hospital. How are you feeling?" she asks me again.

"Better now."

"No more pain?"

"No…what happened to me? Is the baby okay?" The nurse offers me a sweet smile and places her bony, wrinkly fingers on my forearm.

"The baby is just fine. It was in distress earlier when you got here — between the crash, your levels of distress, and the stress triggering early labour, it sent your body into a tizzy, making that little one go bananas. But the doctors got everything back to normal, and it looks like you're in the clear. We're just going to keep you a few days to make sure everything is all right."

A huge crushing weight lifts off me as I hear her words. *The baby is okay.* My heart squeezes with happiness as I rub my little belly.

"There's a bit of swelling and some internal bruising from the crash, but there's nothing to worry about." The nurse walks over to the table by the door, grabs my purse, and walks it over to me, resting it beside me on the bed. "Your phone's been going a bit crazy, all these text messages from a guy named Rhys. Apologies, but we did have to check it to get an emergency contact. We called your parents and they're on their way." She asks me again if I'm okay before leaving me in peace and quiet.

Extracting my phone out of my purse I see about twenty missed text messages from Rhys. The last few are pretty awful.

Rhys: *Fuck you, Riley. You can't do this to me. You can't ignore*

me and shut me out. I'm the baby's father.
Rhys: *God damnit, Riley. If you don't answer me, so help me God I am going to come over to your place and knock down the fucking door.*
Rhys: *Why aren't you answering me? Where the fuck are you? You're not home. You should be home by now, you work in the morning.*

I check the time and it's still in the early hours of the morning, about 7 AM. The last message from him is different, and only from an hour ago.

Rhys: *Please, Riley. Let me know you're at least okay...*

I type out a quick reply to Rhys.

Me: *Sorry. I don't appreciate all those messages you sent. Elissa and I were in an accident on the way back into town...we're at the hospital. I'll talk to you when I have a chance.*

The message appears to be read instantly. Dots appear and disappear as I wait for him to respond, but it never comes.

• • •

An hour later, the nurse walks in with my mom and dad following close behind her. Tears well in my eyes and I try to hold them back when I see them. My mother's face is white as a ghost and splotchy from crying. My father's eyes are bloodshot, and his bottom lip is quivering like a leaf in the wind. When our eyes meet, we all break down and sob together, and the nurse bows out of the room.

"I'm so glad you're okay," my mother sobs. "I was so worried about you and the baby!" She collapses her body on top of mine, surrounding me in an embrace. Tears pour down her face, wetting my hospital gown. My father grunts from behind her, wiping his eyes before he walks over to the other side of my bed and grabs my hand.

Suddenly, a pounding set of footsteps comes racing down the hallway, and a familiar voice that tugs at my heartstrings yells my name. "Riley! Riley?!" A flash passes by my room, and then I hear backtracking, and…it's Rhys. He's doubled over in the doorway, heaving massive breaths. His jet-black hair is chaotic, sticking up everywhere. His face is flushed and his eyes are full of worry. "Riley!" He barrels into the room, throws himself over to me — slightly wedging my mother out of the way — and crashes to his knees. His eyes are full of tears and unsaid emotions. "Are you okay? Is the baby okay?" I nod my head, my mouth fails to say anything. I think I'm in shock. I didn't think he'd show up here when I sent him that message.

"Baby," he cries. His hands cup my face as he presses his forehead to mine. "Baby, I am so sorry. For every-thing. I was a dick, and I know it. I was just hurt and dealing with the stress of the company. And I know it's no excuse, but I fucking love you, baby. I am so incredibly sorry. I'll spend the rest of my life making it up to you and the baby, I promise." Tears are streaming down my face, and I can't explain how happy I feel in this moment to hear those words. He pulls away from me and digs in his pocket, then pulls out a tiny leather box. My heart leaps in my chest. *What the fuck is he doing?* "Riley Mikayla Jaimeson, I need you in my life. And I'm so sorry it took me so long to stop being such a jerk. I promise to love you and our baby. I can't imagine my life without you, and I can't believe I almost lost you. Both of you. I need you, Riles. Please, please forgive me. And please marry me."

He opens the box, and my mother gasps. Sitting in the middle of the cushion is a white gold band embedded with tiny little diamonds. At the centre of the ring, a one-carat diamond sits boldly, glimmering brilliantly under the terrible fluorescent lighting. My breath hitches. I am completely speechless.

My eyes find his, and they're pleading with me, begging me to say yes. And, in this moment, I want nothing more than to be his wife.

"Yes," I whisper.

CHAPTER
THIRTY-SIX

RILEY

Rhys' mouth crashes down on mine and my heart swells with so much love, I feel like I could burst. He breaks the kiss, extracts the tiny trinket out of the box, and tosses the box onto the bed. He grabs my hand, placing soft, delicate kisses on the inside of my wrist before turning my hand around and sliding the ring onto my finger.

"A perfect fit," he whispers. His mouth fuses to mine, and he pushes his tongue through my lips, and they dance together. His hand slides up my face and tangles into my hair. A deep clearing of the throat rumbles behind us, and we hastily break the kiss. My father is standing there, looking like he's ready to kill Rhys. There's fire burning behind his eyes, his face is red, and his arms are locked together across his chest.

"Uh, Mr. Jaimeson, sir. I didn't see you there," Rhys stutters as he clambers to his feet. He sticks out a hand for my dad to shake, but he just looks at Rhys' hand and scoffs. Rhys turns to look at me, silently asking me what to do, and eventually lets his hand drop. The nurse walks back into the room, cheerily talking as she enters.

"Well, Riley! I've got news about your friend —" She skitters to a halt. "Oh, you've got another visitor. Well, nice to meet you." But I'm no longer paying attention to anything else. I perk right up.

"What about Elissa?" The nurse looks from Rhys and my family to me and her face softens a bit. My heart drops to my feet.

"Well, she's okay. She's in the ICU. She has a few bruised ribs, but she hit her head hard a few times, and there's…well, there's some swelling. The doctors had to induce a coma to give her brain time to heal."

My world stops.

Elissa's in a coma?

Bile travels up my throat, burning my esophagus as it comes, and I try to swallow it down. My stomach churns and my breathing increases; I feel lightheaded.

"It's perfectly normal for patients who have major brain swelling to be induced. It gives them the best chance of recovery. They'll lighten up on the medication in a few days and see how she's doing." Her words do nothing to calm me down.

"I need to see her," I say, struggling to get out of bed, throwing my legs over the edge. The nurse rushes to my side and presses me back into the bed.

"Riley, please calm down. You're going to distress the baby again. You can see her tomorrow. We can't move you right now; you're on strict bed rest."

"Baby, please lay down," Rhys begs. "We need you to take it easy. *Please.*" I relent, letting my body crash back into the bed, but folding my arms and huffing. They better let me see her tomorrow.

"Does her mother know?" The nurse gives me a smile.

"Yes. Her mother is here and sitting beside her right now with their family friend, Lana."

"We brought Lana with us," my mom chimes in. She steps forward and places a hand on my leg. "Don't worry. Lana will keep us updated." I don't know what Rhys is doing — when I look over, he's slyly backing out of the room, pulling his phone out of his pocket. But there's too much going on in my head right now for me to focus.

"So, Elissa is stable?" The nurse nods her head. *Phew.* "Okay. But tomorrow I'm going to see her." The nurse nods her head again and covers me back up before leaving the room.

My mom and dad leave for the night to get some rest. I gave them the keys to the apartment so they can stay at my place. Rhys snuggles into my bed, curling up beside me with his hand laying protectively across my belly. He presses sweet kisses into the side of my jaw and hairline. His kisses rain down across my face, full of unsaid words and emotions. Months' worth of longing is spoken with every brush of his lips. He strokes my hair, and it feels so good to be tended to, to feel loved. He laces his fingers with mine and gently twists my hand so the ring is facing me. It's the most gorgeous thing I've ever seen. I stare at our connected hands and allow myself to fall asleep.

• • •

The next morning, I spring awake and am slightly confused when I notice it's still dark and gloomy outside. For a moment I think it might be too early, but then a new nurse walks in the room, turning on the light and bringing me breakfast. I shake Rhys awake and he mumbles something before waking up and sliding off the bed. He kisses my forehead and tells me that he'll be back in a little while, that he's going home to shower and change. He smashes his mouth to mine in a soul-stealing kiss that leaves me wanting more. When he breaks free, I notice the nurse is staring awkwardly at the ceiling and her face is beet red, clearly embarrassed by our passion.

"Sorry about that," I mutter. "We just got back together after months apart." The nurse giggles.

"No worries, I just wasn't expecting that when I happened to look over at you guys. Anyway, here's your breakfast. Let me know if there's anything else I can get you."

"Thank you," I say as she leaves the room. I dig into my food, inhaling the bland hospital food like I've never eaten before. *Baby is hungry today.* I chuckle to myself, rubbing my stomach.

"You hungry today, little Kiwi?" I muse to my stomach, wondering if he or she can hear me. "Momma's so sorry about the accident. I'll never let anything hurt you."

After I finish eating, the nurse comes back in with an ultrasound machine and clears the tray away. "The doctor will be with you in a few moments to do a scan."

"Actually, do you mind having the doctor come in an hour, if you can? My fiancé just stepped out for a bit, and I'd like him to be here. This will be his first time seeing the baby." *Oh my God. My fiancé! I can't believe he's my fiancé!* The nurse smiles sweetly.

"I'll see what I can do," she says.

CHAPTER
THIRTY-SEVEN

BRANDT

It's been a few days since I saw Elissa and that guy together at the restaurant, and my blood still boils.

What the fuck is wrong with me? Why can't I just move on?

But I know, deep down, I don't want to move on.

I'm laying in bed, staring at the ceiling, waiting for my alarm to go off. I've been sleeping like shit ever since I saw them together, and every time I close my eyes I see that bastard's hands on her, and her kissing his cheek. I close my eyes and try to get a few more minutes of sleep, but my phone decides to be an asshole and beeps once, then twice, then a third time. I roll over and check my messages.

Rhys: *Dude, get your ass to Mount Sinai right now.*
Rhys: *Elissa and Riley were in a huge accident.*
Rhys: *Riley and the baby are okay. But Elissa is in a coma. I'm not sure if anything else is wrong.*

My heart drops to my toes. *Elissa was in an accident? She's in a coma? What the fuck happened?*

I rip the blankets off me, and they flutter in the air before falling to the floor in a heap. Rushing around the room, I find random pieces of clothing to toss on — a pair of dark grey sweats and a black tee. I zip into the washroom and brush my teeth quickly, run my fingers through my golden-brown hair, and dart to my nightstand to grab my keys, wallet, and phone.

Normally, the hospital is a thirty-minute drive from my place. Today? It takes me all of fifteen minutes, as I swerve in and out of traffic, honking my horn and getting honked at back. I pull into the parking garage near the hospital, park, and sprint as fast as I can. When I reach the lobby I'm panting as I slam my hands down on the information desk. "Elissa…Black's…room," I huff. The lady at the desk looks me up and down like I've lost my mind, and I feel like maybe I have. My clothes and hair are dishevelled, and I'm probably looking like every bit of the mess I feel.

When I finally get an answer from the nurse, I book it to the ICU, trying to get to Elissa as fast as possible. I was such a dumbass for letting anything get between us. How could I have pushed her away? *What if I lose her? Like, lose her for good?* I can't bear to think about that, so I push the thoughts aside and mash the button for the elevator, wishing it would come faster.

As I arrive at Elissa's room, I hear the soft beeps coming from the machines she is hooked up to. She looks fragile and broken. She doesn't look real. Tubes run out of her nose and mouth, and wires are tangled all around her, hooked up to multiple monitors. Her skin is pale, and there are dark circles painted under her eyes. Angry bruises and welts are prominent on her forehead and temple. My heart shatters into a million pieces as I stand there, looking at the love of my life. She's broken, and there's nothing I can do.

I step into the room and a hushed, weak voice calls my name.

"Brandt?" I turn around and it's Elissa's mother, sitting in the corner of the room. She looks like hell. Her bronze hair is greasy and unkempt, her eyes are bloodshot, her nose is red, and her clothes are wrinkled and mussed. There are tissues balled up in her hands, and she sniffles as she stands and walks over to me, wiping her cheeks. "Thank you for coming. I'm so worried." She breaks down, collapsing into my arms and sobbing. I do my best to try and console her, but I've only met her a handful of times, and she's always been distant.

"What happened?" My voice betrays how I feel. It's calm, collected, and confident. Her mother pulls out of my grasp and shuffles over to the chair sitting beside Elissa's bed. She takes a seat and leans forward to link her hand through Elissa's.

"Apparently, there was a driver on the road that cut them off and Elissa hit a patch of black ice. They started spinning out and crashed into the wall of the exit ramp." Her voice wobbles as she speaks. "I...I don't know what to do. I can't lose her, too, Brandt. I just can't. After Harold died, I realized how selfish I've been all these years. I pushed Elissa away to make Harold happy because he never wanted a girl. I know it's not right, but —" her voice breaks and a strangled cry leaves her. "It's no excuse. I was a shitty mother. And I only hope I get a chance to make it up to her now."

I'm floored by what Collette is saying. Never would I have thought that she'd admit to her neglect of Elissa. I guess dire situations really make people think. Just like how I could lose Elissa for good if she doesn't wake up from this coma. How I spent the last month-and-a-half apart from her, when I could have been with her, loving her. I'll never forgive myself if I don't get a chance to apologize to her. To see her smile again, or hold her, or kiss her.

I walk around the other side of the bed and take the other seat. Collette's blue eyes are so familiar, so much like the woman I love. It's hard looking at Collette because Elissa is a younger version of her mother, and all I see is the woman I let down. That I let go.

My hand slips across the bed and finds Elissa's icy hand. I wrap mine around hers and the familiar buzzing between us ignites. It leaves me hoping that she can feel me, and that she knows I'm here. I'll do anything to have her with me again. To have her wake up. I'll never leave her again. *Please, just let her wake up.*

• • •

The week stretches on, and I've spent all my time here at the hospital. I've left a few times to catch a shower and a change of clothes, and to grab my laptop to work from here. Riley and Rhys have stopped by almost every day to check in on Elissa. Riley is a complete mess, but the baby is healthy and she's doing fine physically, other than a few bumps and bruises. She was actually just released the other day and cleared to go home. No more worries about pre-term labour, as the doctors were able to stop it. She still has to take it easy and be off her feet as much as possible for the rest of her pregnancy though.

When Riley rolled into the room for the first time since the accident, the little green monster inside me raged to break free. I immediately noticed the ring on her finger, and every part of me was jealous and angry. How the fuck could Rhys do this to me? Make a happy situation out of something so terrible? How could he get his happy ending when I'm fucking drowning in sorrow? When my heart is constantly in a state of being ripped out of my chest and stomped on? But, over the last few days, the little green monster inside me has simmered down, and I am happy for them. Truly, I am. I'm glad Rhys came to his senses, because Riley deserves to have the father of her baby beside her, and have love in her life. I just wish my love would wake the fuck up.

Friday comes and goes, and I get an infuriating email from the board of CGC. They're expecting me in the office on Monday for the board meeting, and I want to throw my phone across the room. The thought of leaving Elissa right now is inconceivable. I can't just go back to work and focus, not when my mind is here, wondering if she's going to be okay and wake up.

Later in the afternoon, I'm reading the business section of the Toronto Star and catching up on a few emails when a man walks into the room — the same guy from the restaurant who had his hands all over her. My blood boils and I see red. *What the fuck is he doing here?*

"Oh, Theo!" Collette exhales in surprise. "How wonderful to see you!" His Adam's apple bobs in his throat as he looks at Elissa like he's going to cry.

"I heard the news from my mother this morning and thought I'd stop by and see how she's doing." He raises his hand and I notice the bouquet of sunflowers and gerberas, Elissa's favourites. He hands them off to Collette and stalks over to Elissa's bed, gently running the back of his knuckles down the side of her face. Gritting my teeth, I clear my throat and *Theo* steps back, a little shocked. "Sorry, I didn't notice you there," he says, his voice velvety. He walks over to me, hand stretched out. "Theo Greenbelt."

I stand, stretching my hand out and grabbing his with a firm grip — almost too firm, apparently, when I see him squirm from the pressure.

"Collins. Brandt Collins." Theo's eyes widen with recognition.

"Oh, no way! The tech guy? That's awesome. How do you know the Blacks?" *What the fuck does this guy think he's doing? Are we really having a "bro" moment right now?* I clench my jaw and try to let my anger subside.

"Business partners," I growl.

"Cool, man," he says, dropping my hand and turning back to face Collette. "I'm so sorry about Elissa. We were supposed to get together this week and have dinner. I guess that won't be happening now," he chuckles lightly. Collette's eyes light up at his words like it's Christmas fucking morning. Theo beams at Collette and takes a side glance at me, and I see the smile turn into a smug smirk. I thrust my hands into my pockets and my fingers curl into hard fists. It's taking every ounce of strength I have not to pummel the guy into next week.

Theo takes a seat beside where Collette was sitting, and she grabs a vase from the side table, fills it with water, and arranges the flowers, smelling them as she does, with a cheerful look on her face. She shouldn't be so happy right now with *Theo* bringing flowers. I've been beside Elissa this entire week. Sure, I didn't bring flowers. But I've been here.

An hour later, Theo still isn't leaving. As he chats away with Collette, his glances at me become more frequent and curious. I try to block him out and focus on my work, but it's getting increasingly harder to ignore this guy.

"Yes?" I snarl, finally snapping at his constant looks. His face feigns innocence, as his brows quirk curiously. When he realizes I am, in fact, talking to him, he clears his throat, sits up a little straighter, and leans forward onto his legs.

"So, are you and Elissa…a thing?" I grind my teeth, thinking of what to say. We're not anything anymore. My eyes shift to Collette and she's perked up as her eyes shift between me and Theo.

"No," I grumble. A smug smile stretches across Theo's face and he relaxes back into his chair.

"Hmm," is all he says. Folding his arms across his chest, he turns to Collette and starts talking again about his mother and her newest philanthropic venture. I slam my laptop shut and shove it into my bag, planting my feet on the ground and springing up out of the chair. Both Collette and Theo stare at me like I've lost my mind. I punch my arms into my coat, zip it up, and toss my bag over my shoulder. I can't sit here and look at Theo anymore, knowing that she's moving on with him. My face is growing hot and my teeth are losing enamel by the second with how much grinding and clenching I'm doing.

"Well, Collette. Looks like you've got company now. I'll leave you two be. I hope Elissa wakes up soon."

I strut past them and continue on without looking back, because if I do, I might just break.

CHAPTER THIRTY-EIGHT

BRANDT

Ever since I left the hospital, I've been going insane. Not knowing what's going on right now with Elissa is killing me. I feel like I've been separated from my soul. And I have. She's it for me. My other half. If anything happens to her, I have no idea what I'm going to do.

I'm back in the office and I'm trying to focus, but it's extremely difficult. Rhys is still off on leave for a few more days to make sure Riley is okay, and I hate the friggin' bastard. *Okay, so I don't actually hate him, but fuck him. Lucky sonofabitch.* Why did things work out for him and not me? Haven't I been patient enough? I silently send out vibes into the universe, hoping anyone is listening, and that they'll send Elissa back to me.

I hear a knock on my door and I look up to see Liam standing in the doorway. I nod to him and notice his eyes are sad.

"What's up?" I ask. He shifts nervously, digging his hands deep into his pockets.

"Heard about Elissa. I'm sorry, man. Anything I can do to help?"

"Nah, not really. I spent the last week by her side hoping she'd wake up, but I had to get back to reality. Just waiting to hear anything now, if I do…" Liam cocks his head, his brow furrowing.

"What does that mean?" My jaw clenches, and I reach up to rub the tension out of my neck.

"It *means* there was another guy that showed up today and is waiting to see if she's okay. And he seems rather close to Collette, Elissa's mom. So, I doubt I'll hear anything if she wakes up. Especially since we're not together." Liam nods as if he understands. We're both quiet for a moment, but he breaks the silence and asks if I want to shoot some hoops later tonight when I'm done with work. Not really feeling in the mood for it, I tell him I'll text him later, knowing it would only be us two, as Rhys won't leave Riley's side.

He nods, and before he leaves my office he says, "Don't worry, man. I'm sure you'll hear something soon. Elissa's a badass. She'll wake up." I give him a halfhearted smile, and although I appreciate his sentiment, I'm not feeling very hopeful right now.

The longest day drags on and finally comes to an end. I'm loosening the tie around my neck as I walk down the long, dark corridor to my apartment. The days are finally getting longer and warmer now that it's mid-April, but not even that is shifting my mood. I feel like it's still March, when Elissa left me. There's a big, black hole in the centre of me. A piece of me is missing and I can't fix it.

I finally realize that she's moving on with that Theo guy, just as her mother wanted her to. She's still doing things her parents want. Still trying to prove to them she's who they wanted all along, and it's killing me. And as she's moving on with *him*, I don't know if I'm strong enough to let her go. I don't know if I'll ever be able to let her go. It's like my body doesn't know how to breathe or function without her. She's all I see, all I need. But if she doesn't need me, then what point is there?

I kick off my shoes and toss my bag and coat on the front hall table, shuffling toward my room, but making a pit stop in the kitchen. I grab a beer, twist off the cap, and toss it across the counter, where it clinks as it slides into the sink. Walking to my room, I down the bottle of beer and set the empty on my dresser. I change out of my suit and put on some sweats and a tee that clings to my body and shows every ripple of muscle. Running my hands through my hair, I grab the empty off the dresser and stalk back to the kitchen, where I grab another two beers, and then collapse onto the couch. Kicking my feet up on the coffee table, I grab the Xbox controller and turn on Call of Duty to kill some motherfuckers and take off the edge.

I'm about seven beers deep and in a frustrating round of killing zombies when my phone beeps. I look over at it sitting on the cushion beside me and Rhys' name flashes up at me. I decide to ignore it, not wanting to talk to the happy fucker right now, not while I'm stewing in my misery. I flip my phone over so I can't see the screen and also click the button to turn it to silent, wanting to disconnect from the whole world right now. A zombie attacks me at that moment, ruining my streak, and I toss the remote in anger across the room. It smashes against the wall and the battery compartment breaks off, sending batteries rolling across the floor.

I lunge off the couch and stagger to the kitchen to grab another few beers. I haven't drunk like this in a while, but what else do I have to do? Elissa is safe with *Theo* and her mother while I'm here, fucking heartbroken again over this woman. My hand coils around the bottle and clenches until the glass cracks and shatters under the pressure. A sharp pain slices through my palm and I drop the broken bottle like it's a hot pan. I lean over and rip a tea towel off the stove handle and wrap it around my dripping wound, stepping as carefully as I can around the broken glass. Grabbing the other two beers, I make my way out of my kitchen and into my bedroom to drown the rest of my feelings for the night.

• • •

The next morning, my mouth is dry and pasty, and feels like I dumped a bucket of sand in it. My tongue sticks to the roof of my mouth and peels away like wallpaper off a wall. I open my eyes and my room spins. I can't remember how much I drank last night. Using my hand, I try to push myself to sit up and I'm met with a sharp, searing pain in my palm. I blink in confusion and hold my hand up to my face. I see the blood-soaked towel wrapped around my hand, and some of the night comes back to me. I reach over to grab my phone from my nightstand and my hand knocks over a couple of beer bottles and they smash to the floor. I groan, gritting my teeth as my head pounds.

Fuck. I shouldn't have drunk so much last night.

Finally able to grab my phone, I try to unlock it, but it's dead. I plug it in, waiting for it to power up. I don't even know what time it is, or what day for that matter. I think it's Saturday, but I could be wrong. *Fuck, my head hurts.* My phone beeps and turns on. While I wait for it to load my home screen I look around my room to see about a case's worth of beer bottles scattered around my room. *How much did I fucking drink?*

My phone starts dinging, one after another, creating a rapid chorus of notification sounds. Each of them letting me know it's a message or a call from Rhys. Ignoring the messages, I click on my voicemail and wait for it to connect. Rhys' husky voice greets me, and he only says a few words.

"Dude, answer me! Elissa woke up!"

CHAPTER
THIRTY-NINE

Something is gagging me as I come to. The taste of plastic coats my tongue. I finally open my eyes and my mother is hovering over me, sobbing, calling out for help. My eyes shift around the room and I don't know where I am, but it must be the hospital. I try to relax my throat, but between the taste and the uncomfortable fullness hitting my gag reflex, I keep choking on the tube in my throat.

Nurses bustle into the room, pushing my mother out of the way as they work on extracting the breathing tube. My throat is raw, and feels like tiny razor blades have nicked the passageway.

"Now, don't try to talk for a little while," the nurse chides as I move my lips to speak. She nods to another nurse, who disappears and returns seconds later with a pitcher of water and a cup. He fills up the cup and hands it to me, and I take it cautiously, bringing the rim to my lips and tipping it back slowly. The cool water does wonders to soothe my aching, burning throat. I didn't even realize how parched I was until I took that first little sip. "You were in an accident, and you're at Mount Sinai Hospital." My eyes shoot wide open. "The doctor will be in to check on you shortly." The nurse gives me a polite smile and a nod to my mother in the corner as she leaves.

"Oh, Elissa!" my mother cries. "I thought I lost you too!" Purple circles rim her eyes, making it look like she's been punched in the face. Her eyes are also bloodshot and watery. A wave of uneasiness washes over me, because I don't recognize this person in front of me. I don't think I've ever seen my mother show any kind of concern for anyone or anything other than herself or her appearance. *That's not true, she cried at your father's death.* Yeah, but that was the exception. "I am so sorry for everything," she stammers. Her breathing is laboured as her dainty fingers curl around my hand. "I have so much to make up for and I'm going to take advantage of you not being able to talk to clear some of the air." A grumble rises in my throat and my mother clicks her tongue at me. "Don't start with your obstinance, and just listen."

My mother says nothing for a few moments. Her eyes stay trained on me, overflowing with emotion. My body squirms and I feel like I need to shrink, to worm my way out of this somehow, and get away. She must notice or sense I'm restless because she pins me down with a motherly stare I've never seen before, and it freezes me in my spot.

"Now, I know I've never been the best mother," she starts, and a mix of a snort and a scoff erupts in my throat before I can stop it, causing a searing pain. My mother's eyes narrow and her lips press into a firm, thin line. Once she's convinced I'll be quiet, she continues. "As I was saying, I've never been the best mother, and for that I can only say I am sorry. I let my love for Harold influence how I treated you. I tried to be that trophy wife he always pressured me into being. Now, I know this is going to seem like an excuse, but he never used to be like that. There was a time when he was warm, loving, and caring. I know it's hard to believe, but once he found success and saw how the other businessmen ran their lives, your father just wanted to be one of them."

I roll my eyes. She's right — it does sound like an excuse. She's lucky I can't really talk right now. She clears her throat and levels her gaze at me, clearly expecting me to restrain any kind of sarcastic communication.

"Your father was a brilliant man. Ambitious, hardworking, and strong-willed. Much like yourself. I wonder sometimes if he always knew you were too similar, and that's why you never got along. He held a lot of resentment because you were a woman, and that was old-fashioned of him. Let's be honest — the Harold you knew was an ass. But please believe me when I say that change was gradual. As he became more successful, and the people in our society started accepting him, he morphed into the people he emulated. I believed if I loved him through these changes, I would still see the man I fell in love with. But when I couldn't find that man any longer, I ended up changing with him, because it scared me to lose him. He was still Harold, the man I fell in love with, and I convinced myself a part of him was still in there somewhere." My mother pauses and looks down at her lap, twisting a tissue in her hands.

"I just want to say how sorry I am for the part I played in making you feel the way you do. When you bonded with Lana so easily, I was jealous. I suffered from post-partum depression, though I didn't know it at the time. My jealousy consumed me, and the contempt I got from your father for you being a girl…well, it didn't help. Harold withdrew further and further from me, and it broke my heart a little more each time. And I lost a piece of myself every time I saw you with Lana, but your father refused to fire her. I begged him, even threatened him with divorce. But Lana was loyal, she was an excellent housekeeper, and he refused to let someone go over petty jealousy. Which, honestly, I came to admire, years later. He was loyal to a fault. Maybe not to his family, but to his employees."

Tears form in my mother's eyes, and her bottom lip quivers as she stops talking. Her shoulders collapse as she hunches over and pulls out another handful of tissues. She dabs at her eyes and gently wipes her nose before mut-tering an apology.

"I loved him, Elissa. And he *was* a good man, once upon a time. I'm sorry you never met the man I loved. Losing Harold started this wave of revelation within me. Yes, he changed, and our marriage became nothing more than a publicity thing. But I stuck by him because of the man he *was*. And then, almost losing you, without getting a chance to reconcile. Without getting a chance to actually know this incredible woman in front of me —"

My heart is beating at full speed, and there's no sign of stopping. The computer monitoring my heart rate beeps quietly in the background, speeding up to match my racing heart, but my mother and I don't notice it. I'm too focused on what the fuck is coming out of her mouth. *Who the hell is this woman in front of me?* It feels like I'm suffocating. A thousand-pound weight is pressing down on my chest, and there's no way of getting it off me. I've waited my whole life for this apology. This conversation. And I can't say anything. All I can do is listen, and it's killing me. I feel all of my defences crumbling one by one, and all those years of hurt and pain are easing.

"Both your father and I have done a lot of things wrong. I admit that. But you wouldn't be the woman you are if we had acted any other way. That doesn't excuse our actions, I know. But Elissa, despite us, despite everything we put you through, you are…extraordinary. And through all this, I've finally had enough. Losing your father and almost losing you…well, it's changed me. I feel so ridiculous to be that cliché of a woman, but it changed me. And I can only hope you'll give me a chance to get to know you. I don't think for a second that things will be easy, or we'll ever be close like you and Lana. I'm not foolish. But I just want a chance."

She's breaking my heart, and I didn't think I had any space left in my heart for my parents to break. There's a tidal wave of emotions crashing around inside me, and

I'm not sure if I'm strong enough to withstand them. I'm drowning in the rising tide. Each brick of my emotional dam cracks a little more the more she speaks, and I can't repair the wall fast enough. I've waited my whole life to hear words like these, and I always wanted to rub it in their faces that I never needed them. But now? Now, I don't know what to do with these revelations. Her words never stop; it's like she's broken an emotional dam of her own. I choke on my tears, willing them back to where they came from.

"So, can we?" she asks in earnest. My face twists into confusion and my nerves flare up, not sure of what she's asking as I retreat into my internal chaos. "Can we please try?" She inches closer to the edge of the chair, like she's ready to jump off the cliff if she doesn't get the right answer. Her eyes are wide and wild, darting from side to side, waiting for my answer. Tears well in her eyes again and I can see and hear her heart breaking with every second I take to answer. I currently hold all the power in our relationship dynamic, and I'm not sure how I feel about it.

"*Please*," she whispers brokenly, and that one word shatters everything inside of me. The dam collapses and tears spill from my eyes, cascading down my cheeks and soaking the gown I'm wearing like I've been standing out in a thunderstorm. My strangled voice gets stuck in my throat and all I can do is nod. Her dam breaks, too. And just like that, both of us are sobbing as she comes to the bed and cradles me.

•••

A couple of hours later, my mother leaves to get cleaned up and grab a quick nap. She looked like she needed the sleep.

I can't believe my mother was beside my bed this whole time. *Maybe she really means everything she said.*

A light knock sounds on my door and it clicks open. Wide brown eyes peek in the door, brimming with tears. Riley's black hair is sleek and perfect, like always. As she pushes open the door, Rhys follows behind her closely, his arms wrapped around her like she's fragile, his eyes full of concern as he stares at her.

When our eyes connect, we're both sobbing fools. Riley climbs into the bed with me, and I wince as she nudges my ribs.

"I'm so sorry!" she squeals through her tears.

"Fuck off and get over here," I rasp, choking on my laughter and tears. Her arms encircle me and we lay together and cry. It feels like eternity before the last tear dries up. Rhys clears his throat, and his eyes focus on Riley. A silent conversation takes place between them, and I feel sorely out of the loop.

Riley slips off the bed and sits on the chair beside me, propping her feet up off the floor onto my bed.

"What was that about?" I narrow my eyes and glare at Rhys.

"She's supposed to be on bed rest," he grumbles, and I feel a vibration of anger floating toward me. But I don't focus on him, it's Riley I'm worried about.

"What is he talking about, Riles?" She looks away, her eyes filling with…guilt? Or sadness?

"So, the accident? I could have lost the baby. I went into preterm labour from the stress and everything," she raises her hands to halt my interruption. "We're okay, E. Don't feel bad. Everyone is okay. And Rhys has been great with my recovery. He took a week-and-a-half off work to make sure I was okay. And…"

I cock my head at her trailing off, getting annoyed with the pause.

"And?" I ask impatiently. Riley's face blooms with happiness and she holds up her hand. I see the glittering diamond perched on her slim finger. "Oh my God. Are you engaged?!" I'm bewildered more than anything. After all he put her through, they're engaged? My eyes dart between Riley and Rhys, and his arms fold across his chest. I see the whites of his knuckles from his fists clenching, like he's waiting for a fight. "Oh Riles!" I gush. "I am so happy for you," I say, and I see the tension leave Rhys' body. His arms relax and his expression eases, but I squint at him just the same. "Don't fuck this up, Rhys."

He instantly stiffens. "You're one to fucking talk," he mumbles.

"What the *fuck* does that mean?" Raging anger flares inside of me and I catch Riley glancing at Rhys and muttering something. Rhys waves her off, and my irritation grows. They're keeping something from me, and I am about to lose it on them. "Hello??"

"It means you fucked up with Brandt." I'm shocked. *How did I fuck up? He's the one who walked away.* "He's been fucking pining after you for years. Since fucking high school." My mind goes completely blank.

CHAPTER
FORTY

"What do you mean he's been pining for me since high school? We only just met last year, because of my father."

Rhys scoffs.

"Yeah, so you think."

"What the fuck does that mean? Someone fucking tell me." My hand laces around my aching throat, as it's too much talking for me. I saved my words for Riley, but this has taken a turn. Riley's eyes soften and her hand grabs mine, filling me with warmth.

"Apparently, they both grew up in the same town as us," Riley explains. I don't comprehend what she's telling me. I close my eyes and try to focus on what she's saying. "They went to the same high school and everything. Apparently, they were our orientation leaders on our first day. When Rhys told me, it all snapped back in my mind. I remember Rhys being there. Remember that dick that called us out on the first day for talking? That was Rhys…and the broody, quiet guy with him was Brandt."

My mind keeps drawing blanks. *How is this possible? Oh my God! That must mean that the truck I saw down the road from Riley's parents…that must be Brandt's parents, their company.* Things click slowly into place, and I wonder how I never noticed him before. *He's four years older. He would have only been there the first year of high school for me.* This is just way too freaky and too big of a coincidence. And how would he still have been hung up on me? He never knew me, he never even talked to me. *Wait…was this his plan from the beginning when he invested in my father's company?* I'm at a loss for words and I don't know what to say.

My mind floats back to our first meeting — or, at least, what I *thought* was our first meeting — when the guys came to pack up my apartment before we moved to Toronto. Brandt was sitting on my bed, going through my grade nine yearbook. I thought that was odd at the time, but now I know. *Holy shit.* And just like that, I'm transported back to my first day of high school and the brief spark I felt with one of the guys leading our group.

• • •

Pandemonium ensued on the first day of high school. I've never seen so many students crammed into one space before. Students blocking hallways, doorways, and stairwells. They even seemed to clog up the open areas like the quad. There was also a certain hum of excitement throughout the halls, and the teachers seemed animated, having cheerful conversations with each other and students.

I was among the nervous freshmen coming into their first year of high school. Riley and and I were gathering in the quad, where we were to get our class schedules and be assigned to a group designated by colours. There were about thirty-odd freshmen assigned to a group, making for a total of two hundred and thirty-one students. Two senior students were leading each group.

When the warning bell screeches across the lot at 8:10 AM on this warm September morning, a flurry of students scatter across the quad, looking for their assigned groups. The seniors, however, are in no rush to find their student charges — they all stand in a clump, talking and laughing. When the last bell rings, the seniors break apart and find their corresponding groups. The two seniors who stroll over to our group, the green group, have their arms crossed, and their uninterested stares silence the students' nervous chatter. A hush falls over the green group as the taller of the two guys takes control, speaking loudly and arrogantly.

"Listen up," his voice booms. "I'll only say this once. I'm Rhys, one of your guides for this week at school. Welcome to grade nine, losers." He chuckles, and a few freshmen shiver from the darkness in his laughter. My eyes shift to the senior standing behind him, only slightly shorter. His arms bulge out of his uniform shirt, with broad shoulders, golden-brown waves, and light eyes — maybe green.

When his eyes connect with mine, the hairs on my arms and neck shoot to attention, prickling my skin as they rise. A simmering heat warms my body and something inside me flickers. Breaking the eye contact, I turn my attention to Riley and try to focus on what she's whispering about.

Out of the corner of my eye, I keep my gaze on the two men before us. They are definitely men, not boys. Their presence commands silence and attention. Their tall frames are imposing, and their stares are penetrating. Rhys is certainly cocky, and his looks probably don't help. He's tall, with muscular arms and a flat stomach, made all the more apparent by the uniform polo that clings to his torso like a second skin. His pitch-black hair is shorn on the sides with just enough to spike on the top. His eyes are piercing, but I can't tell what colour they are, maybe some shade of blue. But the other guy, who still hasn't been introduced, is different — no less intimidating. But there is something about him that speaks to my body.

He looks strong and silent, like someone who could go a round or two with you. His muscles bulge out of his sleeves, his shoulders almost bursting the seams of his navy polo shirt. The school's emblem on the uniform is stretched across one hardened pec, and the shirt tapers down his waist, leaving me to wonder what ridges lay beneath.

"Look who's got a stick up his ass," Riley hisses into my ear. Giggles burst from us, and the silent, strong one nudges Rhys in the ribs and juts his head toward us. I try to shush Riley, but she keeps mocking him, and I can't stop laughing.

"Ladies," Rhys' voice drips with reprimand. "You'd better pay attention and stop giggling." He calls us out and our faces colour with embarrassment. "You know what? Just come up to the front. I don't feel like babysitting some niners today." He gestures for us to move forward, and Riley links her arm through mine and drags me behind her, swerving through the group. When we reach the front of the group, my skin engulfs in flames as Rhys' silent friend stares me down, his gaze never wavering. My breath catches in my throat and my eyes slide away, trying to look anywhere but at him.

The tension doesn't die down between us even as Rhys continues to talk. "If you have questions about your time-table, don't discuss it with Collins or myself. Just go see the guidance counsellors." His bored tone carries across the quad as he points in the direction of the doors opposite to us, one of a set of four in the quad. A large oak tree stretches to the sky in the centre, a spot that is probably coveted during breaks. The guidance department is closest to the morning bus drop-off area and driveway. But, even as I shift my gaze to see where Rhys is pointing, I feel the heated gaze of Collins on me, never leaving. Not the entire time of the tour, either.

• • •

I remember that year, I always felt like someone was watching me — I often felt the same warm hum that would light my body on fire. During assemblies, in the cafeteria at lunch, or during school performances, when I was on the dance or cheerleading team, there was always this shadow that followed me throughout the ninth grade year. I just thought it had more to do with being "Harold Black's daughter," and was sure it would die down soon enough. But looking back, comparing that feeling that I remember to what I feel now between Brandt and I…it feels familiar. But now it's charged, powerful, and not so innocent.

Coils of regret and hunger collide together inside of me.

A painful pang of need jolts through my body, and my heart screams out for Brandt.

I chuckle to myself in exasperation, wincing as the breath jerks my ribs. Riley looks at me like I've grown a second head. Fresh anger and sadness surge inside me when I realize he gave up on us too easily. *After all those years of waiting for me? Wanting me? And he just gave up at the first sign of trouble?*

My mother saunters into the room, only increasing the room's tension. She halts, looking around the room curiously.

"What did I miss?" she asks innocently.

"Just a minor revelation about Brandt," Riley offers. I shoot her a withering look, but she skillfully avoids my stare. My mother hums and her heels click across the floor as she rounds the end of my bed and takes a seat beside me.

"Oh, and what's that? Could it possibly be that he's desperately in love with Elissa? Any fool can see that." My mother, with her impeccable timing, looks impeccable again, as if the last few hours hadn't happened. She's back to her normal self, fully pulled together, make up painted on her face, and a mask of indifference. "I, for one, think Elissa needs to get her head out of her ass."

My mouth drops open, along with Riley's. Rhys is shifting his weight and looking between Riley and me with confusion.

"Did I miss something?" His low, rumbly voice breaks the silence.

"Only that my daughter needs to get her shit together and make sure she fixes things with Brandt."

I'm floored.

"What do you mean, Mother?"

"Well, he only sat beside you for the entire time you were in a coma, except for when Theo showed up," she huffs. "It seemed as though he thought there was something going on between you and Theo, considering what Theo said." My heart stutters in my chest, stopping me from breathing for a moment.

"What did he say?" I groan.

"Something about getting together for dinner. We all know in our circle that's just idle chatter, but Brandt seemed to think it was more," she says, bored, as she extracts a nail file from her purse and begins sculpting a nail.

I grimace as I force my body to sit up, bracing myself for what's going to be a long and painful recovery, only to possibly be shattered again at the end.

CHAPTER
FORTY-ONE

ELISSA

The next two weeks drag on as I power through my recovery. I've been stuck in physiotherapy for the small amount of muscle mass I lost because of being bedridden for over a week, but also the bruised ribs, which are fucking painful to work through, by the way. Also, I've started attending therapy again — especially after my mother's big speech. I've really spent a lot of time these last two weeks working on myself with my therapist and figuring out why I don't let people in. I mean, I know it's because of my parents, but it's freeing knowing that I'm working past these issues. My mother has even sat in on a few of those sessions with me.

But I'm doing all this because I've got one goal in mind: getting Brandt back.

I don't know what the fuck I'm doing, but I'll figure it out. I've slowly come to a space where there's no denial. I love him. He's the air I need to breathe. These last weeks without him have sucked the life out of me, and it's agonizing, because I still feel the ghost of his touch, his lips, his hands on me. I miss the way his lips brush against my skin, making goosebumps ripple across my body. I miss the way my body fits and molds perfectly withhis, and the way his cock fills me like no one else's ever has. I miss the way saying his name feels on the tip of my tongue as I'm breathless and riding the waves of pleasure.

I'm finally making some progress in my recovery, and I'm sitting in the waiting room waiting for my last session with my physiotherapist. It's a big, wide-open space with treadmills and other various exercise equipment, like weights and stretching bands. One wall is a bank of windows that opens the space up into downtown Toronto, though it's littered with buildings blocking the view. Cars are bumper-to-bumper down in Yonge-Dundas Square, and it's the only thing you can really see outside of the windows.

"Elissa?" I'm finally called back into the physiotherapist's office for a review of my progress. I walk through the workout space, passing people who are huffing and grunting as they do their stretches and exercises. I sit down in the plush black leather chair in her office. "Well, Elissa. After the last round of therapy, I'd say you're almost at one hundred percent. I think I can clear you for work, and you can finally start jogging again — *not* running, but jogging." The bruises on my ribs still look horrible, but they're fading, and they're mostly superficial now. My sides really only hurt if I turn the wrong way too quickly. "I will see you in two weeks, and in the meantime, keep up with the exercises I prescribed."

Overjoyed, I glide out of the office, finally able to get back into the pace of things. To say I was surprised when my mother took over operations at work while I was down for the count is an understatement. And to admit she's done a great job is even harder to believe. Here's this trophy wife who can actually kick ass at business. Sure, there were some fumbles and calls I wouldn't have made, but I guess being with and around my father and his work all the time really prepared her. I dig my phone out of my purse and text Riley right away about the progress I've made and about my last therapy session, and text the board about my imminent return.

My phone beeps, twice. One is a message from Riley.

Riley: *Way to go! Go get him, girl.*

The other is an email from work, and my heart glows.

I rush home, my mind swirling in a tizzy as I bolt through the front door and make my way to my room.

"Riley! Come help me choose my outfit for Monday!" I call out into the silent apartment.

I pull everything out of my closet, things fluttering to the floor, landing on my bed, or falling flat at my feet as Riley shuffles into my room. Her belly has gotten bigger and it enters the room before she does now. It's crazy to think she has just about three months left of her pregnancy.

"What's going on?" she says in a yawn as she rubs her eyes. Her black hair is fluffy and tangled at the back, while her wrinkled shirt shows her little bump sticking out the bottom.

"I just got an email saying Brandt is going to be attending the board meeting on Monday. Riley, I'm going to go for it. I've got to talk to him."

Riley's face lights up, her eyes filling with tears. She cries at everything lately, a side effect of pregnancy, I suspect.

"Oh, I am so happy for you, babe!"

I grin back at her, my smile beaming at one thousand watts. I'm smiling so hard it hurts my cheeks. My fingers and toes are tingly, and my heart is pounding in my chest as I'm heaving breaths in and out. *I'm going to get him back.*

CHAPTER FORTY-TWO

BRANDT

I've officially given up. I can't compete with someone like Theo. I remember the way her mother glowed the minute he stepped into the room. I just can't do it. I've really got to move on.

I know she's woken up. I've heard so many times from Rhys. He's been really irritating, the amount of times he's hounded me to see her, or at least reach out to her. But I can't. It's fucking embarrassing enough that I sat by her side for a week and then Theo saunters in like he's entitled to Elissa. I've fucked up a lot lately, I know that. I was the one who pushed her away, but I can't shake this feeling. I've lost her. And I've lost a piece of myself, and I'm trying to move on.

Every thought of mine encompasses her. What she's wearing, what she smells like, what she's thinking about… if she's thinking of me. Certainly she's heard about me being by her bedside, so why hasn't she called? Messaged? Anything? *Easy.*

She's moved on.

And it fucking kills me.

I can't pretend I didn't do this to myself, but she could have reached out over these last two weeks. I've been suffering, been in agony, terrorizing myself about if or when she'll call. But she hasn't. Rhys said she's just taking time to deal with everything and heal. Yeah, sure. I get that. But she still could have sent me a text, letting me know herself that she's okay.

As I'm wallowing in my self-pity and destruction, my phone dings.

From: *Black, Elissa*
Subject: *Return to Work*

Good afternoon, everyone.
I've been officially cleared to return to work after my accident.
I want to thank my mother, Collette, for stepping in when I was incapacitated and unable to work. I would like to see everyone at the board meeting on Monday, as there is a lot for me to catch up on.
I am doing well and hope to see you all there.
Thank you,

Elissa Black
CEO
Black & Wells Publishing and Press

Tightness restricts my chest as I read her words over and over. This is the closest I've gotten to any communication with her. A fucking work email. It may be petty, but I text my assistant and forward the email to him, asking him to confirm my attendance.

I spend the rest of my weekend in a drunken stupor, lazing around my apartment, nursing a hangover, and repeating that process. I need to drown myself in something else, other than this hollow feeling that's suffocating me. I need to flush her out of my system, so when I see her on Monday, I don't break. I don't crumble. Or at least, she can't see that I'm breaking.

* * *

Monday comes and I'm in no better shape. I contemplate skipping the meeting altogether. She won't miss me, the company board won't miss me. They haven't for the last two months.

The end-of-April air is temperamental. It's chilly in the morning and warm in the afternoon, which makes it a bitch for me to decide what to wear. My smooth, charcoal grey Armani suit is tailored to perfection as I slide it onto my body, the fabric hugging and sculpting my every muscle. My white button-down dress shirt underneath is a soft, light linen, cooling my burning, nervous body. I slip on a navy TAG Heuer Carrera and fasten it around my wrist, then shove my wallet and phone into my pants pocket. My fingers glide and tease my hair to perfection, and I stand gloating at the mirror.

I feel confident and ready to face Elissa.

That feeling quickly shatters as she walks into the conference room, looking more beautiful than ever. Her radiant cinnamon hair falls in loose curls down her back, and my fingers itch to lace my hand through her strands and wrap them around my wrist. She's wearing a white skirt with a slit up the middle, and her black scoop neck tee fits snugly against her chest and highlights the swell of her breasts, teasing me and reminding me how they felt in my hands. My heart thumps wildly in my chest at the memory. Her long, lean legs have lost some of their tone, but look just as delicious as they did before the accident. My mouth salivates as this gorgeous woman clicks her heels around the table, making her way to the front of the room.

When she smiles at the room, it's like everything melts away and it's just us. Time stands still only for us. The beating of my heart pauses as our eyes connect, and I'm swallowed whole by her oceanic eyes. I'm tumbling and twirling in the undertow, her gaze drowning all my senses. My heart clambers to be with her, and it pounds like it's going to leap out of my chest. All I want is to connect with her again. My cock strains against my zipper, pulsing to be near her. My lips ache to brush against her skin and feel the way she shivers when I touch her.

She breaks our eye contact, and my resolve shatters. I'm left a broken mess in the middle of the boardroom, and the glint in her eyes as she looks away gives off a vibe of mischief and…longing? I blink those thoughts away and convince myself I'm just imagining it. The rest of the meeting passes in a haze, because all I can do is stare at her beauty and wonder how the fuck it all went wrong.

"Projections show that stocks are up thirty percent since your recovery," one of the analysts chatters.

"Collette decided we should focus on marketing this quarter…"

"The new division has been thriving under Selena's watch and we think she should be promoted officially…"

All these bits and pieces of news have no bearing on my focus because I'm mesmerized by the enchanting woman in front of me, who looked so fragile two weeks ago but is now sitting in front of me, stronger than ever.

When the meeting comes to an end, everyone rushes up to Elissa to offer their congratulations on her speedy recovery. The board members are clasping her shoulder, offering hugs, and shaking her hand. I hover in the background, their neediness and obsession with flattering their boss grating on my nerves. My skin is buzzing as I wait for the chance to speak to her privately. I know I shouldn't, but everything inside me burns to be near her. As the room clears, the tension multiplies tenfold; electricity charges the air.

It's finally just the two of us left.

Neither of us says a word, but we miraculously gravitate toward each other, like magnets being drawn together, and finally we click.

"Hi," she says in a breathless whisper. My heart stops.

"Glad you're okay," I manage to mumble. My heart starts up again and is ramming itself against my ribcage. I can feel a drop of sweat forming on my brow. It's unbearably hot in here suddenly. It only blazes hotter when my eyes dart down and see her hand brush against the side of my hand and up, where her hand gently clasps my wrist, giving it a light squeeze and sending searing electricity jolting through my arm.

"Thanks for being there. My mother told me," she says quietly. And I shatter.

My hands dive into her hair, pulling her mouth against mine, devouring her whole. My lips feast on hers and I'm instantly hard. Mint and coffee lace her breath and she's all I taste. When I tip her head back, my tongue swipes at her lips, demanding entrance. She complies and moans as our tongues touch, and I almost come. The sound of her moan is so euphoric; it's like the heavens have parted and angels are singing. It tastes like coming home.

My hand drops and presses her lower back into me as I grind my hardness into her stomach, showing her just how much I need her. Her hands grip the back of my neck, her nails biting into the skin as she kisses me harder. Our bodies press together, any harder and we'd become one. I feel her heart beating in her chest, and I notice the subtle pebbling of her nipples under the slightly padded bra she's wearing. My tongue dives deeper into her mouth, exploring every inch, like it's the last time I'm ever going to kiss her. *And it probably will be.* Then reality breaks the moment, clarity seeps in, and I break the kiss, taking a step back.

We stand there, our chests heaving rapidly. Her face is flushed, her hair is a tangled mess, and a pang of regret burrows into my heart for stopping this. Her cheeks burn darker as we stand there, awkwardly gawking at one an-other in this heated standoff.

Elissa clears her throat, running her fingers through her hair.

"We should talk about this…somewhere where there aren't glass walls," she mutters, her eyes sliding to look out-side the glassed-in conference room, where the board mem-bers are standing and staring, wide-eyed and slack jawed. When we both turn to face them, they all jump out of their skins and bump into one another as they try to clear the area as quickly as possible. "Let's go to my office. We need to talk." So I follow her, letting her lead the way to her office.

She shuts the door behind her and leans against the door. One of her legs kicks out and her arms fold behind her lower back. Her face is thoughtful, her eyes mist over, and she looks fragile once again. She opens her mouth to say something, but I stop her.

"No, let me. I'm sorry. That was inappropriate and it shouldn't have happened." Her face falls, her lower lip trembling as her eyes search mine for the truth.

"Oh," she breathes. It breaks my heart, but I have to be strong. For both of us, because there's this unnatural chem-ical reaction that happens between us, making us both lose all rationale. "I just…"

"Just what?" My voice breaks.

"I just thought you changed your mind. That the kiss meant what I thought it did." Her words muddle my thoughts.

"What do you mean?" Her teeth sink into her lip as she debates what she's trying to say. Her eyes leave mine and she glances at her feet, shuffling a bit. She looks like a lost little girl.

"I just thought the kiss meant you loved me too."

Loved. Her. Too.

Too.

Is this her way of saying she loves me? *No, it can't be.*

I must have been silent too long because something inside her snaps. Suddenly she's standing tall and her limbs are stiff like they're bracing for impact. "I love you, Brandt. There it is. Fuck, why is that so hard to say?" She shakes her head and looks away, burying her head in her hands. "I love you. I love you. I love you. Fuck, it's not easy to fucking say. But there it is." Her eyes snap to mine and they're full of love, vulnerability, and hesitation. Like she's expecting to be shut down. Like I'm going to turn her away. *She said she loves you, you idiot.*

I snap out of my dreamlike state and rush toward her. I press her up against the door, my hand caressing her thigh and hooking it around my waist. My hard length presses into the apex of her thighs as my mouth crashes down against hers. My lips greedily take whatever she's offering as I drown in her sweetness. I steal every breath she breathes, revitalizing myself. My tongue sweeps against her lips and parts them, searching for her tongue. They tangle together in a fury of heated passion. My cock throbs against my pants, begging to be so fucking deep inside her. I need to feel her.

"Brandt," she moans. I swallow my name as it rolls off her lips, taking pleasure in how it sounds flowing from her mouth.

"I fucking love you too."

CHAPTER FORTY-THREE

BRANDT

I flick the lock on the door with a click.

The room is sweltering. I'm already sweating, and we've only kissed.

My hand skims up the back of her bare, creamy thigh, and she moans again. I roll my hips against hers, pressing my hard cock into her. She moans again and I don't think I'll ever get sick of that sound.

"*Please, Brandt,*" she begs. The sound of her begging is so sweet it melts my heart and all my inhibitions.

My hand parts the slit in her skirt and my thumb slips under her lacy panties. She's antsy, moving her body to find my finger. The corner of my mouth hitches as I try to bite back a grin. "Impatient girl," I growl. I press my thumb into her clit, rubbing a slow, soft circle, teasing her more. She moans as she presses her pelvis into me to elicit more pressure from my thumb. I withdraw and a devastated groan escapes her.

"Please, Brandt," she moans.

"Please what?"

"I need you. Touch me, please."

I growl as my mouth crashes down on hers and my hand dives between her folds. "You're so wet for me." My dick strains against my pants. Knowing that she's soaking for me and I've barely touched her makes me want to blow. Her hands slide along my chest, pushing my jacket off my shoulders. I let it drop, removing my hand only to toss my jacket. Tugging my shirt free from my pants, her fingers deftly pop open each button of my shirt.

My fingers circle her clit again before I press one finger in. Her breath catches and her movements stop as I curl my finger in her. "Fuck, you feel so good, Eli." She's panting like a cat in heat when I drop to my knees and throw her leg over my shoulder. Bunching her skirt up to her waist, I push her panties to the side and dive into her tongue first. A strangled gasp leaves her mouth as she shudders around me. My tongue swirls and laps at her and I suck on her clit so hard, one leg starts to buckle. She grabs my shoulders for support.

"*Brandt.*" My name leaves her lips as a breathy moan, and it sends shivers down my spine. It feels so good hearing my name coming from her. It feels so good having her come undone at my touch. "Oh…fuck. *Yes.*" Her moans get louder and her hand claps over her mouth, stifling the sounds. If we weren't in the office, I'd demand she remove her hand. I need to hear her scream. Her breathing is laboured, and she's rolling her hips, riding my face. Chasing her orgasm. My tongue plunges in and out of her, harder and faster until she's whimpering.

"Come for me, baby." That's all the encouragement she needs as she shatters around my tongue, riding the waves of pleasure as I lap up every ounce as she comes down.

"Oh, God," she moans. I unhook her leg from my shoulder, licking my lips as I stand up.

"Not God, just me," I quip, unable to suppress my smirk. She grasps either side of my open shirt and tears it off my shoulders, slamming her mouth to mine in a heated kiss. I step back, carefully maneuvering us to her desk, where I rip her skirt, along with her panties, down to her ankles in one swift movement. Her chest heaves and the swells of her breasts jiggle as she breathes hard. My hands make quick work of my belt buckle and the zipper of my pants, and I tug them and my boxers down to my knees as I line myself up to her entrance.

"Fuck me, Brandt," she moans breathlessly. A dark smirk plays on my face.

"Oh trust me, I'm going to," I growl. In one swift movement, I sink into her, fully seated, and she gasps. I take only a moment to allow her to adjust to my size before I move inside her. Fuck, she feels too good. "Your pussy feels like heaven. It fits me perfectly." As I grind into her, the movements become faster and her body jiggles underneath mine, causing little trinkets on the desk to clatter to the floor.

"Oh, Brandt," she moans. Fuck, I love the way she says my name. I grit my teeth, biting back the need to come. *Not yet.*

"Your pussy takes me so well. Look," I demand. Her head lifts off the desk and her eyes glue to where we're connected. "Look at how well your hungry pussy takes me." I slam into her harder, watching my cock slide in and out of her; slowing my movements to make sure she feels every inch of me. My fingers sink into her hips, pulling her closer to the edge of the desk as her legs wrap around my waist to brace herself. Bending over, I place rough kisses on her collarbone, nipping and sucking at her until I leave a faint mark. *God, she looks so good branded by me.*

I angle her hips up, adjusting her until I hit that spot that makes her pant. She writhes underneath me, moaning and whimpering.

"Does that feel good, baby?"

"*Yesssss,*" she whispers. Her brows pinch together, and her eyelids are fluttering with pleasure. She bites her lip, trying to stop the moans from leaving her mouth. Her bronze hair floats like a halo around her, dangling off the edge of the desk. Her lips are red, swollen, and her lipstick is smeared from my kisses. Her hands curl around my wrists, squeezing them with every thrust. Fucking goddamn, she couldn't look more beautiful in this moment if she tried. The sight of her breaking down, coming undone, losing herself at my touch, is something I will never tire of.

"Eyes on me, Eli." My words are gruff as I slam into her. Her eyes snap to mine, shining with pleasure and love. I can see her wrestling with herself, trying to keep her eyes open and not lose herself in the pleasure. *Not yet.* I unhook one of her legs and drape it over my shoulder, then slide her further down the desk until her ass is just teetering on the edge. I sink my cock into her deeper than before, hitting her cervix, and she inhales a sharp gasp. "Fuck, baby. Your pussy is such a hungry girl." I feel her starting to tighten and flutter around my cock, and it feels like home. It's the best feeling in the world.

As she gets closer and closer to the edge, her pussy tightens against me, sucking the shit out of my cock. It feels too good; I might just come. But I need to hold it together; I want us to come together. My dick is slick as it slides in and out of her. She's soaking wet, dripping down her thighs for me. A tingle rolls down my spine, heating me up. A telltale sign I'm almost there. My eyes burrow into hers as I pump into her. "Ready to come, baby?"

A breathy "yes" escapes her lips. "I'm so close, Brandt." Her bottom lip rolls into her mouth, her perfect white teeth sinking into it as she holds back her noises. Circling my hips, I slam into her harder and release one hand off her hip to allow my thumb to find her clit. "Oh," she gasps. The rough pad of my thumb circles and presses into her clit, making her soar higher.

"Ready, baby?"

She's speechless, nodding her head.

"Come for us," I growl. Her pussy flutters and tightens around my cock, eliciting a shockwave across my body as I pump into her, shooting hot cum, filling her up. I buck into her, riding out our highs together until we both come down. "I fucking love you," I say, collapsing on top of her, still connected.

"I love you too," she pants.

A few seconds pass and I pull out of her, pull up my pants, and adjust myself quickly before I disappear into the en suite washroom of her new office — her father's old office — and grab a cloth to clean her up. As I gently wipe away the mess, I picture her face every time she moves, with my cum dripping down her legs for the rest of the day, and a sense of possessiveness overcomes me. *She's mine.*

CHAPTER
FORTY-FOUR

ELISSA

The last fifteen minutes have left me vulnerable, and I feel surprisingly okay about it.

I know Brandt loves me, and he won't hurt me again. Just like I plan not to hurt him again.

We're going to be okay.

I stand up, my skirt falling from my waist as Brandt comes back from the en suite washroom with a warm cloth in his hands. He cleans me up, and nothing's ever felt more intimate than this. When he does the aftercare of us having sex…I've never had that before. Scratch that, I've never allowed for it to happen before, and I'm glad it's with him. He's so gentle and caring. I see the love and adoration that shine in his eyes. The pride he takes in caring for me makes my heart melt. I never thought I'd be here, in this place, with someone else. Never did I think I could give a piece of my heart away in a way I've never experienced before.

I didn't grow up seeing the care and devotion that this man shows me, and I ran away from it before because it scared me. Fuck, it still scares me. But I'm allowing myself to accept it; to experience it. My fears are not worth losing someone like Brandt again. I don't think I could handle losing him again. I'm a master at pushing my feelings aside, shoving them deep down to where they can't be found; letting them go unacknowledged. Even this time, when he walked away, I didn't deal. Not properly. But I didn't allow myself to be open to the possibility of what he meant to me. None of these are really my own thoughts, just things that have been pointed out to me in therapy, and now I can see how it's all connected.

When he's finished cleaning me, a crimson wave of embarrassment passes over my skin. I've never felt more exposed than I do in this moment. My feelings are out there, he knows. And we just *made love*. A sense of nerves and excitement washes over me, dousing all my fears, pushing them away.

He loves me.

And I love him.

There's something about realizing those words and actually processing them. He's chosen me to love. I don't think someone has ever chosen me before. Not the way

I should have been. Someone actually *wants* me. For me. With my baggage, insecurities, all of it.

I look up and find Brandt's eyes trained on me. A flicker of love flashes through them as his pupils dilate and his breath catches. I'm not sure what he's thinking, but all I can think about is how he's mine, and I'm not letting him go this time.

"So," I say, clearing my throat and finger-combing my hair.

"So," he repeats. His deep voice is gentle and fragile. Like he's afraid I'm going to push him away. Not this time.

"No more running? Either of us?" I ask. My voice is barely a whisper as a sudden twinge of nerves tightens my throat and my heart races. His lips curve, always smirking higher on the right side, and it's a quirk about him that I adore. I love his lopsided smile. He steps closer to me and pulls me into an embrace. He grabs hold of my hand, brings it to his face, and presses featherlight kisses against my palm and up to my wrist. A shiver of pleasure passes over my body as my face heats. Something as small as a kiss on my wrist and he has me losing my inhibitions. My clit throbs with need again.

"No more running," he confirms. His fiery gaze ignites something inside of me, and my heart is leaping out of my chest. "This is it. I'm not letting you go. You're mine. And I'm yours. No more of this pushing each other away bullshit. I love you, Elissa. I've always loved you."

I smirk, and a nervous giggle breaks out of me. His face twists with confusion, his brows furrowing and his mouth melting into a thin line.

"I know, Brandt. I know you've always loved me. Rhys told me everything." He freezes. His whole body goes rigid as he stands in front of me, his arms tightening around my waist.

"He what?" My heart sinks as his face drains to white. His eyes are full of worry, but mine shine with enough love for the both of us.

"I'm here. I'm not running. I found you, you know. In my yearbook. I remember the first day of ninth grade. I remember you." His lips part, clearly unsure of what to say. I press my fingers over his mouth, stopping him from saying anything. "I'm glad you loved me for that long. I'm so happy you still love me. No one ever has before. So, thank you."

His eyes shine with unshed tears. I rise to my toes, my heels slipping out of my pumps, and I press a chaste kiss to his mouth. As I break the kiss, his mouth chases mine and a hand tangles into my hair, grasping my neck and pulling me closer to him. His mouth eclipses mine, crashing down, and I part my mouth, ready to accept him. Accept him, his love, and everything he has to offer. And I'm finally ready to give it back. Finally ready to allow myself to be loved, and love in return.

"Elissa, I —" He pulls away, slightly leaning back to stare at me.

"It's okay, Brandt. I'm not running. Not this time." Something inside him breaks, and I see whatever it is crumbling inside him. My hand cups his face and he leans into it, his eyes closing. He turns his mouth into my palm and places a kiss there.

"I love you, Elissa. You're it for me. And there's no going back. You can't run anymore, and if you do, I'm running right behind you. I can keep up with you, and I will not let you get away again. There's only us. It's only ever been us. You're all I need, you're all I've ever needed. And I can promise you this: One day, I'm going to marry you," he says. My heart flutters in my chest and my breathing quickens. My pulse is thrumming underneath my skin and I wonder if he can feel it, if he can hear it. "I'm never letting you go now that I have you. You'll be mine in every way. But I'm not going to rush you because this isn't some deal for me. You aren't a pawn in some crazy game of your father's. I'm going to marry you because I love you. Because I can't see myself with anyone else."

My heart threatens to leap out of my chest. *How is he so perfect?* This gorgeous man in front of me is so calm, patient, kind, and loving. How is he real?

"I love you, Brandt Collins."

"I love *you*, Elissa Black."

EPILOGUE

One year and three months later

ELISSA

Brandt and I pass through the backyard gate of Riley's parents' house. Birds dance and sing in the air as the tantalizing smell of barbecue hits us. I can see my mother and Riley's father over by the large grill, talking up a storm while Mr. Jaimeson cooks the sizzling hotdogs and hamburgers. Over in the corner near the cluttered food and drink table are Rhys and Riley's mom, talking and laughing hard with people who look like they might be Rhys' parents. His father looks exactly like him, but older and with more salt and pepper in his hair. His mother has soft features and is a little on the heavier side, but no less gorgeous, with her chestnut hair flowing in the light breeze.

Brandt gives my hand a squeeze and I look at him, finding his beautiful eyes. My heart flips in my chest as I squeeze his hand back. It took a while to find each other again, but I'm glad we did. I can't imagine my life without this man beside me.

"'Lissa!" I hear a familiar voice call my name. I look and it's Riley, holding the baby on her hip over by the present table, little Kiana tugging on and playing with her mother's hair. Kiana is the spitting image of Riley and Rhys. She has black hair like the both of them, beautiful brown eyes like Riley, and a mischievous little attitude already, which I think she's inherited from Rhys. She also has a light smattering of freckles across her nose, though where she got those from, I have no idea. Riley looks radiant and happy, even in the unrelenting August humidity. She's shaded by a big maple tree, but it's hard to escape the summer heat in Ontario unless you're heading indoors. I wistfully let go of Brandt's hand as I walk over to Riley. Brandt makes a beeline toward Rhys. The warmth his hand provided fades as we walk away from each other, and the longing in my heart grows.

When I reach Riley, she's set Kiana down in the playpen and pulls me in for a long embrace. It's been a while since I've seen her. We talk everyday, but with her raising a family and working on her new business more steadily, and me running Black & Wells, it's hard to carve time out of both of our busy schedules. Her sleek black hair is smooth against my face as we break from the hug, and I bend down to pick up Kiana, her bright face beaming up at me and arms stretched wide.

"Hey Kiwi," I coo. "How's my favourite little lady?" I wriggle my fingers into her belly and she shrieks before letting out a boisterous laugh. Riley and I laugh along with her. The screen door smacks in the background and little feet pound against the cement, then the grass. Little lungs yell out my name.

"'Lissa!" I quickly pass off Kiana to Riley so that we can avoid a disaster as Knox comes barrelling toward me.

"Knox, slow down! You're going to knock someone over!" a very warm and familiar voice calls out. *Lana.* My heart squeezes the moment I hear her, and I look around to find her trailing after Knox. I crouch down, opening my arms wide, and prepare for impact from Knox. He slams into my body, almost sending us both careening over. I steady us and give him a big squeeze.

"Hey bud! It's been a while." I let go of him and ruffle his hair before he runs off to find a toy to play with. Lana finally makes it over and the warmest smile lights up her face. A light breeze blows past us and I catch a whiff of her coconut and shea butter scent. It smells like home. She pulls me in for a hug, and we hold each other for a few moments.

"Thanks for coming, Mom."

"I wouldn't miss Riley's little one's first birthday. She's just as much like a daughter to me as you are." She pulls away and her hands slide down the backs of my arms until they grasp my hands. "Now, I want to see this thing."

She takes my hand and raises it up. Sitting on my left ring finger is the most brilliant three-carat diamond solitaire ring set in 18K white gold. As she turns my hand to really inspect it, it catches the light and gives off a beautiful sparkle. Never in my life did I think I'd be wearing an engagement ring. But for the man that means everything to me, he's worth it.

Lana lets my hand drop and kisses my cheek. "I'm so happy for you, Elissa. He's a wonderful man, and he chose the most perfect ring for you." Her eyes tear away from me to the commotion behind us. "Knox! Be careful with Kiana! She's only a baby…sorry, baby girl, I gotta go get that little rascal." She hurries off to get Knox and show him how to play with Kiana gently.

As I stand and look around at all these people in my life, I finally realize that I do have the family I always wanted, it's just one I had to make — and fight for. My eyes find Brandt, and he's casually standing with Rhys and his parents, chatting and laughing while he sips on his beer. My roaming eyes take in my gorgeous man. His broad shoulders are covered in a grey and white plaid short-sleeve button-down shirt, his ass looks amazing in beige cargo pants, and his golden-brown hair is styled to perfection, like it always is. You'd never know that my hands were running through it ten minutes before we got here. He's literally perfect. Perfect for me, and I'm a little pissed it took me as long as it did to realize this.

It's taken me a long time and a lot of therapy to get here, but I think I can finally be happy. I actually think I am happy. And for the first time, I don't feel like I need to run from my problems or my anxiety, because everything I need to help me is right here.

"Time to eat," Mr. Jaimeson calls out as he finishes pulling the last burger off the grill and places it on a platter, then hands it off to Rhys. He carries it over to the long table that's covered in a pink daisy-printed tablecloth. In one smooth motion, everyone gravitates toward the food, making a small line with their plates. I stare at all the people I love in one place and feel incredibly grateful. It took a long time to come to this point, being able to have everyone together, including having my mother even be a part of an event like this. Before my father died, this is something that would never have happened. It's going to take a while longer, but I think my mother and I finally have a chance at some sort of relationship. We'll never be as close as Lana and I, or like a normal mother and daughter are, but whatever we have now is something more than what we had.

I stand here, staring at all my loved ones in one place, and it warms my heart. Using my thumb, I twirl my engagement ring around my finger a few times and bite down on my lip. I hold out my hand and take a long look at the ring I'm not quite used to wearing yet. But it is beautiful. And just like the brilliant sparkle that shines in the sunlight, it reminds me of that brilliant spring day when everything changed.

ACKNOWLEDGEMENTS

I want to start by saying I can't believe we've reached the end of Brandt and Elissa's story! It's bittersweet for me to be writing this because being a published author and sharing my stories with all of you only ever happened in my wildest dreams.

I want to thank all you amazing readers. Thank you for being here and taking a chance on me. Thank you for taking a chance on Elissa, Brandt, Riley, and Rhys. These characters will always hold a special place in my heart. So, thank you for taking a chance on a little piece of me.

Next, I would like to thank my amazing editors. Lesley-Anne, I appreciate all the work and dedication you put into my work. You always go over and above and I thank you for that. My novels wouldn't be as great as they are without you. And to Kayla Morton, you're fast, efficient, reliable, and fantastic to work with. I'm so glad I found you.

To my wonderful cover designer, Laura Boyle. I love how we seem to be on the same page with artwork and design. You really dive into my head and pull out exactly what I'm thinking.

To my beautiful family and friends. Thank you for supporting me in every step of this journey. Thank you for not being irritated when all I ever do is talk about my books. It is one of the most exciting things to ever happen to me, making these dreams come true.

And especially thank you to my daughter. You're only six right now and don't even know how to read, but the fact that every time we're in a bookstore and you *have* to find my book on the shelves is the best feeling in the world. You don't even know what I write but you're so proud and supportive of me. I can't wait until the day I can be part of your dream.

ABOUT THE AUTHOR

Kate Smoak lives with her husband, daughter, and fur babies in a small town in Ontario, Canada. When she's not writing, she can be found curling up with a good book, playing video games, or camping at the trailer with her family.

Instagram: @katesmoakwrites
Twitter: @katesmoakwrites
Website: www.katesmoak.ca

If you enjoyed this book, it would mean
the world to me if you would leave a review.
Reviews are like tips for authors.

For more goodies and exclusive content,
please sign up for my newsletter!

www.ingramcontent.com/pod-product-compliance
Lightning Source LLC
Chambersburg PA
CBHW011806200726
48289CB00016B/3002